EMPERORS OF THE TWILIGHT

S. ANDREW SWANN

D0003361

DAW BOOKS, INC.

DONALD A. WOLLHEIM, FOUNDER
375 Hudson Street, New York, NY 10014

ELIZABETH R. WOLLHEIM
SHEILA E. GILBERT
PUBLISHERS

First Printing, January 1994
1   2   3   4   5   6   7   8   9

DAW TRADEMARK REGISTERED
U.S. PAT. OFF. AND FOREIGN COUNTRIES
—MARCA REGISTRADA
HECHO EN U.S.A.

PRINTED IN THE U.S.A.

TARGETED FOR TERMINATION—

When she was under the bridge, Evi spared a look behind her. The dog-walker had just turned down 85th after her at a dead run. He was drawing a silenced automatic as he ran. His doberman was already halfway to her. She dived behind one of the pilings that held up the bridge. She could hear growling and claws clicking across the concrete, getting closer.

There was a crack as a bullet chipped away part of the piling behind her. She got to her feet, pulling the SG from her backpack. The SG cleared the pack as the doberman rounded the piling. Evi aimed a kick at the dog's nose. The contact was solid but the dog didn't back off. Instead, the doberman clamped its teeth around her right calf. The carbon monoweave she wore kept it from breaking the skin, but it felt like the dog was ripping her lower leg off. Evi fired a round into its upper chest, spraying pieces of dog on the sidewalk, but the dog stayed clamped to her leg.

The dog's owner rounded the piling and covered her with his automatic. He addressed her in perfect English. "Do we go quietly, Miss Isham?"

He must have been kidding.

It was a contest to see who fired first and she knew she was going to lose. . . .

Dedicated to Dan and Grace,
both of them, through whatever.

ACKNOWLEDGMENTS

Thanks to Jane Butler and Sheila Gilbert, without whom this book would have remained, if not unwritten, definitely unpublished. Also a load of thanks to the Cajun Sushi Hamsters, you know who you are.

CHAPTER 1

At four-thirty in the morning on a snowless New Year's Eve, Evi Isham was naked on a penthouse balcony overlooking Manhattan. She was doing her best to beat the crap out of her weight machine, and the machine was winning. Even after gearing the bench press down to 250 kilos, the reps were still eating into her shoulders. She had just come back from Havana, her first vacation from the Agency, and her muscles had turned to mush.

Great thing to realize first thing on your birthday, she thought to herself. She was thirty-three, allegedly. She could be twenty-nine or thirty-six. She had picked December 31, 2025, as her birthday for simplicity's sake. No one actually knew her real birth date, but the INS didn't like blank spots in their forms.

However old she was, she couldn't slack off on the workouts like a teenager. At least she had three days to catch up before the Agency wanted her back.

She stopped at rep number twenty and grabbed a towel. She was damp with a light mist of perspiration and her breath fogged, leaving little trails of infrared on the air.

Evi walked to the corner of the balcony and looked at her adopted home. The Manhattan skyline cut a glowing hole in the night. The buildings accumulated toward the chrome-blue spine of the Nyogi tower. Red lights from the constant aircar traffic enveloped the city like hot embers. To her right, through the gap between two neighboring condominiums, she could see a forest-green light from the misnamed Central Park Dome. Beyond the luminescent city, the sky was a dead black.

A cold wind drew across Evi's skin, causing an involuntary shiver that seemed to shake open every pore in her body.

Thirty-three, she thought. She was settling down. She had a permanent address for the first time since the war. Even though she'd kept in top condition, it'd been over five years since the Agency had put her in a dangerous field mission. The only running she did was running the computer at the think tank. The only thing she chased now was lost page work and obscure reference texts.

She'd been here long enough that she already had one male resident hitting on her. Chuck Dwyer on the seventeenth floor had given her his apartment number and a raincheck in her second week here.

She'd even had a coworker invite her over for dinner. Dave Price wasn't quite in her department, but they kept bumping into each other. She'd been to his house in Queens and met about a dozen cats. If David hadn't been aware Evi wasn't human, it might have gone beyond dinner.

She was definitely settling down.

Some people would miss the action.

Such people were nuts.

Even though she had been bioengineered for combat, flying a desk was fine with her. Back in '54, when the Supreme Court finally gave the products of human genetic engineering the same rights the 29th amendment gave the moreaus, Evi had even considered quitting the Agency.

But, by then, she didn't have terrorists shooting at her anymore. One shitfire case in Cleveland and she was transferred to an advisory capacity. More than once she'd supposed that dropping her out of the field was someone's idea of punishing her for unearthing that mess.

As far as she was concerned, it was a promotion. For close to six years she'd been working in that think tank. The closest she ever got to "action" nowadays was writing reports about hypothetical alien invasions and less hypothetical projections on possible moreau violence.

She sometimes felt out of place as the token nonhuman expert in the midst of the academics, economists, and political scientists. But the job provided her with a decent living and a human identity. With a pair of contact lenses she could pass for a compact, muscular human, and the Agency helped her maintain that fiction.

Evi padded back to the weight machine and started to reconfigure it for a leg press. She flipped the cover off the keypad and punched in the resistance at 600 kilos. There was a long pause as she listened to the hydraulics of the machine adjust.

She straddled the bench, leaned back, and put her feet in the grips.

The weight machine was at the end of one arm of the L-shaped balcony. It was pointed toward the corner of the balcony and, beyond, toward one of a twinned set of condominiums that bordered the park. The condo she faced was a dozen stories taller, fifty years younger, and about five grand cheaper than the place Evi lived in.

She watched the front of the neighboring building.

No matter how early she got up for her workout, her penchant for exercising in the nude always drew a few spectators. She hadn't yet decided if she was bothered by it or not.

And, even though she had started her workout a half-hour early, apparently this morning was no different.

Four windows up and three to the left there was a

peeper. He gave himself away with the high-spectrum glow from his binocs. She strained to focus on the guy. The peeper's blurred window shot into focus and the rest of Manhattan quashed itself into her peripheral vision. She saw his face, monochrome and sliced into strips by the venetian blinds in his window. She guessed mid-twenties with mixed Anglo heritage. She couldn't see anything of the darkened apartment behind him. He had supplied himself with a pair of military binocs, a pair of British Long-Eighties with night-vision attachments.

Evi's eyes watered and she closed them.

She did a few presses and opened her eyes and refocused on the peeper. December, and the guy was sweating. She could see the stains under his armpits, and light was reflecting off his forehead. There was something wrong about the guy, and not a standard New York wrongness.

She was working up an irritating sweat herself. Her ass was beginning to slide all over the plastic seat. That usually wasn't a problem, but apparently she'd slacked off a lot. She did three more leg presses and stopped to get a towel to lay on the seat.

When she stopped, she strained at her maximum to get a look at the peeper. That's when she noticed that the peeper had an earplug and a throat-mike. She'd missed it at first, because of the blinds and the shadows they were casting. The peeper was also talking to himself.

And while in Manhattan you expect all the pervs and scuzzballs to talk to themselves, this peeper was talking to someone else.

He wasn't subvocalizing, so Evi could watch his lips move. At a hundred meters plus it hurt to make out, but the old Japanese gene-techs had designed good eyes.

Evi didn't make the mistake of staring at the guy. That would have been a tip that she could see him, and the guy would clam up and dive for cover. Even her brief pause in the leg presses might have alerted him. She resumed pumping.

Fortunately the peeper seemed not to have noticed her pause. So, while the peeper was getting an eyeful down her leg press, she tried to read the peeper's lips.

The fact that he wasn't speaking English threw her for a second. It took her a moment to recognize the syllabication as Japanese. *Damn it.* Trying to lip-read a language that relied so much on inflection was close to hopeless. Then he nodded a little and slipped into Arabic. Evi was much more fluent in Arabic than she was in Japanese.

What the peeper was mouthing looked like, "Word is go. The package is on southwest balcony. Team one is the pickup. Two and three, stairs."

It didn't take a tactical genius to figure out what "the package" might be. And, while being raised within the Israeli intelligence community might have prejudiced her against anyone who spoke Arabic, it wasn't too far a leap to decide that the "pickup" wasn't anything pleasant.

She was on rep number twenty, and she had to blink a few times to clear her vision. Once she refocused and had a wider field of view, something glinted in her peripheral vision. At the same time, she heard a whirring chunk. The glint belonged to an open window on the top floor of the building next to the peeper's. The chunk, and the whir she was now hearing, belonged to the penthouse's express elevator.

No one but her was supposed to be able to use the elevator. The other penthouse was unoccupied.

Colonel Abdel, her first instructor and surrogate father, had given her a number of maxims, and near the top was "know your territory." She knew her building, knew its occupants, knew the sounds it made, and she knew that the elevator would get to the top floor in forty-seven seconds.

The French doors were around the corner of the balcony from her. Only fifteen meters separated her from her weapon.

The open window across the street glinted again, and something visceral made her vacate the weight machine and vault to the roof of the penthouse. Behind her something slammed into the bench she'd just left. She heard the crash of tearing metal and the siren wheeze of escaping hydraulic fluid.

"SHIT!" Evi screamed into the darkness. A sniper was firing at her, with something fifty-cal or better. She ran at top speed across the slick solar-collecting surface roofing the penthouse complex. She felt the wind of the second shot breeze by the small of her back before it shattered into the roof behind her. An explosion of ceramic powder dusted her legs as she dived behind the cover offered by the rectangular brick shack that housed the motors for the elevators and the central-air for the building.

She hunched up, shivering, against the brick wall. She could feel the wall vibrate as a third shot slammed into the other side of the shack.

"What the fuck is going on?"

She could hear Abdel telling her to ask questions later. When people weren't shooting at her.

The sniper let up, apparently waiting for a clean shot. She had been damn lucky she saw that glint. If the sight of the peeper hadn't primed her for trouble, she never would have paid attention to it.

That scared her.

What could she do now? The peeper was talking to a pickup team that must be in the elevator now. The team would be there in less than half a minute. The sniper had her pinned back here, and the peeper was spotter on the high ground, broadcasting her movements.

She forced the panic back and tried to think clearly.

In the elevator their radio would be blacked out for

the duration. She looked up at the wall she was huddled against. The door to the shack was facing the sniper, but here, on this side, was a small window. She forced it open. There was a screech of twisting metal, but she was unconcerned by the noise. The pickup team in the elevator wouldn't hear it. The elevators in this place were plush, luxurious, and soundproof.

Inside the room, the only noise was the motor raising the elevator. The place smelled of grease and electricity. She stuck her head under the blackened girders that held up the whirring motor and looked down the shaft at the elevator. If their radios had been working, the emergency exit on top of the elevator would have been open.

The elevator was halfway up the shaft and the trapdoor was still closed. The radio blackout prevented the peeper from telling the team that she was about to land on them.

Whoever they were.

Evi looked at the cables stringing between the motor and the elevator. She didn't want to do this, but taking the offense was the only way she could gain control of the situation. She grabbed a cable and started lowering herself, hand over hand. Dangerous as hell if her grip slipped, but that was only par for the course.

She and the elevator met on the fifteenth floor of the twenty-story building. Her feet squished in the black filth coating the top of the elevator. Her skin was now covered in brown grease, making her wish for some clothes.

She crouched over the trapdoor and listened. She couldn't hear them, but she could smell them. Two of them, and they weren't human. She could identify the smell, canine, both of them. They were most likely Afghani-engineered dogs. Plenty of combat experience during the Pan-Asian war, would have gone merc when the Kabul government discontinued the strain.

She was glad the Japanese gene-techs had avoiding moreaus in mind when they designed her odor profile. Had she been human, it would have been *them* smelling *her.* But they hadn't smelled her or heard her. If she did her job right, they never would.

The trapdoor was just a panel resting in the roof of the elevator. When the sixteenth floor was passing by, she silently lifted it. She looked down, and her guess was right. Two Afghanis. Their shaggy gray fur was the tip-off. Both faced forward, pointing a pair of silenced submachine guns at the chromed door.

Their black noses began to twitch in unison and the one nearest her began to turn. Noise and stale air from the shaft were blowing in.

She straddled the trapdoor and grabbed the sides of the opening with both hands. She heard the metal crunch in her grip, and so did the canines.

The elevator reached floor number seventeen, and both dogs were turning around. *Too slow*, she thought. She shot her legs through the opening and wrapped them around one dog's neck. She hauled the dog upward, pulling with her arms. The other one wanted to shoot, Evi knew, but his partner was in the way.

She yanked the dog halfway through the trapdoor, giving herself some cover from dog number two. She ended up on her back on top of the elevator, the dog still thrashing. He faced her, sputtering white foam on her stomach as he whipped his head back and forth. She grabbed the dog's muzzle and snapped it shut with her right hand. Blood and a piece of tongue splattered warmly on her thigh.

She used the dog's muzzle as a lever-arm to break his neck.

She unscissored her legs and rolled to the side of the elevator. The elevator passed floor eighteen. The corpse lay folded over the lip of the trapdoor. Its head looked back over the right shoulder as if it saw something interesting at the top of the shaft. Evi spared

16

a look to her right, down the adjoining shaft. The neighboring elevator was down by the lobby, unmoving. She swung down and dangled by the side of the elevator.

She'd just cleared the top of the elevator when the second dog started spraying the roof with gunfire. The corpse shook like it was having a seizure, and the shaft rang with the sound of bullets ricocheting. She worried about the cables and the motor.

The dog ceased firing, managing not to hit anything vital. Evi stationed herself across from the trapdoor, bracing her feet in the metal strut halfway up the side of the elevator's exterior. She ducked low and listened. She heard the corpse thud back into the elevator, and suddenly the shaft was filled with the odor of gunfire. She listened. Soon she heard the canine pull himself out of the hole.

Nineteenth floor.

She waited a heartbeat and popped her torso over the edge. The canine was standing on top of the elevator and, predictably, looking up. She sank her right hand into the dog's crotch and lifted him up and off balance. She held on to the roof of the elevator with her left hand as she leaned her body back into the adjoining shaft. The canine had both hands on his gun, so he didn't have a chance. Evi felt the cables brush her hair as she flipped the dog over her. The dog tumbled headfirst down the neighboring shaft.

Inside the elevator, she heard the doors ding open: twentieth floor.

Below her, she heard the dog hit.

She vaulted to the top of the elevator and dropped through the hole. Her feet squished into the blood-soaked carpet. The canine that took the header had done quite a number on his partner. The inside of the elevator was ripe with the smell of wasted canine. She hit the emergency stop before the doors could close.

Evi gave herself fifteen seconds to examine the body.

The dog looked a little too healthy to be from the Indian frontier, so she guessed that he had originally been involved in Persia or Turkmen. Long time since the war, and the canine had since gone independent. The vest was vintage Afghani special forces, as was most of the dog's outfit. . . .

The gun was a different story.

She briefly considered running into her apartment for her own gun. The windows could stand at least one slug from her sniper's weapon. She decided she didn't have time—yet.

She grabbed the dog's gun and the radio that was clipped to one ragged ear.

She pulled herself back up through the trapdoor and maneuvered through the girders supporting the motor. She gave herself another few seconds to admire the gun. Very rare weapon, Japanese make, something that just wasn't seen anymore. It was hard to find Japanese *anything* after the Pan-Asian war. Weapons were unheard of. The small black Mitsubishi SG-2 was mostly plastic and ceramics. The only metal component would be the firing pin. Even without the silencer it was quiet as the devil.

She checked the magazine. Nine-millimeter, plastic tip, antipersonnel. No wonder the cables and the motor survived the dog's salvo. Full clip, thirty rounds.

The earplug she salvaged from the dog wasn't a human model, of course, but the plastic alligator clip that held it on was serviceable. She hung it off her earlobe. The speaker ended up facing the wrong way, but her hearing was good enough to make out the peeper's Arabic. ". . . team one, repeat, package is on top of the shaft. Over."

Then silence.

She ran through the door into the room adjoining the elevator shafts. She spared half a second to wonder what happened to building security as she rounded the green sheet-metal block of the main air-conditioning unit. The room was steaming from the building's forced-air heating system. It used the same ductwork as the air-conditioning.

She looked at the throat-mike and the radio connected to it. The throat-mike and the strap that held it on hung loosely around her neck. The radio itself was a small box that dangled between her breasts. On the box was a small recess with a row of four dip switches. They were the only controls. She figured they were the frequency pre-sets. It was a guess. The radio wasn't a familiar model.

She reached into the tiny recess with a slightly pointed nail and turned on switch number two.

". . . three to north stairs. Team one needs help delivering the package. The package is intact and unwrapped, repeat, package is intact and unwrapped . . ."

Long ago, she had trained her laugh to be totally silent. There were just too many things in combat that ended up striking her as funny. When the adrenaline was really cooking, she could get inappropriately giddy. She was sure that "unwrapped" must mean she was assumed to be, wrongly now, unarmed. However, unarmed or not, she certainly was unwrapped.

She stopped laughing. Abdel, during many training sessions, had told her that her sense of humor was going to kill her.

She set down the SG-2 and turned the bolts on one of the side panels in the massive air-conditioning unit. She was careful to avoid making undue noise. If team three was made up of more canines, their hearing was to be respected, even if the furnace in the basement would cover most of her noise. Another worry was her smell. She had been engineered to avoid, as much as possible, having a signature odor, but she was covered with grease and blood that would broadcast her location well enough. Still, she'd be descending and the air currents were upward. She'd be downwind of them most of the way.

The green panel came loose and she lowered herself into the ancient ductwork. She shimmied down a rectangular sheet-metal aluminum tube. The hot metal burned against her skin and seemed to do its utmost to amplify her every noise. The updraft of stale furnace air made her eyes water.

"Team three to post office, floor eighteen, no sign of package. Over."

"Post office to team three, team one is not responding. Assume they delivered to wrong address, you're to pick up the package now."

She hit a ceiling duct on the nineteenth floor. She trusted her sense of direction to get her to the north stairwell. She squeezed into a narrow transverse duct. By the time she got behind a grille overlooking a landing in the north stairwell, she was squeezing, gun first, through a tube that was barely a meter wide by a half tall. She couldn't back up. She had scraped her knees, hips, elbows, shoulders and nipples raw.

She got to the grate in time to see two canines rounding the stairs. Evi could tell the dogs were smelling something odd blowing out the vents.

She clicked the SG on full auto and sprayed the dogs through the vent, aiming high. Her aim was good. The first bullet caught the closest canine in the face. The dog's face exploded in a mist of fur, blood, and flecks of teeth and bone.

The other one was quick. He had seen the grating on the vent fly out and started firing immediately, but his gun was pointing the wrong way. She swept her gun on the dog. The dog swept his SG toward her.

She felt a spray of cinder block dust as the dog hit too high above the vent. That had been his only chance. She tracked her fire into the canine, plowing shots into his vest. She pulled up slightly as the dog fell back against the railing. The dog's gun ran away, firing into the ceiling, sending down confetti of broken fiberglass acoustical tile. He flipped backward over the railing as she clipped his neck with a shot. The canine merc tumbled down the center of the stairwell.

The peeper was going nuts over the radio. "Team three, come in, team three. Where is the package, where are you? Over."

Evi squeezed out of the vent with some relief. No one from team three was responding to the peeper. Only the two of them. She looked over the railing to see where the second dog had gone.

The corpse was folded backward over the railing on the opposite balcony on the fifth floor.

She flipped the radio to another frequency pre-set. "... two cross over to the entrance to the north stairwell. Package has not been picked up. Team four will join you at the door. Do not pick up the package until team four joins you. Package is now wrapped ..."

That would be at least four dogs. Five if they had an extra in the lobby. This was getting messy. She'd gotten the four so far by surprise and an edge in the skill department. Time to change tactics.

Team four had to make it up from the lobby, and they wouldn't engage now until the two teams linked up. She had a chance now to get her emergency pack and her own gun.

She ran up the stairs, leaving an obvious trail of grease and blood, and slammed through the door into the hall. The hall ran between the two penthouse apartments, and it had a stairwell on either end. It was done up in mirrors and red carpeting. The elevator was open, still stopped on this floor.

She inched up on her door and punched in the combination. It was a risk, but she doubted anyone had made it up to the apartment yet. The lock chunked open. She shouldered the door open and dove into her apartment.

The peeper went nuts again. "The package is in the penthouse! Repeat . . ."

A shot from the sniper tore into one of the bedroom windows next to the French doors. The polymer held, the bullet now embedded in it. Evi's view of the sniper's building was now distorted and prismatic.

That was good, the sniper now had the same distorted view of her.

She kept moving, rolling through the door to her bedroom as the sniper hit the window again. Two slugs now sat in the center of concentric rainbows. The window began to make ominous creaking noises.

She dropped the SG and swept her arm under her bed. She came out with a black backpack.

Evi rolled to the corner of the bedroom and huddled behind the brick pillar that supported the end of the roof. It offered cover from the sniper. Another shot plowed into the window and it finally gave. The window snapped and sprayed pieces of itself all over the bedroom.

". . . repeat, package is in the southwest bedroom . . ."

She pulled her weapon out of the backpack. It was an IMI-Mishkov LR 7.62, an Israeli design for the Russian secret service. She snapped on the extension, lengthening the automatic's barrel by nearly a meter, and flicked off the safety.

The recoilless Mishkov only held six shots, standard 7.62 millimeter rifle cartridges. She used it because it was the longest-ranged and most accurate handgun in existence, even though the extension was so finely machined that the accuracy crapped out after only a dozen shots. As she shouldered the pack, she made a mental picture of the neighboring apartment building.

She silently thanked the sniper for clearing the window out of the way.

Then, with her heart in her throat, she rolled out from behind the brick pillar and aimed dead center, at the window four up and three to the left.

"Hurry, the package is moving . . ."

She fired at the peeper's window. As she rolled away from her firing position, she saw the venetian blinds close as the peeper collapsed against them. Red stains spread along the slats of the blinds. The peeper's windows weren't bulletproof.

"Now maybe you'll shut the fuck up."

She had a moment to hope that didn't go out over the air.

The sniper missed the one shot she gave him. The bullet tore into her bed. Water sprayed as far as the ceiling. She'd just decapitated the hit squad's command and control, partially blinded them as well, and she now had the evil things she kept in the pack for emergencies.

The sniper missed another shot. The slug embedded itself in another window.

She rolled back out into the hall, and the sniper finished off the window behind her. It wasn't until then that she began to feel the cuts from rolling over the broken window. The grease on her skin got into the cuts, making her feel like a feline moreau was using her for a scratching post. She ignored the pain and headed for the south stairway, carrying her emergency pack in one hand and the Mishkov in the other. Teams two and four would be storming up the north stairway. She didn't have much time.

The south stairway was concrete, functional, the mirror twin of its opposite number. On the nineteenth-floor landing there was a vent grating, exactly like the one she had shot two canines through. The duct led straight across to the other stairwell. She could even catch a whiff of the carnage there.

The vent was barely in reach. She set down the backpack and jammed her fingers through the grating, ripping it away, taking some of the wall along with it. She put the gun back in the pack and withdrew a small round grenade. She chinned herself up, wincing as she rubbed her nipples across the whitewashed cinder block wall. She looked down the vent, a straight aluminum tube down to a small rectangle of light, maybe thirty meters. She smelled canine blood, even over the forced air from the furnace. She listened.

They were trying for stealth, but there were just too many of them. Of course, there was the predictable pause by the corpse. There was a slight echo effect as she heard them through the duct and over the radio.

"Team two to post office, we've found team three. Returned to sender . . ."

She'd never been fond of explosives. They were messy, imprecise, and likely to involve people other than the intended target.

Her left arm ached. She raised the grenade in her right hand, pulled the pin with her teeth and made a quick estimate. She waited exactly one and a half seconds before she threw it through the vent. She dropped and rolled immediately. Two seconds later she heard the grenade hit the aluminum vent and roll half a second before falling out the other side. It was a close thing, but the alarm she heard over the radio told her that it had gone out the vent in the opposite stairwell and not into some side passage.

Teams two and four only had an instant to recognize the grenade.

The sound was deafening even though she was on the other side of the building. A belch of smoke came out of the vent preceding a pressure wave that made her ears pop.

Evi hated explosives, but sometimes they were indispensable as an equalizer.

The canine's radio now only broadcast static. She tried the other settings and their combinations. She only got silence. In the best case that would mean she had gotten them all. However, the safe assumption was that the team doing the hit had discovered that their communications were compromised and were running on radio silence.

In any event, the sniper was still out there. Also, despite their precautions—taking out security, using the penthouse elevator and the fire stairs, silenced weapons—the hit was no longer a secret. The fire alarm was going off, half the building would have just woken up, and the top of the building must be pouring out smoke.

Ten minutes and the NYPD, the fire department, and probably a car from the Bureau would be showing up. In twenty minutes, the Agency would take over the Bureau investigation on behalf of the Fed. In a half-hour the vids would be parroting an official state-ment about random moreau violence. It would be a bland, simplistic story that would fit the facts while remaining a blatant falsehood.

She had about that long to leave the building and come in from the cold.

She couldn't get caught up with law enforcement. Standard procedure for covert ops: get caught doing something a little to the left of legal, even by domestic forces—*especially* by domestic forces—the operative gets thrown to the wolves while the Agency cooks up a cover story, usually about rogue agents.

Sometimes she wished it had been the CIA that recruited her. They'd eat a little bad press to save an agent.

Her time sense told her it was four fifty-two in the morning.

CHAPTER 2

What the hell was going on? It had been nearly six years since she had been involved in anything really sensitive. Why was she suddenly targeted by a sniper and a team of Afghani mercenaries?

She was running at top speed down the south stairwell wearing only the backpack slung over her shoulder. Panic was still clouding her thinking. She wasn't ready for this shit.

She could hear Abdel telling her that no one was ever ready for it.

She decided that she had a minute, maybe a minute and a half, before the civilians heeded the fire alarms and started filling the stairwells. When she hit floor number seventeen, she left the stairwell and jogged down the hall. She could hear the civilians waking up behind their doors. In a few seconds, doors would begin to open.

She passed an intersecting corridor and saw a old man, forty-five, gray hair, towel around his waist. He wasn't looking in her direction. She smelled sweat, musk, and someone else in the room behind him. Then she'd passed the intersection.

Evi hoped Chuck Dwyer had given her the right apartment number.

She stopped at apartment 1712 and pounded on the door. She restrained herself. In her state it wouldn't take much to splinter the door frame.

Chuck Dwyer opened the door. Chuck was in the

process of dressing, and Evi could smell a woman back in the apartment.

He couldn't hide his shock. He stood there, staring at a naked woman covered with blood and grease.

Evi didn't have time. She pushed through into the apartment, slamming the door shut behind her. Chuck was trying to squeak out a comprehensible monosyllable and not doing a good job of it.

"I'm using your shower."

She had to get the gunk off of her, or she had little chance of getting anywhere, past anyone. Chuck, still trying to talk, stared into her eyes.

Damn it! She'd forgotten about her contacts.

In his eyes she could see her own reflection, her own eyes. She could see her yellow iris and slitted pupil quite clearly, and Chuck was probably staring at the green reflective glow from her retinas. Cat eyes.

Chuck finally managed to say, "Y—you're a frank . . ."

Frank. In other words, frankenstein. Lower on most people's lists than the moreaus. Lower because her designers had the temerity to actually fiddle with the human genome. It had taken half a century for people in the States to achieve an uncomfortable acceptance of the engineered animals that kept pouring over the border.

An engineered human was still a horrifying concept.

Evi didn't even like the word. There should be a kinder word in general usage. Even the term moreau, arising from nearly the same source, sounded better.

It didn't really matter that Chuck knew. The penthouse was dead for her. Probably the whole of New York as well.

What really bothered her was the fact that a guy who was once actively trying to get into her bed was now looking at her as if she were a diseased animal. Better to not even try giving him an explanation.

"Chuck, does the woman in the bedroom live in the building?"

Chuck nodded.

"Take her back to her apartment. The police will be here soon and it would be good for you if you never saw me. Say you spent the night here."

She went into the bathroom and didn't bother to close the door. She didn't care what Chuck did. It was irrelevant what he told the cops. Her trail of grease and blood would lead to his apartment. Nothing Chuck could say would compromise her position.

She had told him the truth. His silence would be for his benefit. Especially if the Agency was in the mood for disappearing someone.

Three minutes under a cold blast of water and she didn't look like a refugee from a war zone. She hit the dryer and grabbed her pack off the john. In the pack was a one-piece all-purpose black jumpsuit. It was denim made from engineered cotton. It was faded gray in places and didn't look like a stealth number. Its one special aspect was the carbon-fiber monofilament microweaved into it. It would deflect a knife, and while it wouldn't stop a bullet, it could slow one down enough to save her life.

It was also broken in to the point where it didn't feel like it was sanding her skin off when she put it on.

There were a pair of her special contact lenses in her backpack. Unfortunately, during all the running and jumping, their case had popped open. The one brown lens she found had torn in half.

"Damn," She whispered as she flushed the lens.

She took out a pair of chromed sunglasses. If the cops saw her eyes, they would stop her. Her eyes could adjust to the light level. The only problem was that the sunglasses cut out the high end of the spectrum.

Chuck—and whoever the woman was—had split the apartment. Chuck had the New Yorker's sense of self-preservation.

Now all she had to do was get out of the building

with the sniper watching. She doubted a wave of cops would deter the gunman, whoever he was.

The sniper didn't make sense to her. Unless he was supposed to pin her down for the dogs. But it sure *felt* like the sniper was doing his best to kill her. In which case the hit team swarming the building was irrelevant and costly.

Evi had the feeling that if she hadn't seen the peeper, she'd be dead.

Who was behind it, and why the overkill?

She locked Chuck's door behind her and did Chuck a favor. She kicked it in. The door frame split, and the door swung open. Chuck would receive no embarrassing questions about how she got his combination.

Out in the hall there was a slight haze in the corridor that probably only she could see. She could smell smoke coming from the north stairwell. The fire door leading there was flashing its red fire-warning lights. The scene behind its rectangular chicken-wire window was white and opaque. The door was radiating brighter than the heat vents.

She sensed that most of the civilians had taken the stairs. The floor felt empty. The occasional apartment door hung open, and a few stragglers were heading for the other stairwells.

She'd wanted to take out the hit squad, not torch the building.

Evi hated explosives.

She hung back by the unusable exit until the last of the civilians filed away. She wanted to melt in with the civilians and evacuate out the stairs. But it was doubtful she could get by the cops before they realized her part in this chaos. Not to mention that there were at least a half-dozen felonies sitting in her backpack.

Her internal clock told her it was five-ten. The cops would be around the base of the building trying to figure out exactly what happened. The fire-rescue people would be here as well. Probably headed up the north stairwell. She hoped that if there *was* a team five, they had the sense to bug out when the hit went sour. A shoot-out in the lobby between dogs and the NYPD would complicate things for the fire fighters.

Once the floor felt empty enough, she went to the elevator shafts.

She pulled on a pair of black leather gloves as she stood in front of the chromed doors. Then she shoved her fingers into the gap and pushed the doors open. No elevator. The elevator for this shaft was home on ground level, with a dog on top of it.

Evi took some climbing line out of her backpack, hooked a carabiner to the carbon-monofil-strengthened belt on her jumpsuit, looped the line through, and hooked the end of the line to a strut inside the shaft. She tossed the rest of the line down the shaft and watched it unravel. The rope hit bottom without snagging on anything. She started rappeling down the elevator shaft.

She hit floor five and heard the gunshots and the screaming downstairs. There *was* a team five, and it was engaging the cops.

Pretty soon the SWAT team would arrive.

She landed on top of the elevator and looked down at the dog. Little blood, but quite definitely dead. This was going to be the last body they found, so she gave herself a chance to search this one. Ten minutes, tops. She already knew how he was outfitted. She wanted to know what else the dog carried. No wallet, no ID, but she didn't expect any.

The dog didn't have much. He had one ramcard, black and unmarked with the exception of a long number on the top edge. She pocketed it.

The dog also carried cyanide capsules. She let out her silent laugh again.

Ten minutes, her time was up. The gunshots were becoming more sporadic. From the sound, the dogs had a habit of spraying automatic fire. They were probably running low on ammo. With that thought, she spent an extra ten seconds retrieving the dog's weapon and a few clips. The Mitsubishi was a decent gun, and after removing the jumpsuit and the rope, she had room in the pack for it.

She kicked the remaining loop of rope off the top of the elevator and into the neighboring shaft. The elevator there was still stopped at the penthouse, so she could see all the way down to the water that collected in the shaft below the third sublevel.

She lowered herself over the side of the elevator, more dangling than rappeling now, toward the foul-smelling, stagnant water. Even in such a high-class place on the Upper East Side, she could see rats, real ones, small sleek and black, swimming in the muck down there. It didn't bother her much. She used to be squeamish, but that was before they nuked Tel Aviv.

She rested her feet on a girder that crossed the shaft a few centimeters above the water. It was slick footing. The girder was covered in brown slime that smelled of rotten algae. Evi unhooked herself and left the rope. She drew the Mishkov, sans extension, from the back-pack and listened at the door. She heard only the faint echoes of the chaos in the lobby.

She shoved her left hand into the gap and pushed the left side of the elevator door open, using the right half for cover.

The garage was empty of people, human or nonhuman. Evi knew it as soon as the door slid open. Only empty ranks of expensive metallic-painted cars. No odor except for the faint ozone-transformer smell from the cars and a slight smell of smoke. Evi rolled out of the shaft, still expecting to be shot at. Nothing, but she couldn't count on it to last.

She had a brief unprofessional thought about her Porsche. She didn't go in that direction. If it wasn't wired to explode, it certainly had a tracking device in it. In any event, the sniper would start pumping shots into the car the second it showed on the street.

She headed for the far end of the parking garage. In the far corner, across from the entrance to the garage, there was a manhole in the concrete. That was what she was heading for.

The lights didn't reach far back. That entire end of the garage was swathed in gloom. Evi's eyes adjusted to the darkness as she moved toward her destination. As she left the influence of one light, another light began to resolve itself.

A sleek, metallic-blue General Motors Maduro sports coupe was parked back here. The power plant was emitting a barely visible infrared glow. It must have been operating no more than fifteen minutes ago.

And it was parked on the manhole.

She got unreasonably angry. She put her gun away and punched the driver's side window of the low-slung sports coupe. The plastic safety window cracked and collapsed into the car in hundreds of small pieces. The shock of impact started the aching in her overworked shoulder.

The garage echoed with the piercing sound of the Maduro's car alarm. That was a little much. The high-frequency resonance of the alarm made it feel like her enhanced ears were bleeding.

She pulled the parking brake, shifted the car into neutral, grabbed the wheel, and started pushing. Her first intent was simply to move the car off the manhole, but the alarm got to her. She ran down the center of the garage, pushing the coup down a gentle incline. She let go when the Maduro was going at a fair clip.

Right toward her own car.

She hit the ground as the coupe crunched into her Porsche. A bomb was set off by either a proximity or a vibration switch. The explosion killed the Maduro's alarm and set off every other one in the garage. She heard pieces of the black Porsche fall by her and skate across the floor. She looked up in time to see a momentary ball of flame engulf three cars.

The sprinklers came on.

Someday she was going to have to control her anger. But while she had wasted the Maduro, she had also saved the innocent bastard who would have gotten too close to her Porsche.

She had to vanish quickly now, before the firemen got down here to clean up the mess. She ran back to the manhole, hooked two gloved fingers in two separate holes and lifted the metal cover. She set it down, jumped into the darkness, and pulled it shut after her.

A nice thing about Manhattan, in her situation, was the fact that if you wanted to get from point A to any point B, you could do it underground. There was more architecture buried under Manhattan than there was under Jerusalem.

The manhole was access for ConEd, AT&T, Mann-Sat, and a few hundred other data companies to the main comm trunk into the building. She landed in the concrete tunnel and ran, being careful not to slip on the scum of ice that lined the bottom of the concrete tube.

It was five twenty-five. She had been awake nearly an hour. She ran down the comm tunnel, trying to piece things together.

It was obvious that the mercs weren't trained as a hit squad. Their vests and their tendency to spray their weapons made her think that they'd been an infantry unit. Maybe special forces trained for heavy armed resistance, not stealth, not hit-and-run.

Well-trained, expensive, and not what she would send in for an assassination attempt.

The sniper was a different story altogether. If she had stopped moving under the stare of that gun, she'd be dead. If the sniper had been alone, she'd be dead. If she hadn't broken routine by starting her workout a half-hour early, obviously before the sniper had reached position, she'd be dead.

Evi didn't like those kinds of ifs.

She stopped under a grate that was probably three hundred meters away from her entrance. She could hear, echoing behind her, sounds of commotion in the parking garage, probably firemen.

She climbed up a few rungs in the side of the tunnel and pushed the grate up and to the side with her right hand. She winced a little. The strain from the 250-kilo repetitions was getting to her.

The grate was padlocked to a bolt in the concrete, but water and corrosion had done most of her work for her. The bolt came loose from the wall.

She came out into a recess under the subbasement of the peeper's building. She was playing a dangerous game here, but she wanted to know who was trying to erase her. She gently replaced the grate, so, she hoped, the firemen and cops wouldn't hear.

She now stood in a rectangular concrete recess in the floor of the peeper's basement. The walls next to her snaked with cables of every description running from the tunnel to just under the level of the basement floor. To get to the basement proper, she had to push up against a white enamel panel that roofed the recess.

This panel was unlocked, and it levered up with a hydraulic hiss. Evi crawled out and closed it behind her.

This basement was cleaner than the one to her building. Stark white modular panels were everywhere. Air-conditioning, communications, heating, power, everything was behind square panels that were flush with the walls. All of it sat in a cavernous room indirectly lit by soft fluorescents hidden near the tops of the walls.

The elevator was easy to find. It was a newer maglev design, and the gigantic toroidal magnet housing filled half the basement. The elevator door was recessed nearly two meters inside the outer wall of the magnet.

There wasn't a keypad. So Evi called "Up?" in the hope that the elevator was voice activated. It was. The green up arrow lit above the door.

The elevator hushed into place with a tiny whoosh. The games she'd played in the shafts across the street wouldn't work here. No cables. No real shafts.

"Twenty-four," she said as she walked into the cylindrical elevator.

Ding. It heard her. The elevator's response had a slight English accent. "Going up."

Once she got to his floor, she'd be able to find the peeper's room. She would smell the blood.

She felt a brief two-G acceleration, and an even briefer deceleration. The doors slid open on a plastic-white corridor. The carpet was a stain-resistant splatter-brown pattern that made the walls appear whiter than they actually were.

She saw three cameras, covering the three axial corridors visible from her central location. She wasn't too concerned about them. This building wasn't very security conscious, as shown by her easy access. Also, the guards here would be lazy and probably paying more attention to the chaos across the street.

As she'd thought, she smelled the peeper's blood. Three doors down, she could tell. The door was ajar.

She ran up to the door and listened. Nothing. Evi wanted to take out the Mishkov, but the cameras were watching. She pushed the door open with her foot and tried to look casual for the cameras while still using the doorjamb for cover.

The blood-smell was ripe in the room. She'd plugged him in a major artery. Blood had soaked into the carpet by the chair, a pint or two, and the blinds on this side were practically painted. The British Long-Eighty binoculars lay on the ground by the chair, the slight green glow from the LCD eyepieces the only light in the room.

The peeper, however, was gone.

Evi ran in, carefully avoiding stepping in the blood, and checked all the rooms in the apartment. The apartment was empty of both bodies and furniture. The peeper's corpse was gone. Someone had to have taken it. Even if the peeper had survived, he certainly wouldn't be ambulatory. Evi grabbed the Long-Eighties. There was a ramcard in them. Maybe the peeper had recorded something useful.

She looked at the carpet by the door. She could see a faint bloody impression. A human shoe, size 14, large person, probably male. The nap was already returning to an upright position. It didn't *look* like the guy was carrying a body.

Evi felt her nostrils flare. She could barely see the blood on the brown carpet in the hall, but she could follow the smell. She broke into a silent run, bent over in a crouch, following the trail.

CHAPTER 3

She followed the trail of the peeper's blood with a growing incredulity. The building here might not be as security conscious as hers, but she did pass a dozen cameras as she followed the smell of blood down a flight of stairs and into a parking garage adjoining the building. She couldn't believe someone carrying a corpse would have been ignored by the guards.

However, they had been. The peeper's remains had made it down the stairs, up three levels in the garage, and to a parking space reserved for apartment 2420. When she reached it, there was still the ghost-smell of burning rubber. The vehicle feed was still emitting some infrared.

That was it then.

What she had to do now was get to a public comm. Everyone who worked for the Agency had a number to call when the shit got real thick. She'd memorized hers a dozen years ago. She'd never used it before.

But then she had never gotten caught with her ass hanging this far out. The Agency would have to bring her in.

She walked out the front of the parking garage with a practiced air to make it look like she belonged. The ramp was out of sight of the sniper but on a street in common with her building.

Her guesses had been good. SWAT was there, and since the gunfire had ceased, she assumed that they had mopped up the last of the Afghanis. The firemen were going in now, they'd been holding back because of the guns. She saw three unmarked Dodge Havier sedans, Bureau vehicles, parked down the street.

She turned down the street and started walking away from the scene. She wanted to stay and watch. It wasn't normal in the States to walk away from a knot of cop cars and fire engines. There was a perverse rubbernecking instinct in Americans that made anyone walking away from such a scene an object of suspicion.

She had to risk looking suspicious.

If she walked toward the chaos, like everyone else who was out on the streets this early, she would walk right under the sights of the sniper. She hoped he was going to cover her building until he was damn sure that she wasn't in it anymore.

She turned south on Fifth Avenue, crossing the street to the park side. The sniper was facing her building, the opposite direction, and on the park side of Fifth she'd be in the shadow of the peeper's building.

She wished it were a few hours later in the day and there was a crowd to get lost in.

She ran. She still had no idea if there was anyone else lying in wait for her. She had to get away and lose herself. She ran south, along the massive concrete wall that contained the park and formed the foundation of the "dome."

Only one other person was on this side of Fifth. A tall man in his mid-twenties, walking a nasty-looking, but apparently un-engineered, doberman. Before she reached the guy, she turned into the East 85th Street entrance to the park. Five steps under the dome and the temperature rose by a half-dozen degrees. Humidity stuck to her skin after the December chill in the street.

She kept running, hoping that she looked like a jogger.

Ahead, a new bridge spanned the street, and running across it was a man who instantly made her suspicious. Short, stocky, balding, gray mustache, and in his mid-forties. The build under the yellow jumpsuit showed constant conditioning; the jumpsuit was loose in the top, and Evi could swear that he was wearing a shoulder holster. It didn't look like he was jogging.

The man actually looked down and locked eyes with Evi for a moment.

But he kept running.

When she was under the bridge, she spared a look behind her. The dog-walker had just turned down 85th after her at a dead run. He was drawing a silenced automatic as he ran. The doberman was running, tongue lolling, and was halfway to her.

The embankment was too steep. She dived behind one of the pilings that held up the bridge. She could hear growling and claws clicking across concrete, getting closer.

The doberman was a trained attack dog. In some ways it was more dangerous than its intelligent Afghani cousins.

There was a crack as a bullet chipped away part of the piling behind her.

She got to her feet and listened as she pulled the SG from her backpack. The dog was almost to her position, and the guy with the gun was following. The dog reeked with excitement and blood lust. It was probably barely controllable in the best of circumstances. The guy was using the dog to flush her and give him a clean shot.

The SG cleared the pack as the doberman rounded the piling. She aimed an improperly balanced kick at the dog's nose. The contact was solid and she felt the soft tissues give, but the dog didn't back off or shy away. It should have, simply by reflex.

Instead, the doberman clamped its teeth around her right calf. The carbon monoweave kept it from breaking the skin, but it felt as if the dog were ripping her lower leg off. Evi lowered the silenced SG and fired a round into its upper chest. The bullet sprayed pieces of the dog on the sidewalk and knocked it over.

Despite a hole in its chest she could put a fist into, the dog stayed clamped on. It felt as if waves of fire were shooting up her leg. The dog was still alive and still biting down. A few more seconds of this and the monoweave would give. She lowered the barrel and wedged it between the dog's eyes. That's when she saw that the dog didn't have eyes. It stared back at her with a pair of slightly disguised video cameras.

She pulled the trigger and prayed for her leg. Parts of dog brain and circuitry flew away from her. Fortunately, the bullet missed her leg. She kicked and the dog's corpse fell off her leg, dead now. A dull ache throbbed in her calf in time to her pulse.

The dog's owner had rounded the piling and was covering her. She could now see he was armed with a silenced nine-millimeter Beretta. His face was permanently etched on her brain. Straight black hair, Japanese features, and irises so black that Evi couldn't see the pupils.

The gunman addressed her in perfect English that, had he been two decades older, she would have assumed was the benefit of a corporate education. "Do we go quietly, Miss Isham?"

He must have been kidding.

It was a contest to see who fired first, and she knew she was going to lose even as she started to raise the SG from the dog's corpse.

She was caught by surprise when the gunshot she heard wasn't the soft hammer of the nine-millimeter but a cannon shot from something forty-five caliber or better.

Most of the gunman's head evaporated. There was a soft crack as the Beretta blew away more of the dog. Evi rolled away as the gunman collapsed on the doberman. She whipped the SG around to cover the area behind her where the shot had originated.

Evi found herself covering the jogger in the yellow jumpsuit.

"Who're you?" She didn't fire, though every instinct was screaming at her to do so.

"Colonel Ezra Frey, USMC retired—"

Evi recognized the voice. *"Aerie?"*

Frey reached down and helped her up. "We better leave before the local law follows that gunshot. Too bad they don't make silencers for the old Smith and Wesson forty-four. Can you keep up on that leg?"

Evi nodded as she put away the SG. Frey holstered his weapon and started jogging off into the park behind the Museum as if nothing had happened. Evi followed, trying not to limp.

Frey had just thrown her a massive curve. He had been, she could tell from the voice, her controller in the field for the first eight years after the Agency recruited her. He was a few leaps upward in the Agency hierarchy by now. She hadn't heard his voice manning the Aerie since '53, nearly six years ago. Evi had never seen his face before, and, until now, she didn't have an alias for him other than Aerie.

Damn it all, what the hell was he doing here? He couldn't be with the hit squad, or she'd be dead . . .

It *couldn't* be a coincidence.

They jogged through Central Park for ten minutes before they spoke again. She knew they were hunting for a tail, either cops or black hats. None showed. The only people were the homeless who clogged the domed park, especially in winter. A good quarter of the ragged population were moreaus. Evi kept an eye out for heavy-combat strains, like the mercs that'd attacked her. She didn't see any. The moreaus they passed were, for the most part, rabbits and rats from Latin America.

The sky was lightening beyond the moisture-whitened

surface of the dome, and other joggers were beginning to pass them.

"What the hell are you doing here?" Evi asked when they seemed clear of eavesdroppers.

"What happened back there?" Frey asked, avoiding her question.

"A hit on me. Afghani canine special forces. At least ten mercs. One human coordinator. A sniper, didn't see him. As well as the suit with the doberman."

"Christ." Frey shook his head, whispering to himself. "A fucking shitstorm. Price was right." Before she could ask him what he meant, he asked her, "Have you called in yet?"

There was such a desperate urgency to the question that Evi didn't prod him about what David Price might have been right about. "No, I just got out of there."

She didn't trust the situation. But the agitation she began smelling on Frey was hard for a human to fake. Especially since he kept a professional front that didn't let it show in his face or his voice. "This mess, I'm sorry you're stuck in the middle of it. I'll take you in, a safe house in Queens."

They jogged along a few more minutes, past an empty playground, in silence.

After a while, Frey asked, "What's the status of the hit team?"

"The sniper's the only one undamaged."

"Damn." Frey shook his head. "You didn't get a look at the sniper?"

She shook her head no.

"Gabe, you bastard," Frey whispered to himself, subvocalizing. Evi doubted if he knew she heard him. She restrained herself from asking who Gabe was.

After they left the dome and rejoined Fifth Avenue, she asked again, "What were you doing there, just when I needed you?"

Frey ran a hand through his slate-gray hair. They were waiting for the light, even though there wasn't any traffic. "Call it an embarrassing streak of curiosity." He removed a small plastic box from his pocket and she saw that it led to an earplug in his left ear.

"Police scanner," he explained. "You and the Afghanis caused one hell of a ruckus. I was on my way to see what it was."

Curiosity, hell, she thought, *you were running full out.*

What was he hiding?

Frey lived in a condominium close to Central Park South, about ten blocks away.

She got to his apartment, fifteen floors up, and the situation was still very wrong. Having Frey show up in the nick of time strained credulity.

Frey punched in the combination and let her in. "I'm going to put the call through. We have a secure line here."

She nodded as she walked into the apartment. It wasn't as large as her penthouse, but it could've been as expensive. The Agency tended to reward performance.

The impact of the sunken living room, with its modern black lacquer furniture and glowing holo-table, was ruined by stacks of white plastic boxes scattered at random.

One was spilling Frey's underwear on a couch.

Frey weaved through the boxes and headed for a flat, compact-looking comm hanging on the wall. "Pardon the mess."

Frey paused and said, "Comm. On."

The rectangle on the wall flickered and came on. Evi heard a seductive female voice from the glowing white screen. "Your comm is active, Colonel."

The voice was an artifact of the comm, but she could swear she heard the synthetic voice lick its non-existent lips.

"Load program. Label, 'Secure Line.' Run program."

"Searching . . . I found it, lover."

Evi arched an eyebrow as Frey responded. "Love you, too."

Frey noticed her reaction and explained. "Security code requires the response." Then he shrugged as if it wasn't him that programmed the thing.

She decided that you really didn't know anyone until you saw his or her home life.

Frey looked at a text menu that had come scrolling up on the comm. He was shaking his head. "It'll take me awhile to contact the current Aerie. After I set up a meet to take us in, we won't have much time. Go in the bedroom and find yourself some protective coloring."

"Like what?"

"Cover that jumpsuit. Looks like Agency issue. It also shows off your physique. Any description of you is going to emphasize that. Not too many women built like you."

She supposed not.

She walked into Frey's bedroom and her ears picked up on his subvocalization. "Pity."

That almost made up for Chuck's reaction.

Everything still felt wrong. Too much of a coincidence. However, Frey couldn't be one of the assassins, or she would be dead. If Frey had turned, he was after something else. She'd have to roll with it.

Evi looked around the bedroom. Black and red furniture, indirect lighting, no boxes lying around. She wasn't surprised by the mirror on the ceiling. Looked like it doubted as a holo projector, damn expensive. She wondered if the room came furnished, or if it was Frey's decor.

She slid aside one closet door, and she decided that it was Frey's decor.

Neatly hung up, taking up most of the space in the closet, were women's clothes. An incredible variety of sizes and styles. Cocktail dresses, negligees, evening gowns in red and black, blue jeans that no way could fit the Colonel, a peasant blouse in paisley, T-shirts, one executive suit, skirts, it went on. Some clothes were old, way out of style, some weren't. She could smell at least six or seven different women in the closet.

She wondered if Frey was going to make a pass at her, then shook her head. Things were going too fast, and her mind was beginning to wander.

Besides, Frey was too much the pro.

She found a few items that broke up the appearance of the jumpsuit. She wasn't going to lose the monofil. It had already saved her leg, though the bruise was getting tender and hard to walk on now.

She chose a leather jacket, removing a few of the chrome chains and studs so she could achieve a semblance of stealth in it. There was also a belt in the closet with a brushed-steel death's head on it. It seemed to go with the jacket. Lastly, she undid the velcro tabs that held the jumpsuit's integral sneakers on and replaced them with a pair of engineered-leather boots. The boots were black, like everything else she'd chosen, and had a fringe at the top.

She considered pulling one of the pairs of jeans over the monofil, but she didn't want to restrict her movement that much.

She wished Frey was using the voice interface in the other room, secure communications or not. She wanted to know what he was doing.

There was a full-length mirror in the door to the bathroom. She appraised the look for verisimilitude. She had to admit that little else in the closet would match the way her hair got tousled. With the jacket, the tangled wind-dried look seemed intentional. She ran her fingers through her hair as she tested the jacket for mobility. The jacket wasn't a perfect fit, but it didn't catch her arms. That was good. Some clothes looked like they fit her until she tried to flex her arms and wound up splitting the seams on the arms or the back. She zipped the jacket up and had to stop halfway up her chest. She had small breasts, but they were on well-developed pectorals.

While the jacket hid the physique of her upper body, the formfitting jumpsuit still showed her legs. She decided they weren't that noticeable. The legs of a marathon runner, but not abnormal.

She looked like a street punk or an art student.

She reached under the jacket and zipped open a specially tailored pocket in her jumpsuit, under her left arm. It became a holster. She slipped the Mishkov into it, and she slid the barrel extension into a long pocket on her right leg.

In the mirror, the jacket was tight enough on her upper body to show the bulge. She unzipped the leather to the waist, until the gun disappeared. Magazines for the Mishkov went into other pockets. The only other things she took from the backpack were a selection of false IDs, a roll of twenties, and the black ramcard she'd looted from the canine.

When she put the twenties in one of the jacket's pockets, she found a pearl-handled switchblade. She shrugged and put the money in another pocket.

She took off the shades and looked into her own eyes. Golden-yellow eyes glowed green through a slitted pupil as they looked back.

What was going on here?

She wasn't engaged in any sensitive work for the Agency. She wasn't working on anything remotely dangerous. Her job was cooking projections on the geopolitical situation and forming contingency plans. Her last "fire" assignment had been six years ago in Cleveland.

The four aliens had been sucked into the black section of the U.S. government, and the effects of that had worked themselves out a long time ago, hadn't they?

That had been the last time she'd heard Frey's voice manning the Aerie ...

Frey walked into the bedroom behind her. She replaced the sunglasses.

"Good job," Frey told her.

"What now?"

"In five minutes, six-fifteen, we'll start walking down East 60th. Between here and the Queensboro Bridge, a remote cab will pull up next to us. We get in, stay down. That's it."

Five minutes was pretty quick reaction time for the Agency. She could hear Colonel Abdel telling her to trust her instincts, and her instincts were telling her that things were rotten.

What could she do about it?

She walked back into the living room. Frey didn't follow her immediately. She glanced back and saw he had straightened out the closet of women's clothes she'd rummaged through. Frey's back was turned and he was picking up the sneakers she had abandoned. She expected him to return them, but, instead, he placed them neatly next to a pair of red stiletto high heels in the closet.

He turned and caught her looking. There was an embarrassed half-smile under his mustache. "Some people collect coins." He shrugged and stood up.

"Your shoes are a more than fair trade for Shelly's jacket."

She wondered exactly how Frey figured that. She also wondered who Shelly was. Frey closed the closet and walked toward the door where she still stood watching him.

Instinct was telling her that the situation was wrong, but instinct was also telling her that Frey hadn't turned. Instinct also told her that, once this was over, Frey *was* going to make a pass at her.

She could sense it building in the man. A civilized and very earnest lust that didn't seem to belong to somebody who was about to toss her to the wolves.

But he was still a part of what was going on, and he was hiding something.

Just before they left, he asked, "When was the last time you talked to your superior?"

"You mean the Aerie?"

"No, that's the field office. I mean Hofstadter, the man you report to now."

How the hell did Frey know that? "The week before my vacation."

"In person?"

"Yes."

"Did he seem ..." Frey seemed to search for the word. "Worried? Preoccupied?"

She thought back, but the only image she came back with was the picture of Hofstadter smiling to himself as he told her about her upcoming vacation. The plump German economist telling her how much she'd earned this, while all the time he seemed to be laughing at some private joke. She told Frey.

Frey's reaction was another subvocalization. "I should never've gone on vacation."

It had been five minutes, and Frey led her out of the apartment. He called to the elevator, "Down."

She had to confront him. She backed away from him, confident she could draw her gun faster if shit happened.

"Doesn't you being here, within a few blocks of me, strain coincidence?"

Frey seemed unconcerned. He remained facing the elevator door, tapping his foot. "The Agency tries to spread their agents around, but I'm on vacation. If I were on duty, I wouldn't be anywhere around—"

"*I'm* on vacation." Evi backed a little farther down the hall. There was an emergency exit to her immediate right, next to the bank of elevators.

Frey stopped talking.

"They hit me in my new penthouse—"

Frey turned to face her. "I'll clear this up when we get to the safe house."

Evi began to reach for the door.

Frey took a step toward her. "I need your help—"

The elevator doors opened, releasing the overpowering smell of human blood.

Frey turned toward the elevator and said, "Oh, shit!"

Evi dived at the door to the stairs, screaming at Frey to run. Not because of the smell of blood, but because the lone occupant of the elevator wore a familiar face.

Somehow the peeper had survived.

CHAPTER 4

Evi was on overdrive, rolling out into the stairwell to the sound of gunfire. She was still figuring out what she had seen.

The peeper had been in the elevator, wearing a blood-soaked trenchcoat. As the elevator doors opened, he had swung a Vindhya 10-Auto out from under his coat.

The Vind Auto was Indian make, a ten millimeter submachine gun. It could empty a fifty-round clip in under two seconds. No one made a silencer for it.

She never saw Frey move. He was a long time removed from the field. He had long ago been promoted to command and control. High enough up in the Agency to be far removed from the danger. His reaction was too slow, much too slow.

The fire door closed behind her, muffling the jackhammer spray of the Vind. She concentrated on running as fast as she could while pulling the Mishkov out.

She started going down, but she could hear boots on the concrete steps below her. She could smell at least one canine.

Damn it.

She started running up the stairs.

She stayed close to the wall and made five floors before she heard the peeper explode into the stairwell, yelling in Arabic. The canine was running after her. That was bad. The Afghani dogs were fast, faster than most other moreaus, as fast as Evi. She'd have trouble outdistancing one even without the bruised muscle on her calf.

She could see the shadow of the canine four floors down.

Ten more floors and she looked again. The canine's shadow was three floors away. The dog was gaining.

How the hell did they find her?

Frey turning didn't make sense. If he was working for the black hats, his own team just blew him away.

Only the canine was following her now. She couldn't hear the peeper, and she should have been able to smell him, covered in blood as he was. The peeper must be trying to get back on the elevator, to get above her and cut off her escape. Her options were rapidly diminishing. The doors out of the stairwell weren't offering much, the halls had no cover, no doors that opened into anything but dead ends. There was a good chance that the canine would catch up.

The peeper was trying to be quiet, but she heard the pneumatic hiss of a door on the thirtieth floor. The canine was closing on her; it was only two floors away by the sound and the smell, and she had no time to stop and think.

She could hear the peeper start down the stairwell.

She rounded a landing on the twenty-eighth floor and faced the peeper. From his expression, he didn't expect her to be this high up in the building yet. The echo of her Mishkov set the iron handrail resonating. She had been aiming at the peeper's head. She didn't want him getting up again.

She had to be satisfied with hitting him in the neck, under the adam's apple.

She was already passing the peeper before he fully realized he'd been shot. He was slumping against the wall, clutching his throat. As she passed him, she hooked her left hand under an armpit and pushed him down the stairs. She hoped to give the canine some second thoughts.

On the fortieth floor, the stairwell terminated in a solid red fire door.

She hoped they didn't have people on the roof.

She slammed through the door, setting off the fire alarms. She was getting sick of the sound of sirens.

She emerged on a flagstone terrace overlooking Central Park. She could hear the canine behind her, only a couple of floors away. The roof was flat with no cover for fifteen meters in any direction. Empty pool, tennis court, penthouse on the other end of the roof that she couldn't make before the canine drew a bead on her.

"Shit." The curse came out in an uncharacteristic puff of fog. She was pushing the edge of her endurance. The canine was going to have to be slowed, somehow.

Her left hand shot into her backpack and withdrew another grenade. She pulled the pin and tossed it down the stairs. She wished she had another frag grenade. In her situation it was common to wish for everything from a minigun to tactical air support. For now, tear gas would have to do.

She slammed the fire door shut while the grenade was still in the air. What now? The dog was still just going to stumble up to the other side of the door. It was only a matter of seconds.

Evi pulled the barrel extension for the Mishkov out of its thigh holster and did her best to wedge it between the door and the jamb. It didn't want to go. She forced it and heard the screech of bending metal.

Then she ran like hell toward the penthouse.

She had only gotten three meters before she heard pounding on the other side of the door, but the door stayed shut. If she was lucky it would give her enough time to get into the house and behind something.

She rounded the end of the empty swimming pool

and saw someone moving behind the French doors of the penthouse. He was in his mid-thirties, wearing an expensive-looking robe. He had the door halfway open by the time he noticed her running at him.

She reached the door and dived through the gap, tackling him. At the same time, there was the sound of tearing metal back by the fire door. Evi felt microscopic wisps of tear gas rip at her sinuses.

She had her arms wrapped around the civilian as the back of his legs hit a low-slung couch. They both tumbled over it and into a sunken living room that was the twin of Frey's. The canine opened fire as they hit the ground. The windows ripped apart behind them, and the couch started shaking from multiple impacts. She could tell the shots were going wild. Even with only a few seconds of exposure to the gas, the dog would be in sad shape.

She was thankful that the canine mercs had the habit of spraying their weapons. She waited until the dog swept his fire past the couch. When she heard windows tearing way off to her left, she whipped off her sunglasses, popped up, and braced the Mishkov on the back of the couch.

The tear gas was invisible to ultraviolet.

She took a second to aim.

The Mishkov barked once. The canine's head jerked up and to the left, as if someone had just cracked its neck like a whip. The dog fell backward, its Mitsubishi continuing to fire uselessly. The dog's body followed the motion of its neck, turning to the left and falling into a heap. Its right leg jerked, once.

The Mitsubishi stopped firing.

Evi waited for another target, but for now it seemed that the dog was it.

A sudden breeze carried away the tear gas. It brought with it the sounds of sirens and the smell of the East River. The sky to the east was beginning to lighten with the coming dawn. The light did nothing to lift the chill in the air.

It was twenty after six.

Underneath her a voice spoke in a very restrained monotone. "What do you want?"

She looked down at the civilian and revised her original age estimate. He was a well-preserved forty, maybe forty-five. His hair was colored, but not his mustache, and he kept himself in shape. She figured him as a veep for some corporation or other. A fairly important one, she thought. She could read the guy's expression and tell that he'd been in at least one exec terrorism-hostage workshop. He was following the numbers on how not to get yourself killed. She admired the guy's self-control. She could smell that he was on the verge of a panic attack.

She replaced her sunglasses and got off. She kept the Mishkov aimed at him as she backed away. "Get up."

He slowly got to his feet. The hostage training showed. No sudden moves, and he kept his hands in sight without being told. He didn't even move to close the front of his robe. Evi gave him high marks. In some situations, modesty could get you killed.

"Now what?" The same monotone, but she heard the fear resonate in the man's voice. She was pretty sure this guy expected to die.

"Do you have an aircar parked up here?" If he was really a veep, it was a reasonable expectation.

He nodded. The air was cold from the broken windows, but he was sweating.

"Company car or private?"

"Private . . . A Ford Peregrine."

The sirens were becoming louder. She wanted to go over the canine's body, but there wasn't going to be enough time to find out anything new. The sooner she got out of here the better. "Well, I am afraid that I am going to have to trouble you for a lift."

* * *

The Ford was a luxury sedan. Any aircar is a luxury item by definition. It had oversized leather seats, vat-grown wood paneling, and a nearly soundproof cab. Evi sat in the rear seat, concentrating on covering the veep with the Mishkov. The Peregrine slid into the noncommercial air corridor without any squawks over the vehicle comm, so she assumed that her veep hostage hadn't done anything stupid.

Once they hit two-hundred klicks per, shooting over Manhattan, he finally spoke. "Where are we going?"

"You have an office and the codes to land there, correct?"

He nodded. "Security will call the police. I can't prevent that."

The veep seemed to be calming down. That was good. She would prefer to avoid civilian casualties. "Just land. The rest is my problem."

The Peregrine slowed and started a slow turn toward Brooklyn. For the first time some emotion showed in his voice. "Do you know who I *am?*"

Evi shook her head. "You're someone who needs to take a humility pill."

The Ford slowed and started descending toward the blue chrome obelisk of the Nyogi tower just as a sliver of molten orange sunlight started slicing across the eastern horizon. The aircar slid in on a prepro-grammed approach and landed three levels down on the topside parking garage. No welcoming committee, and practically no cars either.

"Don't kill the engine, just open the canopy and get out."

He got out and started shivering immediately as the wind whipped his robe around. He was four hundred meters up in the open air with nothing but a silk bath-robe. She felt a little sympathy, but not much. In about ten minutes, his problems would be over. Evi had a feeling that things were just starting for her.

"Open the hood."

"But the engine—"

"Open it." He might be speaking more freely, but he remembered who had the gun. Once the hood was open, she motioned him away from the car and got out of the back seat. Her bruised leg was thankful, even though she had only spent ten minutes in the back.

She moved around to the front. With the hood up, she had to raise her voice to be heard over the flywheel. "Don't move."

He didn't.

She looked next to the flywheel housing. There was no mistaking the bright orange plastic that housed the transponder and the flight recorder. She turned the Mishkov around in her hand. Then she slammed the butt of the gun on one corner of the sealed plastic box. The shock of the impact started a throbbing in her right shoulder. She could hear a slight pop over the whine of the flywheel.

Out of the corner of her eye, she could see the veep wince.

She leaned over and saw a stress fracture halfway around the heat seal of the lid.

She braced herself and brought the butt of the Mishkov down on the opposite corner.

There was a much louder pop, and the slight hiss of pressure equalizing.

She holstered the Mishkov and pried off the lid of the housing. Once it was removed, she was greeted with a black and fluorescent-yellow warning label that announced that unauthorized tampering was a felony. The label adorned the lid of a brushed-gray metal box. Four bolts held the lid on. Each was sealed with a thin coat of clear plastic.

Evi looked at her gloves and wished she had a wrench.

She gave the veep a cautioning look as she grabbed

a bolt in either hand and turned. The plastic seal made an audible tearing sound, even over the flywheel. It took her nearly three minutes to loosen all four. Under the lid there were two panels. Red for the transponder, green for the flight recorder.

Her gloves were shredded, so she took them off. Then she reached in and pulled the handle on the red panel. It slid out easily, along with the attached circuit board. The engine died immediately.

She slammed the transponder unit on the concrete of a neighboring parking space. The board shattered with the slight smell of ceramic dust. She followed with the flight recorder. Electronic shrapnel went everywhere. She picked a small wire out of the wasted electronics.

When she reached in and jumped the socket for the transponder, there was an obliging spark and the engine resumed operation.

She turned around to face the veep. "Go."

He backed away slowly. He seemed unsure if he was getting away that easily.

"Go, call the cops before someone else calls you."

He could take a hint. He made for the elevators.

She slammed the hood shut and jumped into the cockpit. Five minutes seemed an inordinate amount of time to spend hot-wiring a car. But at least now, without a transponder, someone would have trouble tracing her movements.

Evi lowered the canopy and engaged the fans. The Ford obliged and slid out into the onrushing sunrise.

Manhattan unfolded beneath her and she dropped down between the skyscrapers. Illegally low, but not low enough to draw attention. She was safe, for a moment.

However, without a transponder, if she hit either river, NYC Air Traffic Control radar would tag her like a signal flare. She didn't want to mix it up with the NYPD. She was committing a dozen felonies by being airborne in this thing.

A cloudy-white dawn light was catching the tops of the skyscrapers around her.

She couldn't believe what had happened to her. It still made no sense. A sniper *and* the merc team?

Wait a minute ...

The realization struck her so forcefully that she shot by the U.N. Building and had to pull a tight turn to avoid shooting over the East River.

The mercs didn't want her dead. They were trying to take her alive. They went in when she was most vulnerable, and the overkill made sense if they were aiming to take her without a fight. None of the dogs fired at her, except in self-defense.

The guy with the doberman paused to talk when he should have shot her. And what he said, asking if she would go quietly, had more than one interpretation.

Abdel reminded her that the sniper *was* trying to kill her.

She turned left around one of the cranes disassembling the Chrysler Building. Scaffolding shot by underneath her as she flew through where the eightieth floor used to be.

Did the sniper necessarily have anything to do with the mercs?

Two separate hits, simultaneously, was as bizarre a coincidence as Frey coming out of nowhere to save her. Unless they were somehow related.

"What if the mercs wanted to take me alive, and, for some reason, the people running the sniper didn't want that to happen?" she asked as she pulled a leisurely loop over Union Square.

That would make sense if the sniper's timing was dictated by the mercs' operation. She had just returned from vacation, and this had been her first vulnerable moment.

That still didn't explain Frey.

Enough looping around the city. No one was following her, and the longer she stayed in the car the more likely a cop would tag her. She descended toward a parking garage near Times Square.

She'd cook the autopilot and send the car out over the ocean. Then she'd go to ground somewhere and call in to the Agency herself.

CHAPTER 5

It was bad. Evi was only sixteen, and she had never felt so alone.

She was on the wrong side of the front, and somehow she had lost her team. She hugged a crag of desert rock, and less than fifty meters away she could see an endless column of moving armor. According to the briefing, it wasn't supposed to be there. She and the rest of her team were supposed to take out a Jordanian observation post, preparatory to an air strike on a few small units of infantry.

There wasn't supposed to be any Axis armor anywhere near this position. It was supposed to be massed up north, in Lebanon.

Worse, the armor was moving. The sound of the moving tanks merged in a single deep bass note. Evi's crag resonated, and she felt the sound deep in her chest.

She hoped the rest of her strike team got a chance to use the uplink. Somehow intelligence had managed to misplace at least two divisions of Arab armor.

The armor stopped.

An infinity of sand sucked up the noise from the column. The only sound that carried to her was a radio from somewhere. It broadcast someone counting down in Arabic. For some reason, she felt an urge to look up into the moonless night sky.

A huge black glider flew in low, soundless, and incredibly fast. It was only in sight for a second or two, but she could tell, from the sloped lines of the thing, it was a stealth aircraft.

The count was on one hundred.

She told herself that air defense was going to get the damned thing.

Silently, the infantry that was accompanying the armored division took cover down on the ground or behind the tanks. The tanks themselves began to button up.

The glider was pointed at Tel Aviv, so of course air defense was going to get it. No Arab aircraft, all through the war, ever got that far into Israel.

The count was on fifty.

Evi had a very bad feeling.

Twenty.

She resisted the urge to look back to where the glider had gone.

Ten.

She felt warmth on her cheeks. She whispered to herself. "Please."

One.

There was a blinding flash of white light from the west, behind her.

She jerked awake.

She wiped off her cheek and looked around the darkened theater. Little had changed but the movie.

It was still the same overheated musk-filled dark. The atmosphere made her feel sticky. She could smell three different species and counted seven other people in the seats. Only one of them, a ragged-looking moreau rat whose fur was coming off in patches, had been there when she'd ducked in the place.

A large and slightly blurred holo screen was showing an impossibly endowed canine moreau who was loudly and sloppily sodomizing a hefty human woman who was similarly endowed in corresponding areas.

There was much rustling of fur and rippling of naked flesh.

Not all the moaning was coming from the screen, and the musty smell of fresh semen certainly didn't come from the dog.

She squinted at the screen. She could tell from the short brown coat that the dog performing up there was probably Pakistani. The way his ear was flapping, she could almost make out the tattoo that would place the dog's unit.

What the hell was she doing?

She closed her eyes and rubbed her forehead. Who cared what unit a porn actor used to belong to?

She wished she could have risked flying the Peregrine off of the island. But by now the aircar had topped out at its maximum ceiling and followed Seventh Avenue out past the Statue of Liberty. Where it should have found its rest, safe under the waves of the Atlantic.

She'd been in the porn palace for at least two hours before she had fallen asleep. She'd been waiting for the black hats, but the only thing that had caught up with her was fatigue.

That meant the NYPD, the black hats, and anyone else involved were still sorting through the mess and trying to figure out what had happened. Just like her.

She massaged her leg and winced. Her calf was beginning to swell, and she felt as if she had just run a marathon. It seemed as if someone had used a belt sander on parts of her body.

She owed her life right now more to luck than to her own skill, and if she didn't figure out what was going on, she would end up dead.

A human male was sitting two rows in front of her. He was grunting, and his seat was banging rhythmically. That was where most of the fresh musk was coming from. Wet sounds came from in front of him, out of Evi's line of sight.

She tried to tune the guy out as she thought.

Assume two teams, the sniper's team and the peeper's team. The peeper's team might only want to capture her. They could afford to hire those Afghani dogs as their front line. The Mitsubishis and the cyborg doberman showed they had access to old Japanese technology. The peeper had been speaking Japanese to someone. From the looks of things, to the guy with the doberman.

The cyborg doberman worried her. All the neural interface technologies were supposed to have been lost or destroyed by the Jap megacorps when the Chinese nuked Tokyo. That was twenty-some years ago.

The sniper's team wanted her dead, period. The sniper's team would have set the bomb in her Porsche.

That didn't explain Frey. He showed up out of nowhere. He was living too damn close to her own address. He was too unconcerned about the coincidences.

Frey had known something.

Frey had obviously had some contact with David Price. "Price was right," Frey had mumbled to himself. Price was a member of the domestic-crisis think tank she worked for. He was the one member who had deigned to meet with her socially, despite the fact that she wasn't human.

Price was a political scientist. He specialized in conspiracy theories.

And Frey was worried about Hofstadter, her and Price's boss. A German economist, of all things.

She couldn't shake the feeling that Frey knew what had happened to her. He had been running flat out to the scene. What really bothered Evi was the fact that he seemed to know what was going on, and he was the *only* one running toward Evi's building. He should have called in some Agency support before he dived in.

"Is the Agency involved?"

It came out in a whisper only she could hear over the grunts from the screen.

That was a frightening thought.

There was only one way to find out. She had to call in.

She put on her sunglasses, gathered the pack up from under her seat, and walked out of the theater and into the lobby.

The manager was sitting behind the concession stand. Huge and buddhalike, he watched her with jaded eyes. Then he bent to return his attention to the card reader in his hands.

The atmosphere under the yellow lighting was as moist and sleazy as that in the theater. A public comm squatted next to a magazine rack that held packs of garishly labeled ramcards. A sign above the rack read "NH/IS." She noticed titles like "Animal Lovers," "Lapdogs," "Morey Love," and the creative "Sex, Sex, Sex." She slipped into the half-closet that housed the comm. From the smell, the place wasn't just used for outgoing calls.

Someone had drawn a rather anatomically detailed erect penis on the screen of the comm. She didn't figure the Agency would care. She slipped in one of her false bank cards and called the emergency number.

The screen stayed blank after she gave the number. It didn't even show snow or a test pattern. Even with the dead screen, she could hear the soft electronic sounds of a connection being made.

"Aerie," a voice announced. One she didn't recognize. That wasn't suspicious in itself. The Agency rotated controllers, often without notice. It had been six years since she'd contacted the field office. Of course she'd be unfamiliar with anyone who manned Aerie nowadays.

She started with her code designation, "Bald Eagle—"

"You're on a proprietary comm channel. Where did you get this number?"

What? "This is Bald Eagle—"

"There is no Bald Eagle."

Oh, shit.

The transmission was filtered, but she heard a voice in the background. "I DL'd her data image. Cut the comm before the channel is compromised. We don't wan't any sampling of our encryp—"

There was a blue phosphor wink as the comm was cut.

The Acrie didn't know she was an operative. She *couldn't* come in.

"What the fuck is going on?"

For once, she was at a loss for what to do.

She looked out from the public comm booth and into the lobby of the theater. It was suddenly a totally alien environment. The artificial yellow light reflected off the pictures on the racks of ramcards. Contorted bodies took on the aspect of hieroglyphics. Transparent cases held devices of undecipherable purpose and origin. Evi stared at the leather-clad man perusing the "Bi,TV" rack of ramcards. He had slick leather boots that came to mid-thigh, a studded leather vest over a bare chest, a ring through one nipple, and a bulging codpiece. He resembled an inhabitant of another planet.

"Get a grip Evi." She echoed Abdel's mental voice.

What was she going to do?

Price, she thought. Frey had mentioned his name, and Price knew her. She knew his address, she could call him. Would he be home? It was New Year's Eve, of course he'd be home.

Evi called Price.

The message came back that Price's home comm was not accepting any incoming traffic.

She slammed her fist into the side of the comm in

65

frustration. The buddha manning the desk looked up from his card reader.

She called the think tank, Hofstadter's private line. The office comm would forward the call to Hofstadter, wherever he was. She was leap frogging over proper procedure, but Aerie was supposed to handle things like this. If Aerie didn't acknowledge her—

Hofstadter was in his office. Behind him was a man she didn't recognize. "Isham, what're you doing in Times Square?"

The way he said it made her suspicious. "I'm safe, but all hell's breaking loose—"

"I know, I know. Have you called in yet?"

"Yes, but the—"

Hofstadter was reddening. "Damn, damn, *damn*!"

The man behind Hofstadter leaned over and whispered into his ear. "Gabe's last report puts him ten minutes from target's position—" She wasn't supposed to hear it, but humans had a tendency to underestimate her capabilities.

Hofstadter pushed him back roughly, "Shut up, Davidson— Isham, get over here, to the think tank. We need to debrief you."

She was backing away from the comm. *Hofstadter?* Frey had said "Gabe, you bastard," when she'd mentioned the sniper. Gabe was the sniper, and her boss and this man Davidson were running him.

"Isham—" Hofstadter was saying as she backed out of the booth.

As she headed to the theater doors, she could still hear him talking. "Davidson, you idiot, the frank heard you."

Hearing Hofstadter call her a frank finally made the panic clamp on. She backed up to the doors feeling a hot iron band grip her sternum. It felt as if the world were collapsing in on her.

She could hear Hofstadter cut the connection.

She leaned against the black-painted lobby doors

and went through the relaxation exercises that Abdel had taught her. She breathed deeply and closed her eyes.

Behind her she could hear the city noise over the moaning in the theater. The door rattled with the traffic on Seventh, the workers readying things for New Year's, the sirens . . .

Sirens?

Evi opened her eyes.

Sirens were *the* ubiquitous city noise in New York, but these were getting louder, closer, and there were a lot of them. It could be anything.

But in her line of work, paranoia wasn't only an occupational hazard.

It was a survival trait.

She opened the door and looked outside. The sun was a cold white spotlight that sucked the edges off the people on the street. The rows of porn palaces seemed to go on forever with their yellow signs and ranks of almost explicit holo displays that kept showing the same five frames, over and over.

And shooting down Seventh toward her theater were three NYPD aircars in tight formation, flashers and sirens going.

She slammed the black-painted door shut. The sirens kept getting louder. It wasn't just the three cars either. She could pick out at least four more by the sound.

Gabe was supposed to be ten minutes away—

No, this wasn't the sniper.

Could the NYPD be after her, too? She didn't intend to stick around and find out.

However, Seventh was out.

Looking for an exit, Evi's gaze passed glass cabinets of dildos, vibrators, and devices less comprehensible, as well as the endless racks of ramcards.

The manager was still watching her. The volume

was peaking on the sirens, and the crowd noise was intensifying outside.

She was rapidly being cornered. She had two choices: go back into the theater or go up the stairs to the restrooms, balcony, and, presumably, an old projection booth.

The leather queen was staring at her, too.

She ran up, away from the stares. She was hoping the restroom had a window. She rounded the landing at the head of the stairs and pushed through the first door she came to.

The smell was overpowering. Five flavors of human and nonhuman excretion. She had to sidestep a drying pool of vomit on the rust-stained hexagonal tile. However, at the end of the short line of stalls, there was a small black-painted rectangular window. She made for it.

Outside she could hear the whine of feedback from someone opening the channel on a PA system.

She raised one foot and set it on a radiator that shed rust and flakes of white paint. Her nose passed in front of a piece of graffiti asking for volunteers to ride the hershey highway.

Outside she could hear a too-amplified voice "... TESTING, ONE, TWO—" It degenerated into more feedback.

With her head even with the small window she scratched some of the black paint away from a corner with her thumbnail. Taking off her sunglasses, she put an eye to the hole in the paint.

Outside, the PA system squawked, "Attention. You have five minutes to release your hostages. Throw out your weapons and come out with your hands in plain view."

She saw another window in a brick wall. It was about three meters away. She looked down, and there was already a group of cops swarming the alley below.

That was damned quick for New York. What the hell was going on?

And what was that bit about hostages?

All she knew was that one of her calls must have triggered the cops. But this response time was unheard of for the NYPD.

Unless all those squads were already there, primed and waiting for a call.

She sat down on the radiator in frustration. For the first time she noticed the row of urinals. She'd stormed the men's room.

She had five minutes to decide what to do.

The patch-balding rat ran into the restroom carrying a large bag of something. He slid in the vomit, almost fell, and ducked into a stall, all without noticing Evi.

Over and over he was saying, "Damn, damn, damn pink cops . . ."

There was a rustling sound, and then the rat started flushing.

There was ringing feedback from the police PA system. "You have four minutes, come out with your hands in sight."

If her time sense was right, the cops had just cheated her out of twenty seconds. Must have fast watches.

She took the silenced Mitsubishi out of the backpack and prayed that she wouldn't have to use it on a cop. The rat came out of the stall without his package. He saw her and threw himself on the ground, groveling.

"Don't shoot, harmless me, do nothing, don't shoot." The rat kept babbling, facedown on the filthy floor. Evi passed him and smelled the strongest concentration of flush she had been near since she'd been in Cleveland. The hallucinogen, flush, had the unmistakable smell of spoiled cherries.

As she slipped out of the bathroom, leaving the rat prostrate, she thought that it was an appropriate smell for the john in a porn palace.

Her silent laugh hit her involuntarily.

CHAPTER 6

"Okay, Evi, the good news is that real cops don't shoot human-looking people without warning."

She covered the hallway with the Mitsubishi. No one in sight. The hallway led straight through the building, with a stairway at either end. It was bathed in red half-light that nearly hid the cracked plaster. The speckled-red carpet was worn through in places to the black rubber underside. Five doors, all on her right, toward the theater. The door at the other end of the hallway had to be the women's room. The door in the center, the old projection booth. The doors flanking it must lead to the balcony.

"The bad news is, they've warned you."

She made her way to one of the balcony doors and pushed through.

She made her way down the aisle and asked herself, again, *now what*? She had a slight edge in the dark, but she wasn't trying to hold her position, she was trying to retreat.

Below her, chaos was brewing.

On the screen the Pakistani dog was spurting toward the audience, helped along by the tongues of his human partner and a female vulpine. The spectators down there weren't paying attention. They seemed to have just realized that the building was surrounded by cops.

Two humans were fumbling toward the lobby in the dark. The guy who'd been sitting in front of Evi earlier was busy trying to get his pants on. Getting up from the floor next to him was a morey fox who bore a passing resemblance to the vulpine porn actress who was now licking the semen off the dog's fur. Two human women were running down the aisle toward the emergency exits.

Of all of them, the vulpine seemed the calmest. She was dressed like a streetwalker, and Evi supposed she'd been through raids before.

All of a sudden, Evi heard a gunshot.

Who the hell was shooting? That shot was going to bring the cops down on the theater faster than the actresses were going down in the movie here.

Over the PA system, as if in response to her thought, she heard, "FIRE!"

She heard the breaking of glass from the direction of the lobby and above her.

Below, the leather queen she had seen in the lobby ran into the theater. He was waving a gun, a matte-black ten-millimeter H&K Valkyrie. What she saw of his expression made her guess he was a regular customer of the rat back in the men's room. He was screaming, "Fascist pigs! You'll never take me back!"

He fired the gun again, at the screen.

The Pakistani dog had the most explosive orgasm in cinematic history. For a split second, the image distorted, turning upside-down and backward. Then the scene flipped inside out around the bullet hole. An arc of electricity shot out from the screen and hit a chair in the front row. The colors separated, and the screen exploded.

Evi dived to the ground too late to avoid being hit in the shoulder by a flying piece of mirror.

She slowly got back up, fully intending to shoot the nut with the Valkyrie. Unfortunately, the leather queen was nowhere to be seen. She could hear him, off somewhere else in the building, threatening to bugger any cop that came within ten feet of him.

Great.

Without the holo movie, her eyes took a moment to adjust to the dark.

By then, the fox was bolting away from the smoking wall where the screen had been, and the guy with the pants was struggling to get up off the ground. The other humans had made it out already.

Outside again, she heard "FIRE!"

She heard more breaking glass.

She began to feel the telltale sting of tear gas in her nose and eyes. Her left shoulder felt warm. She looked and saw a sliver of silver metal the length of her finger sticking out of the leather. She gritted her teeth and pulled it out of her shoulder.

The tear gas was getting worse. It was only a matter of seconds before the police stormed the building. She had no desire to fight it out with a well-trained SWAT team. At the moment she felt as though she'd have problems with a fifteen-year-old kid.

She rummaged in her pack. She had been equipped with a tear-gas grenade, and she had a mask to go with it. One of the eyepieces on the compact, black gas mask had cracked with all her running around, but the seal still looked tight. Evi took off her sunglasses and put it on.

She had one grenade left, a smoker. It gave off gas that was opaque to UV and IR. Unlike the tear gas, she wouldn't be able to see through it. Neither would the cops if they were equipped with vision enhancement systems. If she dropped it, she might be able to slip somewhere unseen.

But where could she go?

The guy with the pants stumbled out an emergency exit. She could barely hear a cop outside order him to hit the ground with his hands in view.

She looked around the theater. The holo screen was a smoking hole in the wall smelling of charred insulation, gunpowder, and mercury. The walls were covered by heavy red velvet drapes. Tear gas was beginning to seep down from the gaps in a suspended ceiling.

The ceiling.

Evi dropped the grenade into the theater below and grabbed a handful of red velvet. There was a sharp pain from her wounded shoulder as she pulled herself up the wall. She tried to ignore it.

As she climbed, the theater filled with smoke. The dead-white smoke from her grenade hung heavy to the ground, building up like a fog bank. At the same time, the semitranslucent tear gas billowed in from the lobby and down from the ceiling. Soon she was enveloped in it.

The mask prevented the gas from becoming disabling, but it still felt like hell. It caused godawful itching all over her skin, especially her crotch. It drove daggers into the open wound in her shoulder, and her view out the cracked eyepiece was blurred and watery.

The white smoke from her grenade caught up to her and wrapped her in a gray fog. The smoke sucked up sound, but she could hear the muffled noise of the cops pouring into the lobby.

Her head bumped something. She looked up and saw a fiberglass acoustical tile, painted black. She held tightly to the drape with one hand as she pushed up on the tile. It gave, with a shower of black grime and a billow of tear gas. A fresh dagger twisted into her shoulder.

She pulled herself into the hole and pushed the tile back after her. It was a good thing she didn't weigh much. The skeletal armature she rested her hands and knees upon was producing some ominous groans. For a while, she didn't dare move. She just stayed still and hurt.

How long?

She could hear the cops storm in. They came in from all corners, the lobby, the fire exits, the balcony. She could tell when they hit her smoke; their movements became cautious. She could hear them talk, but between the smoke, the tile, and the mask, it was hard to make out more than a few sentences here and there.

"—ver the exits. Wait for the sm—"

"—ed and extremely dangerous—"

About half a minute, "—Bureau in five—"

The FBI? Something real big had been twigged onto her. She did a few more breathing exercises.

Where was the nut with the Valkyrie? She hadn't heard any more gunshots.

The gas was dissipating, making it easier to breathe. A lot of the itching had stopped, but her left eye was nearly swollen shut.

"—clearing some—"

"—no sign of sus—"

The voices were becoming louder. They were on the balcony directly underneath her. The tear gas was letting up, and so, by now, was her smoke. Fortunately, she had calmed down enough that her metabolism would be cutting down on her heat signature. IR enhancers wouldn't pick her up.

Evi started looking for an escape route.

"—back. Upper floors have cleared." Pause, then, "None of the terrorists seen leaving the building."

Terrorists?

"Yes, sir," the same voice responded to something she couldn't hear. "This is for *everyone,* hold your positions and wait for the Fed."

There was grumbling from at least five sources down there.

"*Orders,* damn it!" The cop didn't sound pleased. How long? Four minutes? Three?

How do you get out of a building ringed by police, in broad daylight?

Forget the building. Where could she go from here?

A light shower of plaster dust rained down on her head, accompanied by a creaking floorboard. Evi looked up at the original ceiling of the theater. There was a good reason for the suspended ceiling. The old plaster arches above her were, for the most part, crumbled and fallen away. She was looking at a study in dry rot and faulty wiring.

What was left in her pack?

Not much. Some bugging and surveillance devices, a tool kit, the peeper's Long-Eighties, a spare barrel for the Mishkov, a medkit and airhypo with a few dozen illegal drugs, and a military stun rod.

She pulled out the stun rod. She had carried one ever since that weird business in Cleveland, the business with the aliens. The rod measured a half-meter long, was dead black, and doubled as a billy club. It delivered a charge that would turn a hundred kilos of muscle to jelly for about fifteen seconds. She pressed the test button and a green LED winked at her.

The floorboard creaked, and more plaster filtered down.

This could work.

If you're totally silent, if he's not in radio contact with anyone, if you're right and no one else is up there right now . . .

Abdel, she asked her mental voice, *you got any better ideas?*

Abdel didn't.

She shouldered her pack and slowly, very slowly, raised herself into a squatting position under the creaking floorboards. She made sure to brace each foot next to one of the wires that supported the framework of the suspended ceiling. The last thing she wanted to do was try this only to end up pushing herself through in the wrong direction.

She wished she had a pair of morey ears. Her hearing was good, but the engineers could only go so far and have the ears remain human-looking. Eyes were easier to hide.

She was relying only on her hearing to place the

target, and that was very iffy. It was her one chance, and it was a slim one. She braced herself, grabbing an exposed beam with her left hand. Her fingers sank into the rotting stud that ran under the floor above her. She waited for the floorboard to creak again.

It creaked.

She brought the rod up with her right arm, putting everything she had into the swing. The rounded end of the rod hit the center of a floorboard. The board gave with an anemic crack that still ignited a shivering wave of pain all the way down her arm. The rod shredded some carpeting and kept going upward. For an agonizing half-second she feared that she had misjudged and wasn't going to hit a damn thing.

The rod hit something and there was the telltale buzz of a discharge. She caught a whiff of charred fabric as something very solid thumped to the floor above her. More plaster rained down.

She wanted to wait to hear if there would be a reaction from other cops, but she didn't have the time. She pushed two more floorboards up. They cracked much too loudly for her taste. She scrambled through the hole and the torn carpeting, wrenching her abused shoulder again. She bit her lip hard enough to taste blood.

She found herself in a dimly lit interior hallway. Sprawled on the cheap gray carpeting was a cop done up in riot gear; vest, gas mask, boots. The rod had hit the cop halfway up his inner thigh. The point was marked by a circular burn and a halfway-melted patch on his trousers. Evi withdrew the airhypo from her backpack as the cop showed signs of coming around.

The hypo was a high-pressure model that could shoot right through thin fabrics, which was good. Evi had no time to roll up a sleeve. The cop looked close to sitting up when Evi put the hypo against the stun mark and tranked the cop to high heaven.

No commotion, no pursuit . . .

No partners?

Shut up Abdel, it worked, didn't it?

Evi pulled the gas mask off the cop.

The cop was a short-haired oriental woman. Even better, the cop was about Evi's size. There wasn't time for a complete makeover, but Evi could manage the pants and flak jacket over what she was wearing. With the cop's gas mask she could pass at a distance. She hoped that would be all she would need.

She was rushing for dear life, pulling the stuff on, but she couldn't avoid seeing the giant orange "FBI" on the back of the flak jacket.

The cops downstairs were still waiting for the Bureau. What was an agent doing here?

What was an agent doing up here, alone and with no backup? She had a bad feeling about that. The agent was oriental, female, about her size . . .

Evi pulled up one of the agent's eyelids. The agent had been wearing contacts, and one had slid aside. A deep, almost iridescent, blue iris was beneath the brown contact, and there was no mistaking the reflective green retina. Evi could tell that the pupil was slitted, even when fully dilated.

Evi had always known that the Jordanian project's technology was bought from the Japanese prior to the war. However, she had never expected to meet one of her oriental sisters. The pool of her species was so small that the agent was almost certainly a blood relative.

It was just as certain that the agent was there to make sure Evi was taken out. Evi didn't know if she belonged with the peeper or the sniper, but it didn't really matter right now.

She grabbed the agent's ID. It read "A. Sukiota, Special Agent, FBI."

" 'On loan,' I bet," Evi whispered.

Evi'd been " 'on loan' " to the FBI before. There

was a good chance that Sukiota belonged to the Agency.

She recalculated the dosage on the hypo and tranked Sukiota enough to keep her out of the picture for the next six hours. Then she lowered her through the hole in the floor, carefully so the cops below wouldn't hear.

The sounds of more sirens came from outside. Must be the real FBI agents. Evi counted on a little inter-agency jurisdictional chaos to distract the players. Because, right now, there was no avoiding a blatant walk in the open.

She made it to the stairs, turned a corner, and almost bumped into a cop in full gear. Their gazes locked. She hoped that the jacket with the ID clipped to it would be enough. She also hoped that the cop didn't know Sukiota ...

Oh shit, her eyes! The cop was staring directly into her eyes. She'd forgotten about her sunglasses, and she didn't have contacts like Sukiota.

However, the cop was just staring. He didn't call out on his radio, he didn't ready his weapon, he just stared.

Evi felt a wave of deja vu crash over her. She had played FBI for the Agency before, and while in that situation it was procedure to follow the forms and pretend you were human, almost always the people you were working with figured it out. If Sukiota had been working with the NYPD for any length of time, there must already be rumors she was a frank.

It probably had yet to pass the cop's mind that he wasn't looking at Sukiota.

Evi hoped her mask muffled her voice enough. "Problem, officer?"

"No, none." He said too quickly and broke eye contact. He avoided looking at her now, keeping his eyes down toward the corridor he was watching. Better and better. Evi headed down the stairs.

Three flights she went down. She passed two more cops guarding the exits. She pretended to belong here and clamped down on the panic that was brewing inside her. The cops nodded as she passed, and she was thankful that no words were exchanged.

The stairway ended in a doorway under the marquee, to the left of the lobby exits. She looked outside and saw at least a dozen black-and-whites screwing the traffic up and down Seventh. She could pick out six snipers stationed across the street and wondered if one of them was Gabe. A half-dozen Dodge Haviers with flashers out were pulling up behind the NYPD, in some cases pulling onto the sidewalk to do so. Civilians were poking their heads out of windows, climbing onto parked cars, crowding traffic cops who were trying to keep the spectators at a reasonable distance.

Three aircars from the major NY vid news channels were hovering over Times Square, screwing the air traffic as much as the cops were screwing the ground traffic. All eyes were on the entrance of the theater, and she'd be walking out, center stage. She didn't have much time to decide what to do next. Sukiota bought her some time and protective coloring, but she might only have a few minutes before someone found Sukiota.

She went through the pockets of Sukiota's clothes, searching for inspiration. She came up with a small remote control with the GM logo on it. A host of buttons sat above an oval thumbpad. Where was the car?

Wait a minute.

She examined the control more closely. It belonged to a GM Maduro. A sports car like that was hard to miss, and no Maduro was parked outside.

She placed her thumb on the pad. If the car was anywhere around, the alarm should start going off. No alarm sounded. She suspected that this remote belonged to a metallic-blue Maduro that was now smoldering wreckage in a parking garage on the upper east side. Her hand clenched around the small remote control and she could hear plastic cracking as her knuckles whitened.

Somewhere, someone screamed.

She looked out at the commotion ringing the front of the theater. A knot of plainclothes NYPD was arguing with a similar knot from the FBI. They were standing, partially covered from the front of the theater by a SWAT van. They were all turning to look up, toward the marquee.

A cop to the rear, manning the police line keeping the civilians back, turned in response. The poor guy was nearly swamped by the crowd he was holding back. He was holding back a ten-foot line of potential riot all by himself.

She could hear the leather queen. He was the one screaming.

The snipers started to open fire on the marquee, and all hell broke loose.

The lone cop who was swamped at the thinnest part of the police line took a running step, and his chest blossomed in a spray of blood. Evi couldn't tell if it was the queen with the Valkyrie or a stray shot from the cops who were now firing unreservedly at the marquee.

The civilians moved. They were panicking. The cop who'd been shot fell over the curb, and suddenly a hundred civilians found themselves unconstrained. They wanted to go back, but there were too many of their fellows crowding behind them. They had only one direction to run.

The police line evaporated. Blue uniforms were swamped.

The leather queen either jumped or fell into the crowd.

Now or never.

Evi slipped out the door and ran for the riot and waded into the sea of leather, business suits, hard hats and fur, all the time feeling a sniper's cross hairs focused on her back.

CHAPTER 7

She ditched the FBI flak jacket somewhere in the midst of the crowd of civilians, and the gas mask ended up in a waste kiosk on 42nd Street. Evi didn't bother to retrieve the dollar or so the kiosk credited her.

The crowd returned to normal intensity by the time she reached Bryant Park. She turned off Broadway and eventually came to rest under the one remaining lucite-enclosed lion by the steps to the library. The weak noon glow from the white sky was dimming, and a few flakes were filtering down.

As she looked at the sky, three police aircars escorted a helicopter, going north, headed for the commotion up by Times Square.

She sucked in gasps of air, trying to relax, to think.

The only thing she could think about was how much her leg and her shoulder hurt.

Every instinct was calling out for backup. She needed to come in out of the cold. But there was no longer an "in" to go to. A large part of Evi's carefully structured universe had fallen into a black abyss, and suddenly *everywhere* was hostile territory. It was the Axis invasion all over. She was sixteen again, cut off, abandoned.

She noted the way a few passing civilians eyed her and realized that she had better get inside somewhere and clean up. Evi looked up at the library and wondered if, like the Mishkov, the Mitsubishi in her bag was designed not to set off metal detectors.

She decided not to risk it. The Mitsubishi SG found its resting place in a storm sewer running under Fifth.

Ten minutes in the library's public washroom helped her looks, if not how she felt. Evi stuck her head in a sink and let cold water run over the back of her head and the left side of her face. She had no idea how much her left eye had been hurting from the gas until she flushed it out. It was a relief just to rest her cheek against the cold porcelain. For a few minutes she didn't care if anyone tried to jump her.

No one did. The only people who passed through the bathroom were a pair of bouncing blonde teenagers who babbled around her, apparently doing their best to ignore the leather-clad woman with her head in the sink.

When the girls left, she raised her head and looked at herself in the mirror. Her left eye was bloodshot and puffy, and a circular patch of red irritation marked where her gas mask had pressed into the flesh.

With her eyes squeezed partway shut, she could see her Asian heritage.

She bore a very close resemblance to Sukiota. So much so that the Semitic cast to her features seemed to be briefly overshadowed.

It was unsettling, even if they *were* sisters. They were closer than any blood relatives outside identical twins. Evi knew of at least two living women of the same heritage with whom she shared a DNA signature.

The heritage was Hiashu Biological. Specifically, "General Purpose Human Embryo—Lot 23." The last commercial strain prewar Japan ever produced.

She removed the leather jacket and partially unzipped the monofil jumpsuit. Her shoulder had bled enough to make pulling the jumpsuit away painful. She grimaced as she pulled down the collar, revealing the wound behind her left shoulder. She saw in the mirror that the puncture was small and shallow.

Splashing some water over it cleaned the blood and revealed a dark purple bruise that was spreading down her back. Looking at the bruise reminded her how much her leg was aching.

She dressed the wound with an antibiotic patch from her medkit. Good thing the damage was minor. She wouldn't be able to fix a bullet wound in here.

She didn't even want to think about getting a major injury in the field.

She zipped herself up, replaced the jacket, and put on her shades.

Now she looked more the street kid than the art student.

She walked out into the hall, limping, soft leather boots squeaking on the new marble. Muffled construction sounds were emerging from behind white plastic panels on the wall opposite the bathroom. It had been nearly six years since the Bronx Bensheim clinic was firebombed, and here they were, still repairing the damage from the moreau retaliation.

'53 had been a bad year all around.

She smiled to herself. If it hadn't been for her work in Cleveland, it could have been a lot worse.

But her leg hurt, and she wanted to sit down.

She found a comm booth in sight of the front door and slipped inside. It was much nicer than the comm at the theater. It still had the new factory smell about it. The booth was soundproofed behind its tinted glass and provided a contoured bucket seat. The lighting was low, and the plastic was a soft charcoal-gray, not the more common glare-white.

Just sitting down made her feel a lot better.

The booth gave her a much needed sense of privacy, despite her paranoid thought that someone at the Agency might be using the Langley mainframes to leach the comm signals from Manhattan for her image. That kind of extravagance would be unlikely. The cost would be hard to explain down in Washington, even with a black budget. Besides, this comm's primary use was to access the library database. She doubted her picture would be out on the net unless she tried to access an outside line.

The comm began flashing a green message at her. It wanted her to insert her card and choose a function. Damn, it wouldn't let her sit there and think. She picked out one of her false ID cards from her pack. The one she'd gotten herself, without Agency intervention. Eve Herman's existence was shakier than the personae created by the Agency, but Eve didn't exist in any file on any member of the intelligence community, foreign or domestic.

Eve logged onto the library database and began an interminable search on the incredibly large subject of "Japan" while Evi leaned back and thought about why she had become such a prize target.

The Agency had turned on her. Frightening, but not unheard of. It wasn't spoken of in the open, but the stories did circulate. The Agency decided someone was a liability, and something happened to them. They stepped onto a transport that never landed at its destination, or they had an appointment with a superior and never returned. Somehow, their mail gets forwarded to some anonymous post office databank, their furniture gets moved to some small dead town in northern Nevada, their cover identities quit their jobs because of vaguely defined "family problems," and their lives dry up and are forgotten.

The past seven hours didn't fit the Agency's M.O. for "retirement." That was despite the fact that her boss, Hofstadter, was the hand behind the sniper. The Agency wouldn't bother assassinating agents in the field when they could simply be ordered to attend their own execution.

Unless there was a time factor and they had to do it now, this instant.

The mercs must have forced their hand. If she was

right and the sniper was there to prevent the mercs from taking her alive, it would almost make sense. A sniper was much more the Agency's style. They didn't want her taken and would kill her to prevent it. That sounded like Agency thinking.

That didn't explain why she couldn't call in.

It also didn't explain Frey. Frey was supposed to take her in, but Aerie didn't acknowledge her existence anymore.

Whoever Frey talked to, it wasn't Aerie.

The screen was flashing at her. The comm had stopped its search at half a million items. It wanted more qualifiers. Eve told it to drop any references prior to 2053.

The Aerie didn't recognize her code. That meant someone had nuked her Agency file.

Why bother?

There was something else going on here.

Then there was A. Sukiota. Sukiota was definitely an Agency creature. Sukiota had been on her heels twice already—once in the theater, once during the chaos in Evi's building, presuming that it was Sukiota's Maduro that Evi had blown up. Sukiota was working with the NYPD, if not running the show.

Both Sukiota and the cops were after her. Evi could understand the cops, but why Sukiota? The Agency already had one sniper after her, Gabe. Were Sukiota and Gabe the same person?

The comm flashed at her.

There were a hundred thousand references to Japan post-53. For the first time she really looked at the search she was running. She had thought she was just throwing the comm into a random search to let her think. Now her choice seemed less than random.

Japan.

The peeper was speaking Japanese to somebody, probably the man with the doberman. The Afghani mercs were armed with Mitsubishis. Evi had blown away a dog, a generic un-engineered doberman that had hardwired bio-interfaces.

What did Japan, old Japan, have to do with her? She was only ten years old when Tokyo was nuked and the Chinese overran the island. But, if anything, the Japan that was touching her now was the prewar Japan, the techno-colossus that had been gone for more than two decades, not the modern little client state that no one ever heard about anymore.

Her job barely touched that part of the world. At the think tank, that was more Dave Price's area. His doctoral thesis was on the U.S. nonintervention in the Pan-Asian war. It was definitely Hofstadter's area. His main area of study was Pacific Rim economics.

In the dozen years she'd worked for the Agency, she'd had only one operation where Japan was even a small part . . .

2053, Cleveland. Neutralizing Hassan Sabah.

Her last "fire" mission.

The last time she'd heard Frey manning the Aerie.

And Hassan Sabah was an Afghani canine assassin, just like the mercs that had overrun her building.

Could all that be a coincidence?

"Hell, no."

She keyed the search to concentrate on Japanese Nationalist activity. That had been Hassan's last known affiliation before he smuggled himself into the States. Evi had tracked Hassan to Cleveland during the steaming August of '53 and had opened a can of worms that had led to the indictment of twenty-three congressmen and the resignation of fifty more.

As far as she knew, that can of worms had nothing to do with Japan. In fact, it originated about as far from Japan as you could get. A few light-years at least.

As far as she knew.

There was a knock at the door to the booth, and it was all Evi could do to keep from drawing her gun. She looked and saw a young sandy-haired man leaning over and smiling through the tinted window. His name tag said his name was Paul. She opened the booth.

"Yes?"

"Sorry, miss, but because of the holiday the library is closing early."

She looked behind him, at a large digital clock hanging over the main doors. The clock was part of the reconstruction and looked a century out of place in the building. The time was 2:53.

"Thanks for the warning."

"No problem. There's an announcement over the PA, but you can't hear it in these things."

The guy still hovered there, smiling. She allowed herself to smile back.

She had the comm download all the Japanese info onto a ramcard while Paul watched. "You know, I wrote my thesis on the Chinese occupation."

She stepped out of the booth and stretched. She tried not to wince at the pain it triggered in her calf and shoulder. "Very interesting, but it's not polite to read over people's shoulders."

Paul gave a lopsided shrug and broadened his grin slightly. She could smell a little lust and some well-hidden nervousness about the guy. "Ask me something."

"What?"

"Ask me about whatever you're searching for," Paul hooked a thumb back at the comm booth.

This was getting a little annoying. "I'm not even sure what I'm looking for."

"Then ask me something at random, and I'll leave you alone."

Why not? "Tell me about Japanese Nationalist activity in '53."

Paul rubbed his chin. "Busy year, but then you probably knew that. Five—no, six—high-level political assassinations. Started with Yang Peng, assistant political director in Yokohama. The NLF hired a profes-

sional assassin, took an antitank rocket to his limo."
That had been Hassan's work, Evi thought. "That was
in March. A ground-to-air missile shot down an Air-
bus ballistic shuttle on takeoff. That killed the Chinese
foreign minister and about a hundred tourists. That
was in Shanghai in May. The director of the State
Office of Science and Technology along with a few
dozen Chinese scientists and engineers were killed by
a suicide car bomb during a Tokyo excavation—"

Scientists and engineers? "What were they doing?"

Paul smiled. He seemed happy that he had finally
piqued her interest. "The Chinese government never
made an official statement, but their State Office is
mostly known for rooting through whatever was left of
the Japanese technological base for their discoveries. I
did some research at the time, and the location of the
explosion is around where the Japanese space agency
warehoused some of their prototypes—"

"Thank you." Yes, it was much more than a coincidence. She turned to go.

"You're welcome." She didn't hear Paul follow her,
and for that she was grateful.

"Hope to see you again."

She reached the door, sighed, and turned around.
"No, you don't." She slipped outside, not waiting for
Paul to respond.

She walked back out on the street, wading through
the press of people. She knew the pieces fit together,
but she didn't know how. What was clear, however,
was that her involvement in breaking up that cell in
2053 was the reason behind what was happening to
her. She didn't know exactly why, but there were too
many parallels between now and five years ago.

Everyone was after her because of the aliens.

She pushed through the crowd, uncaring. She forced
her way past a growling moreau jaguar. She ignored
him. She was barely aware of where she was going,

until a chain-link fence adorned with warning signs stopped her.

She looked up and found herself facing the scaffolding enveloping the truncated tower of the Chrysler Building. The demolition of the tower had halted for the holiday, and she'd been stopped by the fence that crossed 42nd. The Chrysler Building was the only thing standing in a city block of plowed rubble.

It looked like as good a place as any to go to ground.

She scanned the crowd around her on this side of the fence. Scurrying civilians were doing their best to ignore her, the homeless moreaus huddled in the doorways and into each other. New Yorkers all, and not a cop among them. She might as well have been alone.

She grabbed a handful of fence and hauled herself up to the top. The barbed wire was only a deterrent. It wouldn't stop anyone who took a little care in climbing over it. Once she was over the wire, she vaulted into the construction site. None of the civilians commented or looked in her direction.

She limped toward the surreal monument of the Chrysler Building over a small mountain of broken concrete and powdered stone. The land was cleared for half a block in every direction, as if the city had drawn back in rejection of one of its oldest skyscrapers.

She made it to the base of the building, weaving through a dark jungle of scaffolding to reach the doorway. She didn't go inside. She just sat down in the entranceway, giving a casual glance at the graffiti that covered the exterior for three stories.

"Off the pink," read one sentiment. It was a morey phrase. "Pink" was morey slang for human.

It reminded her of Cleveland, and the aliens.

Evi had handed the aliens to DC and Langley.

It still frightened her. No one in the community had

seemed to have had any official knowledge of the cell that had been based in Cleveland. She had stumbled on it while tailing Hassan.

The mission had started out as a simple game of "bag the terrorist." But the people Hassan killed in Cleveland hadn't been killed for political reasons. They'd been killed because they'd known about the aliens. Hassan had eliminated dozens of people to cover up the existence of a conspiracy buying influence in Washington.

She remembered sitting in her Porsche, waiting outside a darkened office building, headquarters to Midwest Lapidary Imports, fuming at the Aerie. Even then, before she realized the origin of the conspiracy, the scope of what she'd uncovered boggled . . .

A cell controlled by some foreign agency operated behind this corporate front and bought billions of dollars worth of influence in Washington.

Congress, the Judiciary, the White House, nothing had been immune.

There were eight thousand employees working for Midwest Lapidary who only existed as bits in some databank. At that point the latest info was that the data trails led back to Langley. As if the CIA could finance something like that. It had been just another fictional artifact engineered by the people in charge of Midwest Lapidary.

If they were people.

Even then, she wasn't sure if they *were* people. She had seen the corpse of one of the creatures that ran Midwest Lapidary. The being had been called a frank, but it was no frank she had ever heard of. She had an encyclopedic knowledge of human-engineered species, and the corpse of John Smith found no home there. The corpse she had seen had been 300 kilos of white hairless blubber that had been only roughly molded into the shape of a man.

And the corpse had melted.

Nothing she had ever heard of did that.

Smith had been killed by a stun rod, so her team had been so equipped. However, she wanted to try and get these things alive. She had a lot of questions. For that reason, the team also had trank guns.

But God knew what a trank would do to a design so exotic.

And the Aerie had just told her to pack it in.

She had a specimen jar on the dashboard. Inside swirled a milky-white liquid, somewhat more viscous than water. A smell of bile and ammonia hung about it. The rest of Smith's "remains" had been at a lab being analyzed.

Hassan had bombed the lab where the specimens had been stored. It was a total loss. All that was left of Smith was the few ounces of liquid sitting on Evi's dash.

But since Hassan was dead now, Aerie seemed unconcerned. Hassan had been the mission.

She had found that a foreign government was in at least partial control of nearly a hundred Congressmen, and the Agency was happy to pack it in now because a local private investigator threw Hassan off the top of a parking garage.

In fact, her new orders were to track down that damned PI. Nohar Rajasthan, a 300-kilo, two-and-a-half meter tall moreau tiger. A descendant of computer-evolved Indian special forces, all fur, teeth, claws, and muscle. If he had any formal combat training, he'd be scary.

As far as she was concerned, that was pointless.

Nohar just had the bad luck to be investigating Hassan as well. He had uncovered the same mess she had. She had thought he was safely under wraps at the hospital. It wasn't the tiger's fault Hassan bombed the place.

Apparently, after the explosion, there was a battle royal between Nohar and Hassan, after which Nohar disappeared. The Agency was still operating under the assumption that Nohar had links to radical moreau organizations.

She was still fuming at the Agency when the comm buzzed her. "Agent Isham here."

"Isham? This is Agent Conrad. We found one of the people you've been looking for. Alive and well."

"Who?"

"Ms. Stephanie Weir, from the Binder Senate campaign—" Weir was the one executive officer of Binder's staff that Hassan hadn't killed.

As far as Evi knew, Nohar was the last person to have contact with her.

There was a muffled cursing and a female voice. "—give me that. Agent Isham?"

"Ms. Weir?"

"Nohar said that the MLI office building is a front, that they're at NuFood—"

"What?"

"—he said they're based on dextro amino acids. He's gone there."

Sitting at the base of the Chrysler Building, Evi remembered that moment clearly. The moment when she knew. She had pulled out on to the street by the time Weir had reached the word "gone." At the time, she thought the ideas running through her head were insane.

But it had made sense.

All those billions had been spent in a largely successful effort to erode the technical base of the United States. Especially in defense and space. The phony corporation of Midwest Lapidary was backing dozens of senators that would scuttle NASA's deep-space probe project once it came to a vote that session.

And John Smith didn't match any gene engineering project that Evi had ever heard of.

And Weir had just said Nohar Rajasthan believed they were based on a mirror-image biology.

"Agent Isham? What's that *mean?*" Weir had asked.

Nearly everything alive on earth was based on levo amino acids. A creature based on a dextro amino acid biology wouldn't be able to metabolize any food on the planet. Except the exotic dietary foodstuffs that NuFood produced. For the first time, Evi had realized that these were things that hadn't been born on this world.

Evi's response had been, "You don't want to know."

Six years later, she still shivered at that realization. She was more frightened of the idea of otherworldly beings manipulating the government than she could ever be of the Agency.

And, since the library, she had realized there'd be other cells. The aliens, wherever they came from, were interested in preventing anything from Earth interfering with "their" worlds. However, the Untied States hadn't been the only nation planning interstellar probes.

Prewar Japan had been much farther along. So had prewar India.

There *had* to be cells in Asia. If the Nippon Liberation Front bombed a Tokyo excavation of space-probe prototypes, it was a good bet that they were backed by the aliens.

There were two players she was running from.

The sniper was Agency material.

Could it be the NLF that was behind the others? They employed Afghanis and had access to old Jap technology, and they had a possible link, though circumstantial, to the aliens.

But why her, and why now? It wasn't as if she were the only one who . . .

Evi realized that Nohar was the only non-Agency person who knew about the aliens.

CHAPTER 8

The last time Evi had seen Nohar, he had been in a hospital bed. She had dug him, and the four aliens, out from under a warren under NuFood. He had been in sad shape, and the Agency more or less forgot about him. She'd never emphasized Nohar's role in the whole mess.

When she felt safe, and the night had wrapped around the city, she left the wreckage of the Chrysler Building and walked to a public comm. It took Eve Herman nearly ninety minutes and two hundred dollars to find Nohar Rajasthan again.

All the time Evi was thinking of aliens.

Her thoughts kept returning to the aliens' lair under the NuFood complex. Organic shaped tunnels of polished concrete that had smelled of sulfur, burning methane, and aliens. The aliens emitted an evil bile-ammonia odor that she would never forget. The four creatures she'd captured made her think of white polyethylene bags of raw sewage.

She finally found Nohar at some New Year's Eve party in Hollywood. On the other coast it was seven o'clock. If anyone was interested in Nohar, they hadn't done anything about it yet.

What she hadn't anticipated was how difficult getting to talk to the tiger would be, even when she found out where he was. It had been a long time since she had dealt with the real world.

The blonde who answered the comm was stoned

out of her mind, and it took Evi nearly fifteen minutes to explain to her that the call wasn't for her. At which point the comm was abandoned, leaving Evi with an oblique view of somebody's expensive chrome living room filled with nearly equal numbers of moreaus and humans.

She had nothing better to do, so she waited for somebody else to answer her call while she looked out at Third Avenue expecting the city to collapse in on her.

Both snow and traffic were getting worse.

Occasionally she shouted to get the attention of somebody moving close to the comm. Eventually, that worked. A pudgy lepine moreau noticed her yelling at the comm. Third generation, she thought. A Peruvian rabbit, probably a mixture of a half-dozen strains. But he didn't look stoned.

"Hello?"

Finally. "I need to talk to Nohar Rajasthan."

The rabbit cocked one drooping ear toward the comm. *"What?"*

Between the traffic on her end and the party on the other, she had to shout. "Nohar Rajasthan, I need to talk to Nohar *Rajasthan!"*

The rabbit nodded. "Rajasthan, right."

The light at the end of one tunnel at least.

She watched the rabbit melt into the party and waited for Nohar to show up.

She didn't expect the black-haired woman who ended up sitting in front of the comm a few minutes later.

"Stephanie Weir?"

The woman grimaced and read Evi's alias off the screen. "I know they don't recognize it in New York," Stephanie shouted over the party, "but the name is *Rajasthan,* Ms. Herman."

Evi should have noticed the ring on her finger. "I wanted to talk to your husband."

Stephanie smiled. "That was good. I didn't even notice a wince when you said that."

Evi sighed. "Can you get him for me?" She decided that Stephanie was one of those women who became excessively catty when she'd had a few drinks.

"No."

Abdel, what do I do when I can't throttle her? "It happens to be an emergency."

Stephanie nodded. "Matter of life and death, do or die, now or never—You'd be surprised how common that is, Eve. They're *all* emergencies. But it's New Year's. You're going to have to wait until Thursday."

There was a broad smile on Stephanie's face. She was obviously enjoying what she was putting her through.

"It can't wait—"

"Then I'd say another detective is in order."

"Mrs. Rajasthan, there's a good chance that someone is going to try and kill your husband if you don't shut up and listen to me."

Stephanie lost the smile. "You look—"

Evi wanted to punch in the screen. "You look! Tell Nohar his life is in danger—" Evi whipped off her sunglasses. "*Get him!*"

Stephanie looked as if she was about to make another comment. Instead she just stared at the comm, color draining out of her face.

Nohar had told her. Probably a long time ago, but Nohar had told her. Evi could read it in her face. She had never met Stephanie face-to-face, but she had made an impression on Nohar. Any description he gave would have included her eyes.

Stephanie backed away from the comm. "Damn," she whispered as she pushed back into the crowd.

Now she was getting somewhere.

It took less than a minute for Nohar to get to the comm. The tiger was an impressive figure even on the comm's small screen. The party was blocked by a wall

S. ANDREW SWANN

of yellow and black fur, all shoulders and face. Nohar
had wrinkled his muzzle in a grimace and was emitting
a low growl. She noted a few gray hairs around his
broad nose.

"You." Nohar made it sound like an accusation. It
probably was.

She could understand how he felt, but the attitude
still annoyed her. "Six years ago, I promised my good-
will if you helped me out. I'm paying you back."

"Point is?" Nohar was not one for a lengthy
monologue.

"Point is, the company I work for is trying to assas-
sinate me."

There was a subtle transformation in Nohar's face.
If she weren't an expert in reading moreau expressions
she might not have noticed that Nohar had stopped
displaying his teeth. The way his feline cheek was
twisted, it would still be called a grimace. "What
happened?"

"There's a good chance I've been targeted because
of what happened in Cleveland. Because of the
'franks' who ran Midwest Lapidary."

"Shit." Nohar let out a long breath. "That
means—"

"Only maybe."

She could hear Nohar's claws rake the chair he was
sitting on, even over the noise of the party. "What do
I do?"

"Disappear. Go on a real vacation, pay cash, don't
tell anyone where you go, leave the country for a
while."

Nohar shook his head. "Asking a lot."

"I'm not *asking* anything. What you and your wife
do is up to you."

"When will things be safe?"

"I don't know."

"You're not making things easy."

"I didn't have to call."

98

Nohar let out a low rumbling sigh. "I owe you one."

"You did my job for me back in Cleveland. Consider it even."

"Not quite. You're one up on me. Let me give you something." Nohar typed on his comm's keyboard and text began to appear on her screen. It was an address. Evi knew enough about New York to know that it was deep in the Bronx, Moreytown. Nohar also typed "G1:26."

Nohar gave Evi a close-lipped smile. "You might be able to use that."

Nohar cut the connection.

What the hell was "G1:26" supposed to mean? Numbers separated by a colon. Greenwich mean time?

Evi used the memo function to record the note on Eve's card. She'd ponder it later. Nohar obviously assumed she'd know.

She left the booth and started walking down Third, away from the Chrysler Building, away from Central Park, away, she hoped, from the more intense searches for her.

She kept walking south, hiding herself in the eternal press of New Yorkers. It was getting close to nine, and traffic was grinding to a stop. Half the cars she passed had out-of-state plates. Aircars buzzed above, their red landing lights like embers caught in an updraft.

She kept walking, at random for the most part, keeping close to the buildings. She kept one eye open for the police. There, again, the holiday was working in her favor. The NYPD was understaffed to begin with. New Year's in Manhattan overloaded them by an order of magnitude.

Why her and not Nohar?

She kept mulling over that question.

She was pretty sure, despite her warnings, that if the people who were after her were after him, they'd have gotten to him long before she'd called. For some reason, she was more valuable.

The only difference she could think of was the fact that she worked for the Agency, and Nohar was a civilian. The peeper's team, the NLF, seemed to want her alive. And it seemed that the Agency was willing to kill her to prevent it. That extreme reaction by the Agency would make sense if it was something about the Agency itself the NLF was after.

She shook her head. If that was so, then where did the aliens fit in? They had to be involved, there were too many links.

And it still didn't explain why the Aerie emergency number didn't acknowledge her existence. If the Agency was trying to keep her out of the hands of the NLF, it was *stupid* to prevent her from coming in.

And who the hell was Frey talking to when he pretended to talk to the Aerie?

He was Agency, why didn't he shoot her?

She walked south down the axis of Manhattan, her mind traveling in circles over the same set of facts. She managed to avoid crossing paths with any cops.

It was a few blocks south of Canal Street, right in front of the marble pagoda of the Chinatown Memorial, that she heard an aircar do a low flyby and realized that fatigue had made her careless.

She backed to the memorial and leaned against a brass plaque listing the dead from the '42 riots. She was confronted on one side by post-riot buildings. Sleek security condominiums, shades drawn against the empty street. Behind her was the monument to the riot and five square blocks of inadequately lit park that had once been a business district.

The crowd had thinned a little, and the street here was mostly empty of traffic.

The aircar had buzzed by, and she suddenly realized that one of her engineered survival traits could be a severe liability. Her body's metabolism had a very low thermal profile. It was supposed to help her hide from infrared imaging. However, that unusual heat signature would single her out of a crowd of normal humans . . .

The protection the crowd was offering her was illusory.

She stood out like a beacon.

She should have realized how tired she was. She must have been asleep on her feet to walk into a scene this perfect for an ambush. Abdel volunteered that she should have chosen a spot and gone to ground until she figured out what to do.

But she was still here and hadn't been blindsided yet. She rubbed her aching shoulder and noticed that her hand was shaking slightly.

The snow was painting a thin cover on the ground, and she was beginning to feel the chill in the air.

While she was still in the midst of deciding where to go from here, she heard a car coming down Center Street. She didn't want to take any chances. She faded into the shadow of the pillar bearing the memorial plaque and put her hand on the butt of the Mishkov.

The people walking back and forth down the streets ignored her.

The car, a white late-model Jaguar, jerked to a stop, double-parking almost directly in front of her, pointed the wrong way. She was so tense that she nearly shot the driver before she heard the voices. The voices from inside the car were a relief. They all sounded drunk. The car held a man and two women.

None of them sounded like a threat.

One of the women wobbled out of the passenger side door carrying what appeared to be a magnum of champagne.

Evi was about to holster her weapon when she realized she was hearing another engine, above her. The aircar was back in the vicinity. She looked up and didn't see any lights. Legit air-traffic *never* cut the lights.

The civilians across the street were arguing.

"I told you we'd make it," the man was telling the one bearing the champagne as he followed her out of the passenger door.

"Sure, and we only have, like, a half hour to go."

The woman still in the car was the driver; she sounded the most sober. "You wanted to go to Desmond's party first."

"We should have stayed at Desmond's. A fucking waste spending two hours in the car on New Year—"

"Girls, girls—" The guy was trying to calm things down. Meanwhile, Evi tried to spot the aircar. She would have been able to see if it weren't for the streetlights. The bright mercury lamps were washing out her ability to see any infrared beyond a few meters. However, from the sound of it, the aircar was hovering.

She was in trouble.

A tiny, glowing infrared dot sprouted too close to her head and Evi ran. A bullet struck the pillar behind her. A chunk of marble shrapnel whizzed by her ear. The gun was silenced. She never heard it fire.

People cursed her as she slammed through the crowd.

Things were going too fast, and she still had no real idea where the aircar was.

She ran at the Jaguar. The trio hadn't noticed the shot or Evi running at them. The guy was leaning in the driver's side door and trying to coax the remaining woman out. "Come on, Kris, we'll miss Diane's party."

Evi bolted across the street and felt more than heard the next shot hit the ground behind her left foot.

"Not until Red apologizes."

Evi was halfway across the street and the infrared

dot leapt ahead of her. She dodged as a bullet plowed out a small crater in the street.

"Come on, Sam, let's leave her— huh?"

The one with the bottle had noticed Evi running full tilt across the street, gun down. She shoved her out of the way and dived into the open passenger door.

"Get out!" Evi yelled. She was pointing the gun at the driver, but only got a blank look in response.

"No, not my dad's car."

"Lady, this is a real gun."

"You're not steal—" A bullet punched through the roof of the Jaguar and split the armrest on the passenger door. That was too close. The driver let out a squeak and floored the Jaguar.

The man barely had time to dive for the safety of the sidewalk.

The woman, who looked barely nineteen, was looking at her. *"They're shooting!"*

Another shot ripped through the rear window, shattering it. There was a shuddering scrape as the Jaguar bucked forward and sideswiped a parked BMW, slamming shut the driver's door.

"Fuck, somebody's shooting at us—"

They were in the wrong lane.

"Get in the right lane, lady!" Evi shouted as she struggled to sit upright in the passenger seat and get the seatbelt on. Then she began to reach out and close the passenger door.

"Name's Kris," said the driver as she swerved way over the center of the road, rocking Evi too far out the open door. Evi had a brief, terrifying, view of speeding asphalt as another gunshot shattered the passenger window. Kris was still talking, eyes locked on the road now, "My dad's going to kill me."

The Jaguar kept swerving to the right until it bumped up on the curb. Evi was thrown back into the car as a fire hydrant rendered the passenger door irrelevant. The door was torn away with Evi's head barely inside the car.

The windshield in front of them shattered as another shot tore through the length of the car. Kris screamed. Snow began slicing in through the window, burning Evi's cheeks. She didn't want to look at the speedometer.

"We're going to die," Kris was saying now, "it's New Year's Eve and we're going to die—"

"We're not going to die—"

Kris somehow managed to slam the Jaguar through an invisible gap in the traffic on Broadway, scraping at least four cars on the way through the intersection. A bullet hit the hood of the Jaguar, and the engine began to make ominous grinding noises.

"Get under some cover. They're in an aircar."

"Who the hell are *you?"*

"Look at the road!"

Kris snapped her head around. The Jaguar had drifted into the wrong lane again. A van was headed right toward them, horn blaring.

Kris pulled a cornering move that shouldn't have been possible. From inside the car it felt like the ninety-degree turn the car did had a point on the corner. The van scraped by the rear of the Jaguar, and Evi heard its windshield shatter as the sniper let loose another shot.

The Jaguar streaked through an alley, plowing boxes and garbage in front of it. Evi maneuvered around in the seat to look out the rear window. She could finally make out the aircar through the snow. It was a faint shadow lurking in the crack of sky between the buildings.

Evi braced the Mishkov on the back of her seat and aimed. The shot was as difficult as it could be, hitting a barely visible high-speed moving target from a moving platform. She gave herself one chance in ten.

She fired the Mishkov and Kris screamed. The

sound was a deafening explosion in the enclosed space, even over the roar of the wind through the broken windows.

The aircar looked undisturbed.

Evi took another bead on the flyer as a bullet plowed into the trunk, about a foot away from her. Before Evi fired, the Jaguar pulled a shuddering left turn back into the open to the blare of a dozen horns.

The aircar could be anywhere now. Evi had lost it in the glare of the streetlights. The Jaguar passed a restaurant window, which shattered as another shot missed them.

Evi looked ahead of the car. The Jaguar shot through a crosswalk, clipping the front of a cab, and Evi got a look at a street sign—

How the hell did they get north on Hudson? There must have been a turn or two Evi had missed. However, that explained the traffic. Their car was shooting by dozens of vehicles.

"Get off of Hudson!"

Kris took a hard left across another crosswalk, crashing through a sign directing people to the Holland Tunnel. A bullet shattered what was left of the driver's side window. Kris was screaming to be heard over the wind. "Damn it! Who *are* you?"

Kris was crying. Her tears were diagonal streaks in the wind.

She jumped another curb and sideswiped another cab getting onto Canal Street. They were heading straight for the Hudson.

Evi kept watch behind them, looking for the aircar. It was still lost in the glare of the streetlights. She thought she saw a muzzle flash, but since the gun was silenced and nothing hit their vehicle that time, she couldn't be sure. "Kris, I'm sorry—"

"You're sorry?"

"I should have pushed you out of the car."

"I'm soooo happy." Another shot plowed into the

hood of the car, and the engine's grinding became an ominous rumble.

Up ahead Evi saw a giant orange detour sign. Kris ignored it.

They passed another sign, unlit, which read, "New West Side Expressway, Southbound." Under it was another sign, blackened with old grime, "CLOSED." They hit an entrance ramp and slammed through a rusty chain-link fence.

The road immediately began to shake the car's suspension apart. The rattling under the car's hood took on an urgent tone.

They passed a third sign, "NY Urban Infrastructure Renewal Project. New West Side Expressway opens May 2048. Your tax dollars at work." The old sign sprouted a bullet hole as she read it.

The Jaguar bumped through a gigantic chuckhole as they passed a last sign, "Expressway condemned. No Trespassing. Enter at own risk."

Now we're going to die, she thought.

Abdel gave her a mental slap for getting fatalistic in combat. *Think that way and you* will *die.*

She tried to ignore it when Kris pulled a shaky U-turn to avoid a hole that crossed all four lanes and fell straight through to the ground, twenty meters or so. Instead, she tried to get another bead on the aircar. Fortunately, on the abandoned expressway there were no active streetlights and Evi could pick out a flying shadow banking low over the Hudson to follow them. There was a point, at the end of Kris' turn, when the aircar seemed to hover for a split-second, almost stationary.

Evi aimed at the brightest infrared source and fired.

Kris screamed, "Shit," at the sound of the gunshot and the Jaguar swerved and sideswiped a guardrail, knocking a chunk into the darkness. But Evi thought she saw the flying shadow sprout a spark near its midsection. She'd hit it . . .

Unfortunately, the aircar showed no signs of slowing down or stopping.

Smoke began to emerge from the Jaguar's hood, carrying the taint of ozone and burning insulation. Red lights began to blink on the dash. The inductor was overheating, the superconductor was losing charge, and the rattle was turning into a scraping whine.

Kris was pumping the gas, and they were still losing speed.

Evi looked up ahead, and they were aiming right for a thirty-meter gap in the expressway.

The sniper in the aircar fired again, and this time Evi heard the shot. It wasn't the gun she heard. It was the right front tire of the Jaguar blowing out and shredding.

"Hang on!" Kris yelled over the screech of the brakes.

Evi could tell when they hit the hole in the road, because the screech of the brakes stopped and the bottom fell out of her stomach.

The Jaguar spent a full second in free-fall, its nose arcing downward. It seemed to Evi that the second washed the night clear of sound. The Jaguar tumbled and she saw, briefly, the crumbling concrete support pillars rush by the front of the car. Then she was looking straight at a pile of rubble that sloped up under the condemned expressway.

There was a bone-jarring crunch, and then all she could see was an airbag. She'd been turning to face forward under the seatbelt. The shoulder belt dug into her left shoulder, and she felt a burning wrench. The car had stopped moving, and for a moment it felt as if the car were going to stay here, vertical, nose-end into the ground. Then, as the airbag began to deflate, she felt the car tip backward.

The Jaguar slammed its wheels into the rubble. She heard the inductor explode under the car, releasing the smell of melting ceramics and burning insulation. She wrestled the airbag out of her face as the Jaguar slid down the grade.

The hole was receding above them as the car slid backwards and stopped.

"Kris?"

Evi looked to her left when no answer came. Kris was leaning back in the driver's seat, eyes wide open. A trickle of blood was running from her mouth, and her head was leaning much too far to the right.

"Shit, no," Evi whispered.

There was no airbag draped over Kris' lap. The cover that housed it had popped off the steering wheel, and perfectly centered on the cover was a bullet hole. The bag had never inflated.

"*No!* She's a damn civilian."

She popped her seatbelt and felt for a pulse in Kris' neck. "Please, I don't want to be responsible for this. Everything else, but not this, too."

As the plastic fenders on the rear of the Jaguar started burning from the heat of the melted inductor, she placed her right fist between Kris' breasts and began pumping. She ignored the shivers of agony that it drove into her shoulder. Five pumps, then she pinched Kris' nose shut and breathed into her mouth. It was like blowing into a hot water bottle, tasted of blood.

No pulse.

Five more, breathe.

No pulse, no reaction.

Five more, breathe.

Nothing.

"Don't die!"

Five more, breathe.

She heard an engine above her.

"Damn it! Not now!" She was shouting now, it felt like someone was driving a hot poker into her guts. Damn them, whoever they were. Didn't they care who got in the way? She bent over and pulled the Mishkov out of the footwell, where she had dropped it.

Evi could see the aircar clearly now. It was silhouetted through the hole, against the night sky. She clutched her injured arm to her chest and braced the Mishkov against the dashboard and aimed at one of the forward fans.

"BASTARDS!" Evi fired.

There was a grinding whine from above her. A shower of sparks erupted from the front of the aircar as a blade from one of the forward fans sheared through its housing. The aircar's nose dipped and its tail began rising. The car became terminally unbalanced. It fell out of the sky, the fans giving it a lateral acceleration toward the river. The nose of the aircar skipped along the side of the slope of rubble and caught on a chunk of concrete. The car flipped on its back, fans still going, and started rolling. It rolled past the Jaguar and plowed into a concrete retaining wall.

Evi lowered the Mishkov and started shaking, watching the aircar.

The aircar's power plant exploded in a flower of sparks, orange flame, and toxic smoke.

The smell of burning plastic finally got bad enough to make her turn around. The Jaguar's trunk was burning now. She unhooked Kris' seatbelt and, gingerly, dragged her away from the car. Once Kris was clear of the wreck, she tried CPR again, not caring if a survivor from the aircar decided to shoot her, or about the agony in her shoulder, or if Kris' blood could be tainted ...

And she knew it was hopeless five minutes before she stopped.

For a while, she just looked at Kris. Kris had been blonde, attractive, nineteen.

"Damn it, what else could I do?" She asked no one in particular.

You can't get soft-hearted in your line of work.

"Maybe I'm in the wrong line of work, Abdel," Evi whispered.

You were drafted, too.

There was a distant sound of popping, and at first she thought it was gunfire. Then car horns began sounding, along with foghorns from the river, and she realized that the popping was the sound of fireworks.

She reached down and closed Kris' eyes.

"Happy New Year."

CHAPTER 9

It hurt to holster her gun, so Evi put it into her pack as she gathered all her spilled equipment. Then she hung the backpack over her right shoulder. She limped up to the remains of the aircar, but within ten meters she could tell that examination was hopeless. The power plant had only smoldered briefly after the explosion, but the cab was crushed against the concrete retaining wall. The only way she'd get to examine her assailants would be to move the whole wreck.

She had been here too long. The aircar would have had to have been in radio contact with someone. Someone who would be on their way now. Even if, for some reason, there wasn't any backup for the aircar, there would eventually be cops, ambulances and firemen to take care of the crash.

She stepped on something and heard cracking plastic.

She looked down and saw her sunglasses. They must have flown off during the Jaguar's descent. She picked them up with her good arm. Most of the lenses stayed on the ground.

There just went most of her protective coloration.

She spared Kris a last look and then limped through a gap in the eastern retaining wall, opposite the aircar. She limped away from the graffiti-emblazoned wall, left arm clutched to her stomach, realizing just how little time she had left. She was hearing sirens, and with the sirens would come more unmarked aircars.

She stumbled through an intersection and saw she had crashed into Greenwich Village.

She pushed through an obliviously drunk crowd of mixed moreaus and humans and nearly passed out when one of them brushed her shoulder. She fell into a doorway after that, breathing heavily and sweating.

Her shoulder had dislocated, and she had to do something to fix it.

The medkit in her bag had some painkiller, but the airhypo had broken in the crash. She tossed the hypo to the ground in disgust. "Just gets worse and worse . . ."

She saw a police aircar fly over her, flashers going. She fell back further into the darkness the doorway provided. She backed until she was stopped by the door itself, a metal security job with bullet-proof glass. She tried the latch with her right hand. It was locked.

A very bad idea crossed her mind. She didn't want to do this herself, but she had to do something about her shoulder.

The handle on the door seemed to be high enough off the ground.

The hall beyond the bullet-proof glass was dimly lit. She didn't see anyone in the building. She hoped it would stay that way. It would be very bad for someone to try the door while she did what she was considering.

She put her back flat to the door and unbent her left arm. It felt as though someone had spiked her shoulder with ground glass. She took deep breaths as she locked her elbow. She had to breathe through her nose because her jaw was clenched shut.

With her arm straight at her side, she unlatched the strap from her pack and wrapped it around the door's latch and her left hand.

She wiped the sweat from her forehead and whispered to another passing police car, "So much for the preliminaries . . ."

She took a deep breath, gritted her teeth, and started bending her knees.

The pain was a white-hot shuddering rush that originated somewhere in her left shoulder socket, raced down her back, and pulsed through her head to spike between her eyes. As she continued to lower her torso and rotate her arm up and back, the fire in her shoulder planted a hot coal in her guts that shriveled her stomach into a small vibrating ember. Somehow she managed to keep her elbow locked as the pain whited out her vision with dancing sparks . . .

There was a grinding pop in her left shoulder and Evi threw up.

She stayed there, on her knees in the snow, for a few seconds as the world returned to normal. Her left shoulder still hurt like hell, but it was an endurable hurt. She slowly untangled her left hand from the door latch and staggered to her feet.

She stood there a moment, slowly bending her left elbow, rocking the arm fractionally back and forth and wincing. Her shoulder seemed to have regained some semblance of mobility. Her engineered metabolism was supposed to take damage like that well.

She didn't want to see it take something badly.

At least it wasn't broken.

No more police cars screamed by. It'd be safe on the street for a moment or two. But she needed to get inside, preferably within the next five minutes.

A pair of people passed close by her door: a black human and a drunk fox. The man had his arm around the fox and was doing his best to keep his moreau friend from weaving. Even in the beginning of a snowstorm, the fox was wearing as little clothing as he could get away with legally. The human was wearing a shredded denim jacket that was covered by hand-lettered slogans: "Fuck the PTB," "Blow the foundations," "Support your local police—from a rope."

She wouldn't be surprised if the guy had the seminal "Off the Pink" on the jacket somewhere, even if he was human.

What caught Evi's attention was the shades the human wore.

Why not? He certainly wasn't Agency material.

Evi stepped out of the doorway, in front of the pair. The two stopped short. Other groups of humans and moreaus began passing around them. She made sure the streetlight was behind her, so her eyes were in shadow.

From the expression on the human, she must have looked like hell.

"How much for the sunglasses?"

"What?" said the human.

The fox reached up and grabbed the glasses, "She wants your shades—" The fox turned and addressed Evi in a slurred brogue, "Fifty he wants, lass, for this prim— premi— quality eyewear."

"Damn it, Ross. Give those back." The human reached for the shades, but the fox had longer arms.

The fox shook his head. "Quiet, Ross is negotiating."

During the exchange, Evi had the opportunity to liberate three twenties from the roll in her pocket. "I'll give you sixty."

The pair turned to face her. The fox lowered his arm and made as if to chew the end of the glasses in thought. "Now, Ross will have to think about—"

The human grabbed the sunglasses and yanked them away from the fox. "They're my glasses, you Irish furball." He looked at Evi, still disbelieving. "You serious?"

She flashed the three twenties.

The guy tossed her the sunglasses and the fox took the money. Then they rushed around her as if they were afraid she'd change her mind. As they receded she could hear the guy say, "Give me the money, they're my glasses."

"Ross should get some. He did all the haggling."

She put on the sunglasses. These were much darker

than her own, not only did they cut out the UV and a lot of the human-visible spectrum, but they chopped out the IR as well. She'd have to make do.

As much as the contacts irritated her, she wished she had them right now.

Another mix of drunk and half-drunk moreaus and humans passed by. They came from a bar two doors down. She guarded her shoulder as the patrons passed. The humans were four males, heavy on the jewelry, leather jackets with more anti-authoritarian slogans. Evi read a button on one that said, "The only thing of value to pass through a politician's mind is a bullet." The moreaus consisted of two female rabbits, a male rat, and another male fox. Like the previous fox, these wore as little as possible. The moreau females even went topless. But then, moreaus didn't have prominent breasts.

From the look of it, she could get by as a patron without too many weird looks. From her reflection in the glass, she didn't look much worse than the positively trashed fox, whom the rat was trying hard to keep vertical.

She pushed through the door with her right shoulder and found herself in the middle of the highest concentration of moreaus in any one place that she'd ever seen on Manhattan. The place was dimly lit and caught in the middle of a New Year's celebration. There was no shortage of the traditional noisemakers and funny hats. In one booth, a collection of humans and morey rabbits, all female, were being led by a white female tiger in a rendition of "Auld Lang Syne."

The mirror behind the bar was also a holo screen that was currently displaying the typical scene of Times Square. She could barely hear the broadcast over the noise from the bar. She led with her right shoulder as she pushed through the crowd of leather and fur. No one seemed to pay any attention to her.

Good, Evi very much wanted to disappear right now.

She decided she needed a drink to blend in with the crowd around her. With that in mind, she slipped through to the bar. Wincing every time a patron brushed her wounded shoulder.

She squeezed into a small gap between two occupied barstools. To her left was a rat sitting in front of a half-dozen glasses. He was wearing the conical paper hat on the end of his triangular muzzle. Someone was finding it funny. To her right sat a female lepus, drinking something red with an umbrella in it.

The bartender, another female white tiger, walked up to Evi. "You're in time for the last of the champagne—"

Champagne was the last thing Evi wanted. "Something strong, please."

"There's strong and there's strong. I mean we have Everclear—"

"I'll take it."

The tiger cocked a blue eye at her. "Anything to go with that?"

"No."

The tiger shrugged. As she turned to fix the drink, Evi noticed a shaved patch under her right ear. On the skin underneath was a white floral tattoo, a very intricate, and somewhat erotic, design.

Evi, not believing in coincidence, turned toward the booth of female revelers. The white tiger leading the singing had a similar patch under her ear.

"I know what you're thinking," the bartender addressed her as she put down the drink.

Evi fumbled in the pocket of her jacket to peel a twenty off the roll of cash she had. "What am I thinking?"

"Is she a friend or a relative?"

The thought had crossed her mind.

The bartender leaned forward and said in a husky

voice that reminded Evi of Nohar, "She's a friend. *My* friend."

Right. She finally managed to liberate a twenty and placed it on the bar. "Keep the change." She picked up her drink and moved to the rear, back in the shadows. Near the door to the bathrooms.

There was nowhere to sit down, so she stood in a corner where she had a good view of the door, through the crowd. That's when she allowed herself to start shaking.

She felt like she was on the verge of a physical and emotional collapse.

She looked down at the drink in her hand; the surface was rippling. Abdel told her that it wasn't a good idea. She should be concentrating on getting out—

Fuck it. Thinking what Abdel would tell her in this situation didn't do a damn bit of good.

She was a professional, she told herself, a soldier, and at one time she had been a trained assassin. People had always died around her, and for a good part of her professional career her life had been in danger. She had been in worse before, and she had come through without having a nervous breakdown.

She had managed to escape from Palestine when any connection to the former Israeli government was an instant death sentence. She had nearly starved before she had gotten to Cyprus.

She had gotten through that.

But what she had just gone through, having a totally innocent person die because of her . . .

Evi wanted to chuck it all right there.

She put away half her drink in one fluid motion. It burned going down, but the pain in her shoulder began to fade.

A female voice addressed her. "You look like you need to sit."

Evi had been keeping her gaze locked on the door

to the bar. She hadn't expected anyone to talk to her. She turned and looked at the owner of the voice.

Sitting next to Evi, in a small two-person booth, was a pale redhead. Her hair spilled halfway down her back. She was wearing a metallic-red blouse and tight jeans that showed off a pair of well-sculpted legs. As if her figure weren't arresting enough, she'd chosen to wear black lipstick that altered the appearance of her skin from pale to cadaverous. Her nails matched; they were painted gloss-black and sharpened to points.

The woman was wearing sunglasses, too. Black one-piece things that hid not only her eyes but half her face as well. For a brief surreal moment, Evi thought she was being addressed by a fellow frank. That thought—Evi wasn't sure if it had been hope or fear—was put to rest when she turned her full attention to the booth. The smell of the woman was definitely human.

She considered ignoring her, or moving away. But she didn't want to be conspicuously solitary. Also, she did need to sit down, and it looked like the seat this woman was offering was the only vacancy in the place. Evi moved into the booth opposite the redhead.

Evi looked around at the standing-room-only crowd. "How come you rate a table to yourself?"

The redhead chuckled. "Is that what this is? Thought it was a comm booth they never finished." She sipped from her own glass. "Leo, the guy whose seat you're taking, just had an urgent call of nature."

"What if he wants it back?"

The redhead shrugged. "I've had enough of his moreau separatist bullshit."

"Well, thanks for the seat."

"You look like you need a friend."

Evi gave her host a sad, silent chuckle. "Suppose I do."

"You want to talk about it?"

"Not a good idea."

"Sometimes it helps."

Evi felt an urge to tell her to go to hell. Instead, she realized that there was genuine concern in the redhead's voice. Evi sipped what remained of her drink.

"I've lost my job, my home, and I've been through some thoroughly rotten experiences today." What was she doing, talking to a stranger like this? It went against all her training . . .

To hell with her training.

"Christ—" Her host said as Evi's appearance seemed to sink in. The redhead removed her own sunglasses, revealing a pair of green, very human eyes. "Are you hurt?"

She realized that the redhead had just noticed her shoulder and probably some marks on her face. "Someone tried to kill me."

Shut up, Evi. She looked in her glass and realized her drink was gone. She had to keep a tighter rein on what she was saying. Why the hell was she spouting off like this? She didn't want to believe that it was because this woman seemed to be the only person who seemed to give a shit.

Damn, was she about to get another innocent person involved?

"Have you called the cops?" The redhead started to get up.

"No cops."

"You can't let someone get away with—" The redhead was standing up now and sounded angry. Evi grabbed her wrist with her good arm and pulled her back down. The redhead hit the seat with a thud and a surprised squeak.

Evi looked into those green eyes, which were growing wider, and addressed her in a harsh whisper. "*No cops.* I said *tried.* They didn't get away with anything. They didn't get *away,* period."

She realized that she was squeezing much too hard. She let go and saw her hand was shaking. "Sorry—"

"Name's Diana." The redhead began rubbing the wrist Evi had grabbed. "Don't apologize. Your business, but I get sick whenever someone gets assaulted, mugged, *raped,* and doesn't even try to put the bastards away. You should call—"

"Diana, the police would probably shoot me."

Diana just stared at her. She seemed to be taking her in for the first time.

The bartender, who had noticed the commotion, pushed through to the booth. "Is there a problem?"

The tiger was addressing Diana.

Diana shook her head without taking her eyes off of Evi.

"Are you sure?" The tiger gave Evi a nasty look.

"Yeah, Kijna." Diana's voice sounded far away. Then she cleared her throat, looked at the tiger, and her voice regained its confidence. "We're fine, thanks."

The bartender left, but kept looking back, through the crowd, at Evi.

Diana sounded apologetic. "Too nosy. Sorry."

"Maybe I should go."

"Do you want to?"

"I should."

Diana shrugged. "If you don't mind, stay."

Evi remembered Kijna and her "friend." "Are you trying to pick me up?"

"Would you mind terribly if I was?"

"I just ducked in here to get off the street."

Diana responded with a funny little half-smile. "Doesn't answer my question."

Evi felt the sad little chuckle return. "You never answered mine."

"Touché."

Diana found a touch-sensitive spot on the table, and a keypad and screen lit up under the fake wood surface. "You want anything more to drink— What *is* your name?"

"Ev—Eve." Damn. Evi cursed herself, she was slipping over her alias.

"Eve?"

"Eve." Evi nodded. Diana was still waiting to hear if she had an order.

She shouldn't, but her shoulder had stopped hurting, the shakes had gone away, and she no longer felt on the verge of a panic attack.

"Order me whatever you're having."

Diana typed in an order. "You have a nice accent."

"Thanks." Evi listened to herself and realized that her accent was returning with the liquor.

"I've heard it before, but I can't remember—"

"It's Israeli."

"Palestinian?"

"No." Evi felt an irrational wave of irritation. *"Israeli."* The drinks came, and she used the opportunity to change the subject. "What on earth prompted you to invite over someone in my condition?"

Diana took one mug of thick beer and sipped. "My friends say I have an attraction to strays."

Evi laughed at that, a real laugh this time, though inaudible. "I'm about as stray as you get."

All the shit that had happened today seemed far away for once. Though she knew Abdel would throw a fit at her right now for drinking and leading on the local lesbians.

Diana must have noticed a change in her expression. "What's the matter?"

"A little voice telling me to have second thoughts."

"About what?"

"The way I'm reacting to the disaster my life has become." Evi drained her mug. She didn't bother tasting the beer. "Also says I'm leading you on." This time Evi typed on the control panel. She ordered something at random.

Diana grinned. "How so?"

"I drive on the right side of the road and have no inclination to jump the median." Though the odd thought did have some appeal. Especially when she thought of how most men reacted to her genetic heritage.

Diana took a second to catch Evi's slightly inebriated metaphor. "You should try it some time. Dodging oncoming traffic can be quite a rush."

They both broke into laughter at that one. Evi couldn't help thinking of the last half-hour of her life, and she was laughing and crying at the same time.

Maybe she'd brought all this on herself, deserved it even. For a long time she'd been nothing more than a glorified assassin. She had a dirty job.

Evi was thankful that her sobs were as silent as her laughter.

Someone came and placed a shot glass in front of Evi.

After a few minutes of silence, Diana said, "To answer your old question. Initially, I called you over because you looked like you needed help, not to pick you up."

Evi watched Diana drink a liberal portion of her beer and asked, "Initially?"

"Well ..." Diana waited until Evi had started drinking. "You *would* make a very attractive dyke."

The comment almost had the, apparently intentional, effect of putting the drink through Evi's nose. The back of her sinuses burned and her eyes watered. Apparently she'd ordered a shot of tequila. She coughed a few times and managed to choke out, "I'm flattered." It felt strange hearing that from another woman.

"If you don't have a place tonight, you can crash at mine."

Evi stopped in the middle of wiping her nose with a napkin.

"It's not *that*. But I do have this thing for taking in strays."

"I appreciate the offer," Evi thought of Kris, "but you shouldn't get involved."

Diana looked down and shook her head. "I shouldn't have. I know what it looks—"

Evi put her hand on Diana's arm. "Shhh."

"But—"

"Shhh, Diana. Don't apologize. You don't understand." Evi leaned forward. "People will be looking for . . ."

Evi trailed off because there was a commotion behind her in the bar. She turned, briefly, to see what it was.

Two NYPD uniforms had just walked into the bar.

Evi turned away to hide her face. "Shit," she whispered.

"Eve, maybe I do understand—"

"Shhh," Evi silenced her.

Evi listened to Kijna confront the cops. Kijna seemed very protective of her clientele. The cops said they were looking for a hit-and-run suspect.

"Diana, is there a window in the bathroom?"

"Yes, but, Eve—" Diana started to move, but Evi kept an iron grip on her arm.

"No, don't. They haven't noticed me yet and I'm only going to have a moment while Kijna distracts them. What's behind the bar?"

"Trash, and alley, fire escapes, but—"

"Thanks. I appreciate the offer, but, Diana, you never saw me."

Diana nodded.

Evi tried to hug the shadows as she slipped into the alcove that led to the bathrooms. The two cops didn't appear to see her before she had backed into the john.

The woman's room this time.

There was a small rectangular window snug up against an upper corner of the far wall. It looked as if Evi could wiggle through it, but just the idea of doing it reawakened sympathetic pain in her shoulder. The window was above one of the two stalls. Fortunately, it wasn't above the one that was in use at the moment.

Evi locked herself into the unoccupied stall and stood on the seat of the toilet so she could reach the window. It was double-paned fogged polymer, clean but painted shut. She took a few seconds to figure out exactly how the thing was originally intended to open.

The curly-haired brunette sitting in the neighboring stall was resting her head against the tile wall and staring up at Evi. For no particular reason, Evi smiled and nodded at the brunette. The brunette responded with a confused wave.

Too much to drink. Her judgment was screwed.

She found the partially hidden handle sunk flush in the top frame of the window. She slipped her right hand into it and pulled.

The paint cracked and the window tilted outward in a shower of flakes. She kept pulling a little too long. The strut that held the open window in place was old and had been unused for a long time. It folded out, then, after a protesting creak, sheared the bolt that held it to the wall. The whole window tumbled out. It was all she could do to keep a grip on the unwieldy thing and ease it to the ground without a massive crash.

There wasn't going to be a question over where she went.

A cold wind blew a shower of flakes into the bathroom. Evi chinned herself up to the sill with her good arm. The brunette gave her another weak wave goodbye.

Evi tumbled through the opening and her feet landed too far apart on a trash bin below the window. She stumbled once, slipped, and fell on her ass in the snow-covered alley.

Definitely too much to drink.

Abdel, where are you?

"Face it. He's just an excuse to talk to yourself."

She stood up and looked around. She was in a long straight alley, with a T-intersection at each end. She needed to avoid the street that the bar was on; the NYPD and less savory characters would be watching it. She also needed to get away from here as soon as possible. Once the two cops reached the bathroom, they'd see the window and put two and two together.

She made for the left end of the alley, running. She nearly slipped and fell on her ass again, twice, but the cold air and the adrenaline seemed to be washing out the alcohol.

As soon as she reached the intersection, she was spotlighted by a pair of headlights turning into the alley from the street. As if to drive the point home, as soon as the vehicle completed its turn, the engine revved and started rocketing toward her.

Evi ran back into the alley behind the bar. What the hell was she going to do? She couldn't outrun the damn thing. With her limping gait right now, there were few *humans* she could outrun.

She began to fumble in her pack for the Mishkov, spilling the medkit.

The car was getting louder as Evi passed a trash bin and took cover behind it. Her breath was steaming and beginning to fog her sunglasses.

Evi braced the Mishkov on top of the trash bin one-handed and fired as soon as the car screeched to a stop at the intersection. The Mishkov clicked on an empty chamber. She had forgotten to reload it.

From the cherry-red Ford Estival, Evi heard a familiar voice yell, "Hey, Eve!"

Evi looked at her gun, and where it was aimed, and shuddered.

CHAPTER 10

The press of traffic made the Estival's progress agonizingly slow. But nobody stopped the car.

Evi's view sucked. She was wedged in the footwell of the rear seat. Anyone observing Diana's Ford would only see the driver, but Evi couldn't see anything but an oblique cross section of Manhattan's skyline.

"Do you have any idea what kind of danger you're in?"

"Some." Diana eased the car out of what seemed to be the mainstream of New York's gridlock. "I counted at least five unmarked cop cars up and down Bank Street."

"Why the hell did you—" Evi kept thinking of Kris. "I could get you killed."

"What's the diff between a cop shooting you in the middle of a pro-morey demonstration and getting blown away helping a quote-terrorist-unquote."

Evi shook her head. She had trouble following Diana and couldn't decide whether or not it was the alcohol. "What are you talking about?"

"I know who you are. Anyone who gives the PTB the shits like you did is okay in my book."

"Powers that be," Evi whispered to herself. "You know who I am?" Evi asked, "Then who am I?" She wasn't too sure any more.

Diana chuckled. "You're a radical pro-morey terrorist. Responsible for an attack on an Upper East

Side condominium that caused at least three million in damages, not to mention a few dead cops."

Evi felt the bottom fall out of her stomach.

"All bullshit, of course, but I'm intrigued by a girl who is in the middle of that much trouble."

"That's sick."

"I never said I wasn't neurotic."

"Is that what's going out over the news?"

Evi studied the side of Diana's face. When Diana nodded, her right earlobe became briefly visible. She wore as an earring a small silver anarchy symbol. Before today Evi would have found such disenchantment with the government hard to relate to.

"You've made the top story on every news channel. Largest manhunt," Diana repressed a laugh and it came out a snort, "in the city's history. Though so far you're an 'unidentified female.' "

This was getting too bizarre, even for the events of the last twenty-four hours. "So naturally, when you realized who I was and that the cops were after me, you decided to pick me up."

"Just funny that way, I guess."

"You're nuts." Evi wondered if she should be looking to jump from the car.

"What, are you complaining because I'm helping you?"

"Yes, too many people have been hurt—"

"Are you going to tell me that the moreau underground is suddenly working with Afghanis?"

"What?" The Afghani canines were mercenaries who cared nothing for politics. They usually worked for humans; the pay was better. "No, but—"

"You going to tell me that the morey underground had suddenly changed tactics and is going after civilian targets?"

"No," Evi said. The main thrust of moreau violence, as little as there was in the past few years, had been "military" targets—communications, power, police. She fell silent.

The Hassan case in Cleveland echoed through Evi's mind. Then, as now, there had been the attempt to pass off the Afghani mercenary activity as part of the radical moreau movement. Evi could see the same people using the same phrases now as they did six years ago. A group of people high up in the Agency didn't want anyone following the canines to their source.

Diane was continuing to talk. "So, are you going to tell me that you really are a terrorist and evil incarnate?"

Evi stared at Diana and tried to make sense out of her benefactor. "I have the feeling if I told you I was the Antichrist, you'd just get excited."

Diana shrugged. "Going to bite the hand that feeds you?"

"That isn't the point."

"What is?"

"The point is that someone could kill you if you hang around me." Evi surprised herself with the force of her protest. Did she really want to have the only person to help her abandon her?

Evi knew that she desperately did not want Diana to end up like Kris.

Diana was silent for a moment before she spoke. "If my name's on a cop's bullet, it was put there back in the forties."

The Estival drove on in silence. It hit a bump, turned down a side street, and stopped. "Speaking of names, is Eve your real name?"

"Huh?"

"You don't look like an Eve."

Evi sat up and winced, she was feeling her shoulder again. Once she was upright, she could see where the Estival had parked. Diana had maneuvered the car into a bare alley between the back end of a line of refurbished brownstones and the blank cinderblock of an old warehouse.

"It's Evi. Evi Isham." Evi picked up her pack and opened the door. "Diana, thanks for the help. But I can't risk you—"

Diana reached over the seat and put a hand on Evi's good shoulder. "Wait."

Evi stopped and looked at Diana. The alcohol was mostly gone now, a benefit of an engineered metabolism. With the haze gone, she could feel some of her judgment returning. She tried to cultivate some of her normal suspicion as she listened.

Diana squeezed Evi's shoulder. "If the cops were going to land on us, they would've already. You aren't going to drag me down unless you want to."

Evi ducked out from under Diana's hand and stepped out of the car.

Diana continued to talk. "I used to have close ties to the nonhuman movement, a long time ago. I know you aren't a part of it. A human as high profile as the news is making you out to be, I'd know—everyone in the Village'd know."

Evi turned around to face Diana. Diana scooted across the front seat and stepped out of the passenger door in front of Evi. "The people in that bar have no love for the cops. Your shadows've been sent off in a dozen different directions. You're safe. I'm safe."

The world was eerily silent, wrapped in the blowing snow. The way the sounds were sucked into the night reminded Evi of the Jordanian desert. Evi felt alone, and she felt that Diana was taking advantage of that feeling. It was a twisted feeling. If anyone was being exploited, it was Diana.

Diana was trying to force Evi to use her.

"Damn it." This was pissing Evi off. She turned on Diana and yelled, *"Why do you want to help me?"*

"You want to know why?"

Evi tossed her pack to the ground and spread her

arms wide, ignoring pain in her shoulder. "Yes, I want to know *why*. Why someone would *choose* to get involved in this shit. This *isn't* your fight!"

Diana shrugged. "In the bar, I saw how you looked. I've seen it before—" Diana looked up into her eyes so deeply that Evi raised her hand to make sure the sunglasses were still there. "Ten years ago. Smuggling nonhuman refugees into the country. Saw a lot of people with that look."

Evi lowered her arms. "What look?"

"Despair, loss, lots of fatigue. The look of someone who's lost everything. Someone who's been running too long— Close?"

Evi could feel her shoulders slumping. She still tried to cultivate her instinct for suspicion, tried to see Diana as a potential foe. But even Abdel was remaining mute on the subject.

"Damn."

"Close to calling it quits, weren't you?"

"You've made your point," Evi whispered. She wasn't going to get out of this without trusting someone. She sighed. "God. I need a rest."

Diana closed the car door, picked up Evi's pack and shouldered it. "The offer's still open, to crash at my place." As an afterthought, she added, "I have a couch."

"Where?"

Diana hooked her thumb at the warehouse and started toward it. Evi followed.

The entrance to Diane's apartment was a decrepit freight elevator that could fit the Estival inside it, but no way could have lifted it. They shuddered up four floors, past converted studio apartments, to the sound of an overtaxed electric motor. Evi smelled grease, rust, and static electricity, and as the haze of alcohol continued to lift, she could smell Diana. Jasmine touched by a hint of sweat and beer. And . . .

The elevator chunked into place and the smell of incense wafted in, overpowering any subtler odor.

Diana opened the gate on an impressive studio apartment. A small kitchenette to their right, a wall of glass block to their left, and, in between, a low entrance hall that opened out into a vast open space. They faced a vast sweep of windows that looked out over the Hudson River.

When they walked out into the room, grudging lights came on, erasing the skyline of Jersey City out the window.

"My place."

"I'm impressed. I didn't think there were places like this left on Manhattan."

Evi walked toward the couch that formed the centerpiece of the room. It faced an old comm that squatted in front of the windows. She rotated, slowly, until she was facing Diana and the elevator. Above the elevator was a loft draped with curtains.

She stood there a moment taking it in.

After an uncomfortable moment Diana shook her head. "I'm being a poor host. Do you want something to eat? Drink?"

Evi ran her hand through her hair and winced when it caught in the tangled mess. "Thanks, but I'd like to clean up first."

Diana stopped in mid-step toward the kitchen and turned toward the glass block. "Yes, of course. The bathroom's over here."

The bathroom was cavernous. The shower could have easily accommodated a half-dozen people. "Leave your clothes by the door, and I'll try to find something clean for you to wear." Diana put Evi's pack down between the john and the bidet. Diana fidgeted a moment or two before she left.

The bathroom was nearly eight meters on a side by five high. Half the walls were tile, half glass block. One wall was faced with mirrored tile; the upper half of the opposite wall was eaten by ranks of windows. The view out the windows consisted of glowing swirls of white flakes against a totally black background.

Evi shucked the jacket.

"I shouldn't be here," she whispered. The sound bounced off a dozen walls and the corrugated steel ceiling before it laid itself to rest.

She emptied the pockets of the jumpsuit, including the clips for the Mishkov, back into her pack. Then, slowly, she unzipped the jumpsuit.

She kicked the boots and the jumpsuit back by the door and walked to the shower, not looking in the mirror.

She'd forgotten how good a long, hot shower could feel. She stood under the stream of water for nearly five minutes before she realized she still had on her sunglasses.

She put them in the soapdish.

Once out of the shower, she looked in the mirror. She expected to look worse than she did, after what she had been through. Again, the benefits of an engineered metabolism.

The bruise on her calf had faded to a dull yellow, while her tear-gas irritated eye was more-or-less normal looking. The shoulder, however, was an ugly sight. The shrapnel wound had closed up, but from the wrenching injury in the car crash, the entire area had turned a dark purple.

Evi tried each axis of movement in her left shoulder and each sent a shuddering wave of pain.

"This could be a problem," she told her reflection. Even with her metabolism, it could be three days before she could even think about using that arm.

She opened her pack. Most of her medkit had fallen out, but the bottom of the bag was littered with items that had spilled out of the kit. The mess was mostly drug cartridges that were useless without the hypo, but she thanked the gods that one of the items that stayed was the heat-activated polymer support bandage.

She strapped up her injured shoulder. Her body heat was supposed to fuse the white bandage into a single tight piece. Her metabolism wouldn't cooperate on that score, but Diana's dryer did just as well.

With the bandage in place she could use the arm, a little. Very little.

Diana had done as promised and left her some clean clothes in place of the jumpsuit and leather. She had been thoughtful enough to leave a number of things to choose from. After trying on a few items, it was clear that Diana had no clothes to fit Evi's relatively compact scale.

She finally settled on a red kimono that would be a racy number on Diana's six-foot tall, robust frame. On Evi it was a modest robe that came down past her knees and covered her rather completely.

Sunglasses . . .

She looked at her reflection in the mirror and at her eyes. The pupils were narrowed in the light. She wished she had contacts.

She put the sunglasses back on. She would rather explain away that than try to deal with the reaction her eyes might cause. She kept remembering Chuck Dwyer's face. "You're a frank." Like she was a piece of diseased meat.

"So, I'm a frank," she told her reflection. "No need to bother her with that fact."

She picked up her pack and the extra clothes and left the bathroom.

"If she asks, it's because I have sensitive eyes."

Diana never asked.

In the kitchenette, she served her tea and some Chinese dish with pork and tofu. Evi ate ravenously while Diana seemed to abort her own attempts at conversation.

She was fully prepared to answer most of the questions Diana should have been asking. But she wasn't asked. After a few false starts, they ate in relative silence. Evi could smell a host of confused jasmine-flavored emotions floating off of Diana. She didn't press.

Eventually, Diana led her to the couch in the middle of the studio's main room. Diana left her there in the dark. Evi took off her sunglasses, wrapped herself in a blanket, and fell asleep instantly.

CHAPTER 11

Something brushed her hair and Evi snapped awake. Her hand had struck out before she was fully aware of what was going on.

According to her time sense, she'd been sleeping for four hours.

Diana was perched on the end of a coffee table, backlit by a streetlamp shining through the growing snowstorm. Evi had reflexively grabbed her wrist. Diana's fingers were barely touching her hair.

"Sorry. I didn't mean to wake you." Evi could see Diana's flush as a slight infrared pattern in her face. The combination of blush, red hair, and reflected light from Evi's borrowed kimono gave Diana a rose glow, as if an internal fire illuminated her.

The black lipstick was gone.

Evi slowly released Diana's wrist. "Old reflex. I didn't hurt you, did I?"

"No," Diana said. She was looking down at her lap and had let her arm fall to her side. All she wore was an oversized satin pajama top.

Evi sat up and looked at Diana, who had perched herself on the edge of the table, long legs crossed under her. The pose showed off her calves. More rounded and shapely than Evi's legs. Something to be said for more than four percent body fat.

Evi realized that the silence was stretching out to an uncomfortable length. "Is something the matter?"

Diana looked up and shook her head, rippling her hair. "I don't know."

That was another thing Evi envied. Long hair was a liability in her line of work.

Her former line of work.

Diana was staring into her eyes.

No!

Evi's hand shot out toward the coffee table and grabbed her sunglasses.

"Evi?" There was a quavering note in Diana's voice.

Damn, damn, damn! The eyes, why did it have to be the eyes? No one was ever going to be able to relate to her normally because of the damn eyes. Evi put on the sunglasses in a vain hope that Diana hadn't seen them.

She was still putting them on when she felt Diana's hand on her own.

"Your eyes—"

Go on, say it. I'm not human. I'm a goddamn frankenstein—say it.

Diana slowly pulled her hand down, along with the sunglasses. She didn't bother resisting the pull. Diana kept staring into her eyes.

Evi wanted to scream.

"Why do you hide them?" Diana's voice was barely a whisper. "They're beautiful."

She stared for a fraction of a second, leaning forward. Then, with a gasp and a violent shake of her head, Diana turned around and fled to the window. Evi was left sitting on the couch, confused, sunglasses halfway to her face.

Did she hear right? All of a sudden she felt very warm.

Diana was standing in front of the windows, arms clutched around herself, staring out at the snow. The white top she was wearing took on a glow from the streetlight. No fires raged now. She looked like an ice sculpture.

Diana's shoulders were shaking.

Evi put down the sunglasses and walked up to the window. Diana was softly crying, leaning her forehead against the glass. Evi put a hand on her shoulder, forgetting that Diana knew she wasn't human. "What's wrong?"

"I shouldn't bc doing this."

"Doing what?"

Diana gave her a look telling her she should be perfectly aware of "what."

She supposed she was. "I really don't mind."

Diana turned around and sat on the floor, back to the window. "*I* do. You said you didn't have any intention of 'crossing the median.' "

She had, hadn't she? Even so, there was no denying the way her pulse was accelerating. It could be despair, fatigue, or the fact she needed someone, anyone . . .

But explaining it didn't make it go away.

Evi shrugged, hurting her shoulder. "There's nothing wrong with trying to change my mind."

"You have no idea." Diana was shaking her head. Moisture on her cheeks threw back frozen glints from the streetlight outside. "I knew this guy once. The sleaze took pride in seducing and 'initiating' poor, naive, young college kids. He *bragged* about the kind of damage he did."

"I'm not a poor, naive, young college kid."

"One of those kids couldn't live with it. He shot himself." Diana shook her head. "I'm never going to be like that man. That evil bastard."

"You're not—"

"You can't. If someone isn't prepared. Not sure." Diana stopped talking and just started shaking her head.

Evi stroked Diana's hair with her good hand. It was

fine, silky, similar to how Evi imagined that satin pajama top might feel. "I know."

They stayed like that for a while. Then Diana said in a low voice, "I don't want to hurt you."

Evi liked the feel of Diana's hair. It had been too long since she'd been close to anyone. It felt good simply to touch another person.

"Diana, what did you say about my eyes?"

"What?"

Evi slid her hand to Diana's shoulder and knelt in front of her. "Tell me about my eyes."

Diana sniffed. "I've never seen anything like them. They, they glow—"

Evi leaned forward and stroked Diana's cheek, silencing her. "I'm not going to be hurt."

Evi placed her lips over Diana's partially open mouth.

She felt the blood rush to Diana's face as well as her own. Evi's metabolism forgot it was supposed to have a low thermal profile. Diana's sharp intake of breath sucked the air out of Evi's mouth, pulling her tongue after it. Evi tasted the remnants of Diana's toothpaste and a slight cherry flavor from some lip balm.

Over everything was the rich, warm scent of jasmine.

The ice sculpture melted.

It was a warm, wet, hungry kiss, and Diana seemed to lie back in a state of shock throughout the experience.

After half a minute Evi drew back, smiling so widely her cheeks ached. Diana just stared at her with a red-eyed expression of disbelief. "I thought you weren't a lesbian."

A small part of Evi's brain was just as disbelieving. What was she doing?

"I'm not." Evi kissed her again, before Diana could object. This time she embraced Diana with her good arm and rolled. Diana wasn't fighting, so she ended up pinned under her.

Evi's combat training was useful for things other than infighting.

Once Diana's lips were unrestrained, she managed to sputter, "But—"

"Objecting?" Evi unhooked Diana's neck and got to her knees, straddling Diana's hips. Not entirely by accident, the kimono fell open.

"No." To emphasize the point, Diana sat up herself and hugged Evi, giving her own gentle kiss. Diana was uncertain, probing, as if still not quite sure she was welcome.

During the lingering embrace, Evi's skin was caressed by Diana's satin top. Every brush ignited a flash of warmth that sank down to the core of her body. Evi wasn't satisfied with the tentative contact and wrapped her good arm and both legs around Diana, pulling her toward her.

Diana's breasts pressed against her, and Evi could feel Diana's nipples harden against her own skin. The satin separating them had become a sheet of silken fire.

They came up for air, and Evi could feel Diana's hands behind her, finding the collar of the kimono. Diana nipped at Evi's earlobe and whispered, "Why?"

While Diana fumbled off the left side of the kimono, being careful of Evi's shoulder, Evi's right hand slipped under the pajama top. She was asking herself the same question. "I'll give you a list."

Diana helped Evi lift her top over her head. Diana's pale skin glowed from both the reflected streetlight and its own internal heat. Evi kissed her cheek. "I'm lonely. I need you. Badly."

Evi kissed the hollow between Diana's collarbone and the nape of her neck while gradually easing them both back to the ground. She lifted her head and traced Diana's jawline with her right hand.

"You helped me . . ."

They were lying side by side now, skin touching. Diana was beginning to breathe heavily. Evi slid down and kissed Diana's left breast, lingering, sliding her tongue around the nipple while her right hand gently brushed its twin.

Diana arched her back and Evi rolled on top of her.

Evi glided down further on a slide of Diana's perspiration. She kissed Diana's navel, sliding her mouth around her abdomen. Evi could smell that Diana was becoming very wet. She looked up. "Most important . . ."

Evi slid down the rest of the way.

"You liked my eyes."

Evi lowered her head between Diana's legs and began to kiss Diana under the silky red hair she found there.

The conversation died after that.

They remained locked together for the better part of two hours. Somehow they managed to avoid breaking anything or popping Evi's shoulder out of its socket.

It was hard to place exactly when the lovemaking evolved into a simple embrace. But that's what it was when the sun began to rise. Evi rested her head on Diana's shoulder as they sat on the floor in front of the couch, wrapped in Evi's blanket. The table had been pushed aside, and Evi was looking past the comm, out the window.

Sunlight was just catching the tops of the buildings across the river. The snow had stopped, leaving the sky a crystalline blue. Somehow, the world looked worth living in again.

Evi felt Diana's hand brushing her hair. "Awake?"

"Yes."

"How do you feel?"

How did she feel? Damn confused, really. Not that she hadn't wanted to. What was strange was that she wanted to in the first place. It was unnerving to realize that she couldn't predict her own behavior.

She did have to admit that sex with Diana had been more gratifying than the sex Evi had had with any number of men. Evi didn't know if that was because she really was a lesbian or because she never gave a shit about the men she'd slept with.

Maybe it was because Diana was the first lover she'd had without the benefit of those damn contact lenses. All the others had been Chuck Dwyers waiting to happen.

"Better," Evi finally told her. And she did feel better. She had needed someone for a long time, since long before all this started.

There was a long pause before Diana went on. "Tell me something about yourself."

Evi closed her eyes. "A lot of it you wouldn't like . . ."

"Do you have a family?"

"No."

"No one?"

Evi thought back to Israel. "I had a family of sorts. About four dozen sisters, one father."

Diana stroked her hair. "I'm an only child. That many sisters sounds like quite a family."

Evi let out with her silent laugh. "We were Japanese-engineered humans, hatched in a Jordanian experimental facility, and we were all captured by a Mossad commando raid. I was raised in something between a boarding school and boot camp."

"You said you had a father?"

"Colonel Chaim Abdel. He ran the place where I was raised."

"What happened to them?"

Evi shrugged. "War broke out. We lost."

"That was a long time ago. How old were you?"

"When they nuked Tel Aviv, sixteen."

Diana didn't respond for a long time. After a while

she said, "I hoped it would be a long time before I heard stories like that again."

"What do you mean?"

"Oh, back in the forties I helped a lot of moreaus into the country. Especially after the riots when the borders were closed."

It was surreal, listening to that. For a long time after Evi made it into the country and was more-or-less forced into the Agency, her job had been busting people like Diana. Talk about strange bedfellows.

"When did you come to the States?" Diana asked.

"Forty-five."

"How'd you manage that? The INS is still uptight about engineered humans."

Evi thought about the round-faced State Department official at her debriefing. He had said that no franks were being let into the country. It was the first time Evi had heard that word. However, if she agreed to work for the government, perhaps he could work something out.

"I had to make a few concessions," Evi said.

"I'll bet."

Evi felt dishonest. She should be telling Diana the whole story, but Evi was suddenly afraid of losing her. How exactly could she tell this woman that she had spent the last twelve years working for the government?

She was also still very tired.

Evi sighed. "I still need to finish that good night's sleep you interrupted."

"Oh." Diana got to her feet and gathered up her top. "Good night— morning."

Diana began walking to the stairs that led to the loft and Evi cleared her throat.

Diana turned around. "What?"

Evi stood, holding the kimono in her good hand. "After all that, I sleep on the couch?"

* * *

On noon of New Year's Day, Evi woke up. She got out of bed carefully, to avoid waking Diana, and went down to the kitchen.

After she'd heated some leftover tofu, she took the ramcard from the library out of her backpack and slipped it into the reader for the comm. The comm took a second to warm up. She dug around and found the remote. It had been kicked under the couch sometime during the night.

A commercial station came on the screen, Nonhuman League Football. The game was halted for an injury and she briefly heard something about a twenty-yard penalty for illegal use of claws.

Evi found the database function on the remote and called up the information on her ramcard.

The N.Y. Public Library logo replaced some unnecessary roughness on the first down.

"Japan," she said to herself, wishing Diana had some more complex functions on her comm.

She spent a few hours going over what she already knew. Assassinations, car bombs, downed airplanes. Sometimes, however, a detail or two could catch her attention.

For instance, at least half of the assassinations the NLF claimed responsibility for were in some way involved with the Office of Science and Technology. The NLF hit hard liners, but a few of their targets were distressingly liberal. Some victims had actually been reformers who wanted to grant some limited independence to occupied Japan.

The NLF also had little tolerance for rival organizations. They were particularly gruesome to anyone who purported to speak for the Japanese people.

From Evi's point of view, she was looking at an organization that, despite its rhetoric, had a vested interest in the status quo.

That didn't mean anything in itself. Any organization was vulnerable to bureaucratic inertia and power games. Even terrorists, especially terrorists, could get so caught up in dogma that they lost sight of their original goals.

However, while the NLF's strikes were doing nothing for the liberation of Japan, they were very efficient in slowing technological development throughout the entire Pacific Rim. Especially in areas where Japan had excelled. In fact, she thought that it wouldn't be far-fetched to presume that the NLF was responsible, in large part, for the Asian scientific community becoming insular and paranoid.

As effective as the aliens' pet congressmen were in passing counterproductive legislation.

That brought her mind back to a line of thinking she'd been on earlier but hadn't followed to its ultimate conclusion.

The U.S. hadn't been the only country capable of interstellar probes. Before the Pan-Asian war, both India and Japan had been far ahead in their space programs.

Before the war.

That war was one of the ugliest chapters in world history. Close to a hundred million human dead. No one knew how many nonhuman. Two decades of fighting. And all the wrong countries won.

Could that have been caused by—

"No."

She didn't want to think about it. Past was past. What she needed now was some line on the NLF that could tell her if it *was* the Nippon Liberation Front after her, and if so, give her some idea why.

Money.

Finances always struck near the heart of the matter. It was the money trail that finally brought down that cell in Cleveland. If she found who put money in the NLF, she might be able to sharpen her focus. She needed specifics, not broad generalities.

Specifics . . .

144

She manipulated the control while she heard Diana awaken in the background. Text flew by as she listened to Diana shower, dress, and fix a pot of coffee.

The coffee smell closed on her, and she felt Diana sit down by her.

"Morning."

"Three-thirty in the afternoon, really," Evi responded.

"Picky, picky. I notice you left off the sunglasses."

Evi automatically put her right hand to her face, nearly bashing the remote control into her nose. The database stopped scrolling.

"What's on the comm?"

Evi set down the remote and looked at Diana. Diana was wearing an oversized sweater that hung on her very well. "Trying to find out who those Afghani mercenaries were working for."

Diana sipped her coffee and asked, "They work for Nyogi Enterprises?"

"Huh?" Evi looked at the comm. It had stopped on a U.S. Newsfax article about a ten-grand-a-plate dinner held by the board of Nyogi Enterprises. The text with the picture insinuated that the Japanese relief effort the dinner was raising money for was really the NLF in a very thin disguise. The article itself was rather low on facts and high on innuendo.

But as far as Evi was concerned, the picture was damning. Sitting at one of those ten-thousand-dollar plates was a face that Evi would never forget.

The peeper.

CHAPTER 12

"Nyogi Enterprises," Evi read, "Established in 2040 by refugee Japanese industrialists and financiers. Corporate headquarters, New York City. Major factory supplier to Latin American consumer electronics companies. Major stock holdings, they say zip. Major stockholders, they say zip. Assets, not specific, but they're compared to General Motors . . ."

Vague, vague, vague. Evi wanted to hit the comm. She thought of calling what's-his-name at the library, the one with the thesis. Except she didn't need to know about Nyogi Ent or its shadowy board of directors. What she needed to know was who the peeper was.

At least Evi had convinced the comm to crop and print out a copy of the peeper's face. "Are you sure that your comm can't be configured for a graphic search?"

"You've got to be kidding. That thing?" Diana started to laugh. Then she choked it off and drew her knees up under her sweater. "Sorry, I'm not being very helpful, am I?"

"If it weren't for you, I wouldn't have a picture of the bastard." *Or be here at this cheap hunk of annoying electronics.*

She ejected the library's ramcard and the comm's screen returned to football.

She looked at the picture she had of the peeper and realized that she still had the Long-Eighties. There was still a ramcard in the peeper's binoculars. He might have recorded something useful.

Evi zipped open her backpack and pulled out the Long-Eighties. They were a sensitive collection of British electronics and they'd been trashed. The video lens was cracked, and the LCD eyepieces showed kaleidoscopic patterns of green snow laced with dead-black nothing. Evi had to pry off the housing to remove the ramcard.

"At least he was recording."

The ramcard went in as a vulpine place-kicker for the San Francisco Earthquakes made the extra point.

She played the card at high-speed, backward. The video started with a blank screen imprinted with a timer and yesterday's date. The time counter started speeding backward as she raced over the all-too-familiar scene of her jumping around in the nude. Evi heard Diana stop breathing and turned to look at her. Diana was perched, leaning forward, on the edge of the couch. Evi watched Diana, who was absorbed in the video, until Diana waved frantically at the screen. "Stop, what was that?"

What was what? Evi started the comm playing forward again. The binocs were focused on a grainy green image of herself, on the balcony, doing her leg presses. Then she moved and vaulted on to the roof. There was a clear shot of a bullet impacting the headrest of the weight machine.

The binoculars didn't follow her.

Their view whipped around for a badly-angled shot of the neighboring condominium. The peeper focused in on the open window in time to see a definite muzzle flash. Briefly, she though she saw a face, and then the peeper whipped the binoculars back on her.

She backed up the video, frame by frame, until she caught the scene that gave a partial view of the sniper's face. She got a printout of that as well.

It wasn't Sukiota.

"Know him?" Diana asked.

Evi shook her head. "I think his name is Gabe."

"A cop?"

"I sincerely doubt it."

She started the reverse playback again.

Evi watched herself back into the apartment early yesterday morning, and then there was an abrupt jump cut to, according to the date on the record, a week earlier.

It was a daytime shot, in color, and Evi recognized the scene.

The peeper was looking through a window into Frey's apartment. Frey was there, with two people Evi recognized from her office. One was her fellow think tanker, David Price. The other was her immediate superior, Erin Hofstadter. The man she had reported to for the last six years.

Three others were in the apartment. One she didn't recognize. One she couldn't see clearly.

The last was the sniper.

"What the fuck is going on?" She froze the scene on the sextet so she could compare faces. The view she had printed of the sniper was fuzzy. There was a slight possibility that she was wrong. She doubted it.

She reviewed the card; there was all of five minutes of Frey's apartment on it. The scene was bracketed by Frey opening the window at the beginning and a jump cut at the end.

She sighed and played the five minutes she had, running the video back and forth and trying to read lips.

Frey opened the window and looked out. ". . . ains, do we bring her in?"

Frey was standing in front of Hofstadter, keeping Evi from seeing his response.

One of the unknowns, an old professor type, spoke to Hofstadter. He was in profile, and she could only

EMPERORS OF THE TWILIGHT

make the words "stupid idea" and "a vacation." Then
the prof put his face in his hands and shook his head.

Price was facing the window and was only partially
obscured by Frey. He spoke across Hofstadter, at the
prof. "Doc, stick to—" Price leaned forward and she
lost the next few words. When his mouth was visible
again, she made out the word "xenobiology." She rewound the video three times to get that word right.

Frey waved them down. He was still looking out the
window. "Cool it. We can't afford internal bickering."

One of the ones she didn't know, one dressed in an
impeccable black suit, spoke up. She could barely see
him from around the window frame. He waved his
hands, but his lips were only in view for the phrase
"I warned."

Price turned a pleading look at the sky and said a
whole sentence she could make out. "You and your
fucking tachyons."

"Shut up Pr ..." Frey turned around and delivered
an inaudible tirade. Then he sat down, facing the five
others across his black lacquer holo-table.

"Agreed," Hofstadter responded to something Frey
had said. Now that Frey was sitting, Hofstadter and
Price were the easiest people to interpret. "But I am
still against it."

The suit said something with a dismissing wave of
his hand. Evi wished he'd lean forward so she could
see his face. The glimpses she was getting of his profile
were tantalizingly familiar.

The suit's speech, whatever it was, initiated a shouting match that started everyone talking over everyone
else. Then the suit leaned into the frame to emphasize something.

She froze the frame and looked at him. She had
seen his face before; he had been the man standing
behind Hofstadter when she had called from the
theater.

There they were, she realized, the majority of the

149

people after her. This guy in the suit, Evi remembered Hofstadter calling him Davidson, Hofstadter himself, and the sniper, Gabe.

If Frey was sitting there, in the middle of it, why didn't he do Gabe's job and blow her away when he had the chance?

She looked at Gabe, standing in the background of the frozen scene. The sniper stood by the door and apparently contributed nothing to the conversation.

She rewound the shouting match and watched each face separately.

The suit leaned in to say, "—against bringing a non-human into the community."

Price was responding. "—in on the beginning, Davidson—"

Hofstadter was saying, "—late date would be counterproductive—"

The prof was saying something out of Evi's view.

Gabe remained close-mouthed.

Frey shouted them down, though Evi couldn't see what he said. He started pointing around the circle.

He pointed at the suit, Davidson. She couldn't see him, he'd leaned back out of the frame

He pointed at Price. "Yes."

Hofstadter. "No."

Evi couldn't see the prof's response.

Gabe. "I abstain."

Frey nodded and the video jumped to a night-enhanced picture of Evi leaving her apartment.

"That's it," she said and ejected the ramcard.

"What was that?"

She looked at the unlabeled ramcard, "I wish I knew, exactly." The card caught the light, which rippled rainbows across its surface. "I also wish you had a better comm."

Evi fished out the last ramcard she had, the one she'd found on the Afghani mercenary in the elevator shaft. It was dead black, with what appeared to be a serial number across the top of the card. It could be anything.

She slipped it into the card reader.

All the memo function would read off it was the message, "Property of Nyogi Enterprises. Authorized use only. Unauthorized use subject to prosecution, ten years imprisonment, and minimum fines of $500,000." Everything else on the card was encrypted and copy protected.

"I'll be damned. It's a card-key."

Evi looked over her shoulder at Diana. "You're right. The dogs work for Nyogi."

Diana got up and stood behind the couch, putting her arms around Evi's neck. Evi pressed the eject button on the remote, and football returned. She pressed the mute button.

She cocked her head back to look at Diana. "What?"

Diana kissed her on the forehead. "I'm just wondering what you're going to do now."

Evi closed her eyes and rested her head against Diana's chest. "I'm not sure. I want to rest and heal up, but there are still people after me."

"Nyogi?"

She nodded.

"They've treated you rudely."

Almost as rudely as the Agency. "They started the whole mess I'm involved in."

Diana's hand brushed against her right breast, and Evi reached up and held it there. She was warm again, and she realized that a repeat of last night could happen very easily. As far as Diana was concerned, she was a lesbian.

"What are you going to do?" Diana asked again. "I might be able to unearth my old contacts from the forties. The moreaus might be sympathetic—"

Evi shook her head. "I need to find out why this is happening before I go running off to the Bronx."

"Are you just going to walk up to a Nyogi exec and ask him?"

Evi opened her eyes and looked up at Diana. The veep she had liberated the aircar from had landed in a privileged space in the Nyogi tower. He had to be high up in the corporation. "Why not?"

She kissed Diana for giving her the idea. When Diana raised her head, Evi spit out some red hair and told her, "I can be very persuasive."

A half-hour on a public comm gave her the veep's name, Richard Seger. She had called his apartment—no way was she getting near that condo again—and been forwarded to Nyogi. She hung up before the call made it all the way through to the veep's office. It had confirmed what she wanted to know: Seger was working this New Year's Day.

At least he was in the Nyogi building.

Evi walked back to Diana's Estival. Diana lowered the window as she approached. "Are you *sure* you want me to leave?"

Evi nodded. "You shouldn't be near me when this goes down. No one can trace me to you. Let's keep it that way."

"The way you're dressed, I'm glad." Diana smiled as she said it. She was the one who had found the androgynous exec suit on such short notice. Diana had borrowed it from one of the warehouse's tenants. Male or female, Evi didn't know. The suit fit loosely, but it let Evi look like a junior corp type, and it hid the Mishkov.

Diana reached into the pocket of her jeans and pulled something out. "Here, before I forget." She handed Evi a pearl-handled switchblade. "It fell out of your jacket."

"Thanks." Evi slipped it into the top of the leather fringed boots she still wore. Then she leaned forward and kissed Diana good-bye. "You'll hear from me."

"I expect to," Diana responded as she drove away. *So I'm a lesbian*, Evi thought.

She put on her sunglasses and walked back to the limo she'd rented. She had wanted a less conspicuous vehicle, but the limo company was the only place open today that would take cash. She had rented the thing for only six hours, and her roll of twenties had been reduced to a small wad.

It was closing on six o'clock, and she was parked across Eighth from the entrance to the Nyogi parking garage. She could see the Empire State Building, down 33rd. After its recent refurb it outshone the glass and metal obelisks that swamped it. Unlike the Chrysler Building, people had spent money to fix up the old skyscraper. Steam belched from a chuckhole a car-length from her limo and Evi had the cynical thought that the Empire State Building was the only thing people spent money to fix up in this town.

She passed the time by popping the cover off the dash and disabling the collision-avoidance systems on the limo.

The sky darkened from a crystalline blue to a dark purple. She kept watch on the exit from the garage, as well as on the passing traffic. For more than an hour, nothing left the garage, and the cars that passed her were, for the most part, taxis.

By seven-thirty the sky was dead-black beyond the streetlights. According to the dash clock, and Evi's time sense, it was exactly seven-thirty when a car pulled out of the Nyogi parking garage. In the back, she could see her friend from the penthouse. She'd been right about him not being able to replace that Peregrine so fast.

Driving the Chrysler Mirador was a huge Japanese. Evi supposed that the chauffer doubled as a body-guard. She let the sedan get a few car-lengths ahead of her on Eighth before she pulled the limo into the traffic behind it.

As they drove past the mid-forties, she passed the Mirador. She made sure she pulled in directly in front of the veep's sedan. She slowed the car under the speed limit as they came to the red light at 56th. The light changed to green as she approached, so she accelerated.

As soon as the Mirador picked up speed to follow her, she slammed on the brakes in the limo.

The chauffer and the Mirador's computer tried to keep from rear-ending her, but the snow and the distance between them made sure there was a satisfying if undramatic crunch. Both cars slid to a stop midway into the intersection, and every taxi in New York City used it as an excuse to lean on the horn.

Evi smiled to herself, cut the engine to her limo, and got out of the car.

"What've I done?" She put on her most innocent tone.

The driver getting out of the Mirador looked unsympathetic. The huge Asian was round, solid, easily 200 kilos and two meters. She couldn't help but think of videos she'd seen of old sumo wrestlers. She smelled the taint of the modified testosterone in the driver's veins. He had a bald scalp and a deep shadow on his chin that she knew no amount of shaving would eliminate.

He was a frank. She knew what brand, too. He was one of Hiashu's early combat models. The first one they started playing glandular games with. They weren't known for their intelligence.

"Lady, what the fuck did you think—"

She walked up to him, shaking her head. "Look, I'm really sorry about this. It's my fault." She put her good hand on his shoulder. "I'll pay for the damages. Do we have to get the cops involved?"

She brushed his cheek, and she could smell a wave of overpowering lust sweating off the man. He couldn't control it, not after what the Hiashu engineers had done to his gonads.

He looked indecisive.

She slammed her knee up between the man's legs.

His eyes widened and he gasped. His arms began to move into a defensive posture, too late . . .

She kneed him again, and his eyes rolled back into his head. With her right hand she gave him a shove that guided his collapse. The man lost consciousness as he fell on his side in the snow next to the limo.

Oversized glands made a convenient target.

The Mirador's engine was still going, and Evi walked to the still-open driver's door and got behind the wheel. She backed away from the limo and turned onto 56th.

That went smoothly.

She glanced back at the veep, who was still looking back at the limo. He turned around to face her with a look of stunned disbelief. She smiled at him. "I won't ask if you remember me."

Evi headed for the Queensboro Bridge.

CHAPTER 13

The lower level of the bridge was undergoing repairs. The work had stopped for the holiday. Evi drove the Mirador through a few sawhorses and past a few detour signs to get on the lower thoroughfare, where she could have some privacy.

She drove past city vehicles, dumptrucks, and silent construction equipment. She slowed as she went on, and the Mirador started vibrating as she hit the old concrete. To her right, the guardrail abruptly disappeared. She shut down the car, leaving it in gear.

The only sounds were now the wind and the rumble of traffic driving by above them.

She drew the Mishkov and pointed it at the veep. "Get out."

"But—"

"If you're cooperative, we can get through this without any bloodshed."

The veep spread his hands and let himself out of the back of the car. Evi followed, keeping the gun trained on him. With her left hand she reached into her pocket for a pair of handcuffs she'd liberated from Diana's bedstand. It hurt her shoulder, but she wasn't about to lower the gun.

She tossed the cuffs to the veep. "Cuff yourself to that." She waved the gun at the scaffolding at the near edge of the hole in the side of the bridge.

The veep looked at the velvet-lined cuffs and arched an eyebrow.

"You're right," Evi said when he didn't move immediately. "Maybe I should just shoot you."

He moved, cuffing himself to the scaffolding. "What—"

Evi put the gun away and walked to the edge of the bridge where the guardwall should have been. She looked down over the East River. Then she walked over to the Mirador and picked up a loose steel reinforcing rod.

"What," he repeated, "are you doing?"

"I'll get to you in a moment," Evi said as she slammed the windshield with the rod. She hit it a few times to clear out most of the glass. She did the same to the rear window.

She dropped the iron rod and turned to the veep. "Don't want any trapped air keeping this thing afloat."

She reached through the driver's window and turned the wheel toward the hole in the side of the bridge.

"You're not . . ." he said.

She pushed the Mirador toward the edge, until the front wheels left the pavement and hung over empty space. She looked down again; still no boat traffic.

She got behind the car and kicked it in the ass. There was a short scrape, and the rear end bounced a little. She kicked it again, and there was a longer scrape. The rear end bounced some more. This time the rear wheels came a centimeter off the ground.

She stood there and looked at the precariously balanced sedan. Then she looked at the veep, hooked her right hand under the bumper, and lifted. She rocked the car up to the point where the rear wheels were a meter off the ground, and gravity took over.

There was a sickening scrape as the chassis slid against the edge of the bridge. Then the rear wheels hit the edge and they rolled, silently pushing the car off.

A few seconds passed before she heard a splash. Then she walked up to the veep, smiling.

He was staring at the river. "Someone saw that. They'll call the police."

"No lights on the car, no lights under here, and if someone did see, police response time in this city is fifteen minutes, minimum. Long enough." She stopped a half-meter from the veep. "Now, will the cops find you cuffed to the scaffold?" She jerked her head in the direction of the river. "Or when they dredge the river for that car?"

"What do you want?" The veep hugged the scaffold and kept looking down at the river. The Mirador was drifting by, and sinking as it did so.

"In the aircar you asked, 'Do you know who I am?' I decided to find out, Mr. Seger."

"All I do is acquire real estate for Nyogi Enterprises."

"Like the building you live in?"

"Yes."

"Like other condos up and down Fifth?"

"Yes."

"Like condos that got plastered with dead Afghani dogs?"

Seger choked. "Yes, yes, damnit."

Nyogi owned her building. Nyogi had owned Frey's building. This had been going on for a while. She was on the right track. Evi ran her hand across Seger's face. He had a day's growth of beard, and it looked like he'd slept in his thousand-dollar suit. He had lost all vestiges of his hostage training. She ran her fingers through his hair and balled her hand into a fist. She yanked his head back. "Why is Nyogi after me?"

"I don't know."

She leaned next to Seger's ear. The smell of his sweat overpowered the East River. "You've spent over a grand on hair replacement. Don't risk that investment by lying to me."

Seger tried to shake his head. "I don't."

Evi let his hair go and pulled out the Mishkov. She placed the barrel on his temple. "Who instructed you to buy those properties?"

Seger swallowed and stayed silent.

She raised the Mishkov and whipped it across Seger's face. "I'm not playing games here!" Blood trickled down from a cut she'd opened in the veep's cheek.

"Okay ..."

"Good. Now—" Evi ran the barrel of the Mishkov down Seger's cheek, under his chin, and used it to turn his head to face him. "Who told you to acquire those properties?"

Seger swallowed again. He was drenched with sweat. He was even more scared than he'd been when she stole his aircar. Seger sputtered, "Hitaki, Hioko Hitaki."

"Nice Jap name. Works for Nyogi?"

Seger took too long to answer again.

"That should've been easy, a simple yes or no question."

"Are you trying to get me killed?"

"That's a stupid question to ask with a gun in your face. You're stalling."

Seger nodded violently. "Yes, yes, damnit. He works for Nyogi. He's Special Operations—"

That was a familiar euphemism.

"He also works for other people, doesn't he?"

Seger nodded, weakly.

"Japanese Nationalists?"

Seger froze, looking down. She jabbed the barrel of the gun into the flesh under his jaw, forcing his head up.

"Yes or no?"

"If I told you—"

She smiled. "That's enough of an answer. I know who to thank for the Afghanis who tried to kill me. Now we come to the million-dollar question—"

Evi leaned in until they were barely a centimeter apart. "Why?"

"I just handle the real estate. They don't tell—"

"I'm going to ask you again. Why? If you say you don't know, I'm going to put a bullet through your head and toss you into the East River."

Seger sucked in a breath and started shaking. Evi could hear him subvocalize, "Where the hell are they?"

"Where the hell is who?"

Seger looked her in the face. He was on the verge of panic. "No one—"

That's why he was stalling. Evi backed away from Seger, pointing the gun at him. "Where is it?"

"What are you talking about?"

"The tracking device, where is it?"

The color drained from Seger's face. "They made me eat it."

She kept backing away. "I should blow you the fuck away—"

"Damn it, you think I wanted this? Do you know what those creatures are like? I was treated like an *animal*—"

"*WHY?*" Evi yelled at him. Her gun was shaking.

"They want their people back—" He was interrupted by the sound of an approaching aircar. He looked out over the river. Evi could see the sleek black wedge of a Chrysler Wyvern.

Seger started waving his free hand and shouting. "Here, over here!"

She could see what was about to happen. She got on the ground behind a city truck and yelled, "Seger, get down!"

Machine gun fire strafed the lower level of the Queensboro bridge. She looked out from under the truck and saw Seger jerk backward and lose his footing. He ended up dangling from one velvet-cuffed arm.

EMPERORS OF THE TWILIGHT

A bullet came too close, blowing out the truck's tire opposite her.

Damn.

She wedged herself between the truck and the concrete median, her back to a rear tire. She was pinned where she was. She could hear the Wyvern hovering on the other side of the truck. Was the driver going to try to slide into the hole in the wall?

Damn it, he was. She could hear the whine of the fans change in character as the Wyvern made its approach. She could smell the electricity off its inductor. Then a breeze started blowing around her as the aircar began to dust the concrete.

Evi swallowed and checked the Mishkov.

She had six shots and the switchblade in her boot. She wondered if it would be enough. She doubted it. The hit on her condo had been a costly mistake, a mistake that people like the NLF rarely made twice.

She could smell the canines now, more than three of them.

She had two choices, sit or bolt.

If she bolted, they'd shoot at her. She didn't like that idea. So far she'd avoided getting a bullet in her. She'd like to keep it that way.

Perhaps now was the time to test the hypothesis that they wanted her alive.

Someone hit the underside of the Queensboro bridge with a spotlight. What had been the sound of a slow advance behind her became running and scrambling. The night was sliced open by sirens and the sound of helicopters.

An overamplified voice over a PA system ordered, "Step away from the aircar."

There was the sound of machine-gun fire from behind her, the distant sound of shattering glass, and the spotlight went out. She heard the Wyvern rev up.

The cops opened fire.

She pulled herself into a little ball. Concrete chips

flew by her. Bullets ricocheted off the truck she hid behind, carrying the smell of sparking metal. Two more tires blew out.

There was a loud pop and the smell of molten ceramics as a bullet clipped an active inductor. It had to be the Wyvern. She heard the fans die, and the gunfire ceased in time for her to hear the Wyvern splash home.

Another spotlight lit up the lower level, and she could hear cars approaching from both directions. Red and blue began to cut into the white of the spotlight. Short of dashing for the edge of the bridge and diving into the East River, there was nowhere she could go. The Wyvern might have had her pinned, but the cops had her surrounded.

It had been only ten minutes since she ditched the Mirador. She had been overly pessimistic about NYPD response time.

She put the Mishkov on the ground next to her, and when a NYPD uniform ducked around the truck, gun drawn, she spread her hands wide. "I surrender."

The cops pulled her out into the open. Black-and-whites were everywhere. Way too many for deep-sixing a car. Like the cops that had surrounded the theater on Times Square, these boys had come out of nowhere. It was as if there were a whole division of NYPD cops primed and ready to . . .

To what?

The cop bent her over the hood of a new Chevy Caldera cop car. He patted her down and emptied her pockets. Three cops stood by with ready weapons. The cop liberated her wallet, her backpack, and several magazines for the Mishkov.

The cop car was too damn new. The cops also had a pair of helicopters. One swept the East River with a spotlight while the other just hovered with its light trained on the bridge. The cops themselves were too well equipped.

They were also too white.

By the time the cop took her sunglasses and started ushering her to a windowless van, Evi realized that there were only two blacks in a group of nearly thirty NYPD officers, and there were no Hispanics, or Asians . . .

She was roughly cuffed to a bar inside the van as she realized she was looking at a well-camouflaged Agency operation.

They let her stew for two hours after the van stopped moving. There wasn't any light, and there was nothing to do but sit and try not to think about the way the cuffs hurt her shoulder.

Why am I still alive, Abdel?

Obviously, came the reply, *we're guilty of faulty reasoning at some point. The Agency wants something beyond your demise.*

The Agency proper didn't want to ice her. Hofstadter was acting on his own initiative with the sniper. That would explain why Frey was helping her rather than trying to kill her.

It didn't explain why the Aerie wouldn't acknowledge her existence.

It also didn't explain what the peeper had recorded on his binoculars.

It was after ten when the door on the transport opened. She was as far from the door as the chain on the cuffs would allow. The rear of the van whooshed aside and the first thing that hit her was the smell. The New York subway system was the only place where she had ever come across that particular flavor combining the odors of fermenting urine, century old grease, stagnant water, overheated transformers, and dead air.

Somewhere, a train passed by. The noise rattled the walls of the van and made Evi's teeth ache.

The open door faced an anachronism. Amidst the

cracked dirty tile, blackened girders, and crumbling concrete were scattered brand-new comms, electronic surveillance equipment, and dozens of people in NYPD uniforms.

The small command center had taken over an old subway platform, and Evi couldn't see more than ten meters past it because the entire area was lit by extremely bright temporary lamps that hung from a ceiling that was invisible beyond them.

Most of the "cops" swarmed around the equipment and ignored Evi and her van; three didn't.

Two were leveling automatic weapons at the van. They were Agency. The NYPD didn't issue Uzis to patrol officers. As if to drive the point home, the third was Sukiota.

Sukiota climbed into the back of the van. The door remained open, and guns remained leveled at Evi as Sukiota walked in front of her. Sukiota balled her hand into a fist and slammed it into Evi's stomach. It was so fast that Evi had no time to prepare for the impact. She doubled over and started retching.

When she was done spilling pork and bean curd over the floor of the van, Sukiota grabbed her by the chin and lifted her head to face her. "For my car, Isham, and the theater."

A gob of half-digested tofu dribbled out of Evi's mouth. "Sorry," she managed to choke out.

Sukiota slammed her knee into Evi's solar plexus. The pain spasmed every muscle in Evi's body. She shook with dry heaves, and she prayed that she wasn't suffering any internal injuries.

"Want to know why you're alive?"

All Evi could manage was a hoarse monosyllable.

"You're alive because you are screwing with my mission." Sukiota grabbed Evi's bad shoulder and violently pulled her upright. A dagger of fire raced down the length of Evi's arm. *"And I want to know why!"*

She looked at Sukiota, and she began to realize that

something else was going on here. Something she hadn't known, or guessed at.

Sukiota released Evi's shoulder and sat down across from her. "Do we have an understanding?"

Evi nodded. She understood. She knew the type of agent Sukiota was.

Another train passed nearby, the lights outside dimmed briefly, and dust filtered in through the open door to the van.

"Who do you work for, Isham?"

She couldn't stop her silent laugh, even if she was risking being hit again. "Same people you do."

Sukiota hit her with a backhand slap that was more irritating than painful. "Bullshit. I thought of that, when you called the Aerie. You aren't on the database."

"Then I got erased."

"Convenient. You were carrying a ramcard of surveillance footage. Who are the principals in the apartment?"

Evi told her. If Sukiota was on the ball, she knew already.

Sukiota nodded at the names she knew. "Good. Now I'd like you to explain to me how seven *dead* people are screwing with my mission."

"What?" Dead?

Sukiota leaned forward. "Ezra Frey died in an explosion on an Agency mission in Cleveland in August '53. Erin Hofstadter has been missing ever since a State Department fact-finding mission into occupied Japan in December '53. David Price drove his car into Chesapeake Bay in September '53. Davidson, his first name is—was—Leo, burned in his house in San Francisco May 23rd, 2055. The professor-type's name is Scott Fitzgerald, and he was supposed to have fallen from a radio telescope and broken his neck in '53 . . ."

Sukiota paused, apparently to gauge Evi's reaction. Evi knew she must have looked as shocked as she felt.

"I suppose you *didn't* know you were looking at a recording of a room full of corpses? Two more are on the walking dead list, Isham. The guy you called 'Gabe' had the code designation 'Gabriel,' a freelance assassin. He was reported neutralized in '54—"

"You said two." Sukiota had gone through the whole room.

Sukiota smiled and pulled a ramcard out of her pocket and looked at it as if she could read it with the naked eye. "You mean you don't know? Someone invested a lot of time and energy to falsify dozens of secure databanks on your behalf—"

"What the hell—"

Sukiota grabbed her by the neck, choking off her statement, and held the edge of the ramcard a few millimeters from her eye. Evi watched a rainbow shimmer shoot across the edge of the card.

Sukiota shook the card. "Don't play dumb, Isham. The Aerie doesn't respond to dead agents. And you *died,* Isham. In December 2053, a few days after Hofstadter disappeared—"

Evi's eye was beginning to water. She couldn't take her gaze off the edge of the ramcard. "I was transferred," Evi whispered.

"Where."

"We call it the Domestic Crisis Think Tank."

Sukiota loosened her grip. "All these corpses work there?"

"I don't know." Sukiota tightened and Evi speeded up. "Dave Price and Hofstadter I'm sure, Davidson maybe. The others I never heard of before yesterday."

"Who runs the place, and where is it?"

"Hofstadter runs my department. It's all in a building off Columbia. Broadway. 109th."

Sukiota leaned back, rolling the ramcard in her fingers. "That's good. See how simple it is. You answer my questions and bad things don't happen. Now you are going to tell me what happened in your condo."

CHAPTER 14

Sukiota questioned her for three hours. The only thing Evi tried to hide was her evening with Diana. Thankfully, Sukiota didn't seem to care much where Evi spent her night. What Sukiota wanted were details, details about the Afghanis and the NLF, and details about the Domestic Crisis Think Tank ...

Sukiota never once asked about the aliens.

Evi had mentioned the aliens, when Sukiota had questioned her about the scenarios she'd been cooking for Hofstadter. Evi'd responded with the studies she'd written up on a hypothetical invasion.

Sukiota's only reaction had been a condescending smirk. She'd been much more interested in Evi's studies of hypothetical moreau violence.

When Sukiota finished the questions that interested her, she uncuffed Evi and, escorted by five Uzi-toting pseudo-cops, led her back on the abandoned subway platform and tossed her in a holding cell.

The cell was as makeshift as the rest of their headquarters. It used to be a public john. The place had been stripped to the walls. Dead pipes jutted out of the walls. The musty urine smell had stayed, as if it were baked into the yellowing tile, under the cracked glaze. Spray-painted graffiti wrapped around the walls, mostly gang names. The name "Pendragon" seemed to predominate. That and the 130th Street something-or-other. They cuffed her to a pipe in the wall near the floor.

One lit fluorescent tube dangled from the ceiling by a pair of frayed wires. It rattled and blacked out every time a train passed close by.

A pipe near the door dripped irregularly. The echo was irritating enough that Evi thought they had purposely chained her out of reach of the drip as a low-grade torture.

At least she'd learned something about what was going on, although it was depressing to learn that someone had already written her obituary back in 2053.

It was clear that the Domestic Crisis Think Tank had stepped beyond the Agency's purview. Not only that, Sukiota showed no knowledge of the aliens. At the think tank, the aliens were taken as a given. A top secret given, but a given. It looked as though everything that Evi had uncovered in Cleveland had never gotten beyond Frey, who'd been fielding the operation.

Instead of booting the aliens upstairs, Frey must have bottled up everyone involved and siphoned off funds for his own operation. For six years she had been working for some private conspiracy.

A private conspiracy that wanted her dead.

Hofstadter was behind the sniper.

Frey had been surprised at what was going on. Frey had been running toward her building. Frey had asked her about Hofstadter's state of mind. And Frey had mentioned that he had been on vacation himself. The last thing he had ever said was that *he* needed *her* help.

Frey set up the conspiracy that ran the think tank. He had to be the person behind it. He was the only one in a position to bottle up knowledge of the aliens. And the timing of most of the "deaths" had been shortly after the Cleveland mission.

He might have set up the conspiracy, but it looked

as if he had lost control of it. Hofstadter had taken over. That would explain Frey's behavior . . .

She remembered something Frey had said. "Price was right."

If Hofstadter, Davidson, and Gabriel were the forces arrayed against her, perhaps Frey and Price were allies. Frey was dead, but Price might still be out there. He was locking out calls to his comm, but Dave could still be sitting in his house in Jackson Heights.

Queens, Evi thought.

Frey was going to take her to a "safehouse" in Queens.

Evi let out with her silent laugh. Price *was* an ally, if he was still out there. She looked around the pit she found herself in. How the hell was she going to contact Price?

She had to get out of here. She didn't trust the Agency, especially after finding out that for six years she'd been a de facto traitor. She didn't picture Suki-ota allowing her to outlive her usefulness. She might have already passed that point.

She looked at the pipe she was chained to. If she could get free of it, she might have a chance to get out of here. They hadn't found the switchblade in her boot.

A switchblade against Uzis?

Shut up, Abdel.

One cuff was around her right wrist, thankfully her good arm; the other was cuffed around the base of a pipe extending out of the wall. The pipe terminated in a lip that held a large connector that would have attached to some part of a john. The piece was rusted and fused into a single object.

If she could loosen the connector, she could slide off the handcuffs.

The catch was, she had to do it lefthanded.

Evi gritted her teeth and grabbed the connector

169

with her left hand. Just bending her arm to reach it shot a lance of pain through her shoulder.

"This isn't going to be fun," she whispered to herself.

She sucked in a deep breath and twisted the end of the connector as hard as she could. It felt as if she were trying to twist her shoulder out of her socket. She kept pushing, trying to ignore the grinding she felt in her shoulder. The rough, rusty surface of the connector bit into her fingers, and her grip began to slide on her own blood.

She heard a snap, and her hand slipped off the pipe. She fell to the floor and, for a few seconds, thought that the snap had been the bone in her shoulder. But as the pain receded and her breathing returned to normal, she realized that the noise had come from the pipe.

The connector had remained fused to the pipe, but the pipe itself now rotated freely. She pulled on the end of it, and it slid out from the wall. The end that came out from the wall was threaded and polished smooth. The handcuffs slid easily over it.

So far so good.

She wiped her left hand on the exec trousers, leaving a dark stain. Then she pulled the switchblade out of her boot.

If Sukiota stayed true to form, she'd leave the guards by the door when she came. And she'd come in unarmed. Coming in unarmed would have a point when you didn't want the prisoner to steal a weapon. However, it gave the prisoner an advantage if she was already armed.

Evi slid the pipe back into place and folded her body over it and her right arm so they wouldn't see her hand was free. She waited.

It was five-thirty in the morning when Sukiota opened the door and walked into the cell. Two of the pseudo-cops stood outside with their Uzis pointed into the room.

The cops were human; their reaction time wouldn't be quick enough. At least she hoped so.

Sukiota walked into the middle of the room. "We're going to have another little talk."

"You bet we are," Evi responded in as insolent a tone as she could muster.

"You—" Sukiota stepped toward Evi, hand raised.

Evi leapt. She tackled Sukiota to the far wall, slamming her good shoulder up under Sukiota's chin. Sukiota's head thudded against the tile. Evi kept close to her, hoping that the guards out the door would hesitate out of fear of hitting their superior.

They didn't fire, and by the time Sukiota had recovered from the head blow, Evi was pressing the knife against her jugular.

For a second, everything stopped moving. One of the cops, one of the token blacks, had stepped into the room. He froze, machine gun leveled at Evi and Sukiota. Beyond the door, out on the subway platform, the pseudo-cops who were manning equipment at the impromptu command center stopped their activity as they turned to watch what was going on behind them. Even the dust from the last train passing seemed to hang in the air, frozen in the lights.

"Drop the guns!" Evi yelled at the guards, keeping her gaze locked on Sukiota.

The vein bulged from the pressure of the knife. A little more pressure, or a quick slash to the left or right, and even an engineered metabolism wouldn't keep Sukiota from bleeding to death.

"NOW!"

Two guns clattered to the ground. Evi moved around, to Sukiota's right, so she could keep an eye on the gunmen and her hostage.

"This is a dumb move, Isham."

"Don't make any sudden moves. I'm as quick as you are, and younger."

"Enjoy it. You won't get any older."

The two cops, black and white, were staring at Evi, guns at their feet. "You out there, kick that weapon away."

The one outside the room did as she told him.

"And you," she said to the one in the room with them, "kick that gun over here."

The gun slid across the tile to clatter to Sukiota's feet. Sukiota's eyes glanced down briefly and Evi pressed the knife harder. "Your throat'd open up before you were halfway there." Evi put her foot on the butt of the gun. "Not worth it."

She addressed the black cop, "Get out of here."

He backpedaled out of the room, leaving Evi and Sukiota alone to face each other. Sukiota smiled. "Now what?" She asked.

Evi was becoming aware of the pulse in her neck. There was a coppery taste in her mouth. *Calm,* she told herself, *you have a hostage.* She looked deep into her adversary's eyes and came to a realization. "You *enjoy* this shit."

Sukiota smiled wider.

"Get on the ground, face down, slowly."

Sukiota slid slowly down. Evi kept her knife pressed into Sukiota's neck. A small trail of blood had leaked down the edge to form a small bead on the web between Evi's thumb and forefinger.

She put her knee in the small of Sukiota's back and glanced at the scene out the door. Everyone was facing the cell. A few were trying to ease out of her field of vision.

"All of you, down on the fucking ground, now!"

To the last one, they hit the dirt. They knew when it was not a good idea to play games.

Sukiota was wearing a familiar-looking black jumpsuit. Evi reached down under Sukiota with her left hand, which hurt like hell, and unzipped the top about halfway.

Sukiota was maintaining a level tone of voice. "Are you going to use me as a hostage or rape me?"

Sukiota was trying to rattle her, have her make a mistake. Evi almost slugged Sukiota the way she'd been slugged. In Evi's awkward position that move would have been disastrous.

"Put your hands flat at your side."

Sukiota did so, and Evi retrieved her left hand and pulled Sukiota's collar down to her mid-back, restraining her arms. Only after she had Sukiota somewhat immobilized, did Evi reach over for the gun.

It wasn't a real Israeli Uzi. It was an Italian knockoff. It still carried uncomfortable echoes.

She held the barrel of the gun between Sukiota's naked shoulder blades with her left hand as she slowly withdrew the switchblade and pocketed it. Then she switched the gun to her good hand. "You're going to get me out of here."

She backed off of Sukiota, holding the Uzi with her right hand and the collar of Sukiota's jumpsuit with her left. "Get up."

She did so, stripped to the waist. "You can't—"

"Can the speech. Where's my bag?"

"Over there." Sukiota gestured with her head. Evi saw her backpack sitting on a table next to one of the portable comms out on the platform. "You," she yelled at the cop laying in front of the door. "I want you to get up and slowly walk to that backpack. Bring it here."

The cop looked up at them and Sukiota said in a disgusted tone, "Do as she says."

"Finally being cooperative?" Evi asked.

"It's not like you're going to get away."

"Just keep thinking that." The cop returned with the backpack, tossed it into the room, and returned to his spot on the ground without being told. Evi briefly let go of Sukiota to retrieve her backpack. She made sure the gun was a constant pressure between Sukiota's shoulder blades.

"Even if you get out of here," Sukiota said. "I'll be able to find you."

Evi shouldered the pack with a wince. "You know the drill. We're going to move slow, and by the numbers." She grabbed Sukiota's collar again. "Now, walk out. Toward the van."

It was nervewracking, the slow advance toward the police van. The darkness beyond the lights seemed perfect to hide a sniper, and every eye was locked on her, looking for an opening. All they needed was one person with a gun that wanted her dead more than they wanted Sukiota alive.

Somewhere down the length of the abandoned subway tunnel was the echo of dripping water. Closer was the occasional electronic beep from the equipment. One of the comms began to ring for attention, an incoming call. One of the agents looked at the offending comm but didn't move toward it.

"This is a communications hub," Sukiota told her. "You've cut it out of the loop. How many people do you think are converging on us right now?"

Sukiota was right, too right. This HQ might be makeshift, but there were enough agents, computers, and secret encryption and surveillance equipment here to make any compromising event here a national security risk. A priority risk. Red lights would be flashing in DC right now, and the Feds would be mobilizing everything in the immediate area from the FBI to the Coast Guard.

That triggered another thought, one that was even scarier.

Am I being set up? Evi thought. This seemed to be going much too smoothly.

Evi backed against the side of the police van. The

handcuffs chained to her wrist was rattling. She calmed her shaking hand.

"Get in the van."

"It's locked."

Evi didn't like the thought that Sukiota was keeping her cool better than she was. Evi looked at one of the agents hugging the ground nearby. He was the other black guy.

"You, lose the gunbelt."

He looked up at her and fumbled it off. Evi was getting nervous. She'd almost feel better if one of these Agency people dove for a gun. They were being too acquiescent.

But even if it was a setup, what could she do other than what she was doing?

"Come over here and punch in the combination for this vehicle."

She watched him unlock the van door and then had him resume his position on the ground. Evi ushered Sukiota into the passenger seat, fastening Sukiota's seatbelt with her left hand. Between the restraining of the jumpsuit bunched around Sukiota's forearms, and the seatbelt itself, Sukiota was immobilized.

"Where are we?" Evi asked. The view out the front windshield showed more of the subway platform, which ended about ten meters in front of the van. To the right, the platform dropped off to the subway tracks. To the left there was a blank tile wall broken only by a large garage door hanging open next to the nose of the van. That was the only route from which the van could have come.

Beyond the door was darkness.

"There's only one exit."

Evi sighed. "I could, out of view of all the people out there, quietly slit your femoral artery and try and bluff my way through using your corpse as a hostage."

You're letting her get to you, Abdel said, *that's what she wants.*

175

Yes, but someone still ought to bury her.

"We're under East 130th Street."

Evi started the van.

"The hole opens into the parking garage under the new Harlem precinct station." Sukiota wore an evil smile.

Damn. That meant cops, sharpshooters, all waiting for the Feds to show up. That blew her only escape route. No wonder Sukiota was smiling.

Could that be why the Agency people weren't acting? Did they want her to run that police blockade? Was it because they didn't expect her to break through it—?

Or because they thought she could?

Being shot while trying to escape was a venerable method of disappearing troublesome prisoners. That could be it.

Or they could want her to escape.

Evi decided she was getting too paranoid even for the situation at hand. All she knew for sure was that she didn't want to use that garage door as her escape route.

Evi shifted the van into gear, hit the headlights, and gunned the engine. Out of the corner of her eye, she could see Sukiota lose the smile. "What?"

Evi didn't head for the door. She aimed right off the edge of the platform, turning the wheel to shoot the van out on to the tracks themselves. The bone-jarring thud of the impact reawakened the pain in her gut where Sukiota had punched her.

Gunfire sounded from behind her, but none of the shots seemed to hit the van.

While the van was making the abrupt transition from platform to tracks, Evi had a brief fear that there wasn't enough clearance under the van for the rails. After the one big jar, the rail began sliding under the van inside the left tire. Even so, it wasn't a smooth ride. The rotting ties were busy trying to shake the right side of the van apart.

They shot down the tunnel, leaving the platform behind them. The van's headlights cut a hole in the darkness ahead. Concrete walls shot by on the left, while on the right, black grime-coated girders flew by.

The top of the rail that the van was straddling was dark with rust. Evi considered that a good sign.

The speedometer was creeping toward 100 kilometers an hour.

"You're crazy."

She smiled at Sukiota's reaction. "In the last forty-eight hours I think I've earned the privilege."

"You're only delaying the inevitable. Someone *will* catch up with you."

"Think I don't know that? I tried to come in, and I got *you* for my trouble."

"You're not helping yourself—"

Evi felt her pulse race as the scream of a train passed by them. Very close, in a neighboring tunnel. The entire van shook in response, and she had to struggle with the steering to keep the vibrating wheels on course. When she could hear again, she told Sukiota, "I cooperate with you, and I'd disappear. As far as the Feds are concerned, I'm either a rabid terrorist or a great big embarrassment."

"Or a traitor."

A bright light caught the windshield and began to close on them. White washed the front of the van. Evi hit the brakes, for all the good it would do, as the sound of the oncoming train threatened to shake the van apart.

A wall of moving graffiti shot by the van on the track to their right.

She caught her breath, then turned to Sukiota. Sukiota hadn't moved and was looking at Evi in much the same way Chuck Dwyer had.

"You—" She sucked in another breath and looked

at Sukiota. "No. Explaining it wouldn't do any good."
She swung the Uzi up to Sukiota's jawline. "But cut
the 'traitor' shit. I've never turned on anyone."

Sukiota remained silent.

Evi felt her hand tighten on the trigger. "Whatever
was going on, it was Frey's operation—"

"You were recruited by a rogue element of the Executive sometime in '53, and when things went bad
and they tried to eliminate you, you tried to run back
into the fold of the Agency."

There was nothing she could do. As far as the government was concerned, she was fucked. Ignorance
never cuts very well as a defense. Frey and the others
had separated from the Agency and had followed their
own secret agenda.

Why did they drag her along without telling her the
full story?

She pressed the gun harder beneath Sukiota's jaw.
"Do you *know* what happened in Cleveland in August
of '53?"

"The Agency terrorist division attempted to appre-
hend a canine terrorist named Hassan Sabah."

"Who'd he work for?"

"The CIA. They were trying to cover up an operation to funnel money to political candidates."

"The CIA?"

Evi couldn't believe it. The aliens had gotten away
with it. The secret masters, the ones who had controlled the money, had manufactured the CIA story
out of whole cloth. The agents in Langley were no
more in control than the congressmen who were
indicted.

"That was a plant for public consumption. The CIA
was just a scapegoat. Who was Hassan *really* working for?"

Sukiota stared at her.

"You think it was a coincidence that Hassan's last

known affiliation was with the NLF? The same people
the Afghanis you're tailing are working for?"

Evi reached into Sukiota's pockets. She found a wallet, the keys to the handcuff she was wearing, and the
white ramcard that Sukiota had been waving in her
face earlier.

Sukiota stayed silent.

Why didn't Frey and the others bring her all the
way in? Why the hell did they let her be blindsided
by all this?

Anger was beginning to twist in her gut. "Let me
draw you a picture, sister. I look at you and I see
myself back in '53. You're about to tackle something
that's a hell of a lot bigger than you are. You're going
to get too close to what's at the core of Nyogi and
the NLF. You get too close to Frey's little sideline,
and everything you thought you worked for is going
to go south on you—"

She unlocked the passenger door, popped Sukiota's
seatbelt, and prodded her with the Uzi. "Get out."

Sukiota zipped her jumpsuit back up and stepped
out of the van. "You aren't going to escape, none
of you."

"And you are?"

Evi floored the van, letting inertia slam the passenger door closed.

No more trains passed by her, and the tracks eventually disappeared, leaving a subterranean highway of
algae-slick ties and black gravel. She pushed the van
beyond any safe speed because she wanted to beat
any attempt to cut her off.

As she shot through the bowels of Manhattan, she
tried to understand the events that had swept her up.

The first players, the peeper and the Afghanis, were
part and parcel of Nyogi Enterprises. Specifically, the
subsidiary of Nyogi popularly referred to as the NLF.
From what Seger, the veep, said before he was venti-

lated by the Afghanis, an alien cell was running Nyogi. "You don't know what those creatures are like."

"Yes, I do," she whispered.

The second players were Frey and company. Frey had covered up the situation in Cleveland. Instead of reporting MLI and the aliens to the Agency, they had let the phony money trail to the CIA stand. And someone had appropriated the aliens and MLI's assets for their own use.

Those assets exceeded eighty billion dollars.

For the past five years, Evi had been working for an Agency within the Agency. A totally self-contained organization, answerable to no one. The think tank she, Price, and Hofstadter worked for was totally outside the community. She'd known about the aliens, so the conspiracy had to keep her in its own fold . . .

But they had never brought her all the way in.

Evi was beginning to realize why—

It was because she wasn't human.

Hofstadter called her a frank and was trying to kill her. At least she knew why now. She could finger too damn many of the conspirators. Everyone at the think tank, Hofstadter, everyone who had some knowledge of the aliens back in 2053.

Evi growled and floored the van, intentionally slamming the side of the vehicle against the concrete walls.

She'd been duped. For six fucking years she'd been duped. And they didn't let her in, not for security, not because she was a risk, *but because she wasn't human.*

"BASTARDS!" A bright blue spark flashed across the passenger window as she scraped the front fender across the concrete on the inside of her turn. "All of you. Fucking bastards!"

The tunnel dipped down and, up ahead, the headlights were reflected back at her. She was going one-twenty, and the brakes didn't stop her in time. The nose of the van plowed through a scum of ice, throwing sheets of gray water up and out. Evi heard a buzzing zap and the cab filled with the smell of a blown-out transformer. The headlights and the indicators on the dash died.

The inductor had shorted out.

The van coasted to a stop in almost complete darkness. Even after her engineered eyes adjusted, the world was a dark-gray monochrome shadow that ended about ten meters ahead of her.

She sat in the driver's seat, stunned, as icy water began to collect in the footwell. "You're all hypocritical, manipulative bastards."

Evi, a mental voice began to say.

"Even you, Abdel."

I raised you, Evi.

"Even you." She could feel burning on her cheeks. "What the hell was I, ever, but somebody's intelligence asset?"

But—

"YOU AREN'T MY FATHER!" It echoed into the darkness, faded into nothing.

She slammed her fists into the dash, ignoring the pain in her left shoulder. "They said human experiments were atrocities. What were you going to do when you swept through that Jordanian facility? Kill us all?" She shook her head. "No, you couldn't do that. What a waste it would have been. You took us and trained us to be *your* atrocities."

She rested her head against the steering wheel. "Go away, Abdel. It's my life, and I don't want you any more."

Abdel didn't respond.

She was so damn tired. Tired of being a pawn. Tired of being controlled. Tired of relying on a system that pulled the carpet out from under her. Tired of a world that didn't give a shit about her.

The water was up to her mid-calf, and her feet was falling asleep.

Great, all she needed was a case of hypothermia.

She rolled down the window and looked around the tunnel. Halfway up the right side of the tunnel was a rusty catwalk. At least she could get somewhere without wading. That only left the question, forward or back?

There was no way she was going back.

Dawn broke as she kicked away the garbage holding shut the door on an abandoned subway station. The first sight to greet her upon clearing the top of the concrete stairs was a blown holo-billboard, the mirrored surface marred by the painted legend, "OFF THE PINK!"

Evi knew where she was now. The northern tip of Manhattan, past the barriers. The retrofitted slums of Washington Heights crowded around her, trying to buckle the crumbling streets. A few blocks away from her she could smell the Harlem River. Beyond it was the blasted shell of the Bronx.

The Bronx. The war zone. Moreytown.

Some *moreaus* wouldn't step into the Bronx. She set down her backpack, unlocked the handcuffs still attached to her right wrist, and tossed the cuffs in the bag. Then she reshouldered her bag and headed toward the Bronx.

CHAPTER FIFTEEN

Evi walked across the crumbling bridge, weaving through the stray burnt-out cars, and left the human world. She passed under a rust-shot green sign reading, "I-95, Cross-Bronx Expressway." Under it was an ancient grime-coated detour sign saying the expressway was closed for repairs. More of the NY Urban Infrastructure Renewal Project. It was supposed to open the summer of 2045. Someone had spraypainted "abandon all hope" over "your tax dollars at work."

The first thing to hit her as she set foot in the Bronx was the smell. Even a fresh layer of gray snow, which muted odor as much as it did sound, could not hide the smell of animal musk. She was enveloped by the overlapping melange of the three million moreaus who owned the Bronx.

She stepped off the end of a crumbling off ramp.

The view down the street belonged to another continent. Even at this early hour, the street was lined by hawkers at makeshift stalls. A Peruvian rabbit sold gold jewelry out of a white plastic shipping crate. Three leather-clad rats chittering lightning Spanish were selling electronics using a burnt-out Chevy Caldera as a base of operations. Behind a rank of orange cones and old traffic sawhorses, a blind Pakistani canine with only one arm was being helped by a young female vulpine, running skewered meat over over a coal pit in the asphalt . . .

People were everywhere, the highest concentration

of moreaus in the world. In any direction she looked there was an undulating ocean of fur. Short dirty white for most of the Latin rodents, rabbits, and rats. Spotted brown for some rabbits and dead black for some rats. Red to spotlight the British vulpines. Gray, brown, and black for the Middle Eastern and Southeast Asian canines. Brownish black for the slow-moving ursoid mountains and the subliminal flashes of otters and ferrets. Yellow and black for the big cats . . .

She waded into the sea of nonhumans, not bothering to hide the Uzi. The crowd parted around her as the population turned to stare. A barely audible growl followed her like the sound of crashing surf. She got a half-block before she met a portion of the crowd that didn't break before her.

Upon seeing the creature, her first impulse was to file it in her knowledge of moreau strains. He was Russian, ursoid combat strain, Vyshniy '33, first generation.

The bear was a wall of fur reaching up for nearly four meters. The individual muscles that snaked through his forearm were the size of Evi's thigh. Dozens of scars picked through the bear's brown fur; most looked like bullet holes. A diagonal slash originated under one eye and snaked across his muzzle, revealing a slice of raw pink across his nose. The only thing the bear wore was a pair of khaki shorts.

It snarled at her. "Pink."

She leveled the Uzi at the bear. Around her she could hear weapons clearing holsters, guns being cocked. The bear raised his hand and she knew a solid contact from that arm would break her neck.

She tensed to duck and roll to the side. "*Look at me!* I'm no more human than you are."

The bear's brows knit as it stared at her. It took a few seconds for him to lock eyes, a few more to realize what the eyes meant. His arm remained raised. "You're a frank?"

Those words seemed to ignite something in the crowd. What had been a frozen tableau around the periphery of Evi's vision melted back into motion. Motion *away* from her and the bear. What had been something of universal concern now seemed to be a personal matter between the two of them.

The bear was still looking for an excuse. "Not pink, but you can't talk like that to—"

She saw a quiver of motion along the bear's forearm. "Don't." She shook the Uzi for emphasis.

"But—"

"Your backup's gone."

The bear lowered his arm and grumbled, "Thought you were fucking human."

Evi sighed. "Done?"

The bear gave an all-too-human shrug and limped away. For the first time she noticed that the bear's left foot was a makeshift prosthetic.

She continued down the street, keeping an eye out for other potential conflicts. For the first time she saw her nearly human form as a handicap. Everyone eyed her with suspicion, some with outright contempt, but no one else opted for a direct confrontation. With the exception of some yelled obscenities, growls, and one thrown brick that missed her, she passed through unmolested.

But this deep in the Bronx, the only thing that *would* molest her would be the locals. Humans, cops or Feds, wouldn't come down here. The only people she'd have to worry about would be Nyogi's. And then only if they sent the Afghanis down after her. However, there was a good chance that no one knew where she was.

Not an aircar in sight. Not too surprising, since the FAA restricted the airspace above Moreytown. Allegedly because it was too dangerous, but Evi knew better. Both local and federal policy since '42 was to restrict physical access to concentrations of moreau population.

She needed to find a comm. She wove through main streets between modular mass-produced housing, burnt-out ruins, and old unfinished housing projects, looking. It soon became obvious that there was not going to be any operational public comms out on the street. The few kiosks she passed, whether they'd originally been a comm, a bank machine, a trash depository, or a city directory, had all been gutted long ago.

She walked deeper into the nonhuman city as the sun rose. The night was catching up with her. Evi had a headache that was telling her she had gotten too little sleep, and her left shoulder was a deep ache that flashed into full-blown agony whenever she tried to move her arm. She knew that all the movement last night had canceled any healing her arm had done the previous day and had probably made things worse.

She needed a place to rest.

She walked for two miles. She paralleled the valley of the dead I-95, passing abandoned earth movers and bulldozers that'd been stripped to orange metal skele-tons. At eight in the morning, Evi passed an ancient brick structure that hadn't burned. It was wedged be-tween a lot humped with soot-scarred concrete and the girder skeleton of what had, long ago, been an attempt at low-cost housing. The framework stork of the crane still hovered over the project, leaning at an ominous angle over the brick building.

The building's windows hid behind rolling steel doors. The way the graffiti wrapped around, ignoring the division between steel and brick, showed that the front windows had not been opened in a long time. What had stopped Evi, though, was the sign above the open door, "ROOMS."

"ROOMS" was lit in flickering neon that, against all odds, remained intact. The front door gaped open at her, held in place by a granite lion that stood rampant about a meter high. Mortar still clung to the lion's feet, a legacy from whatever facade he'd escaped from.

She needed a place to hole up. "ROOMS" was the best she could expect from this town. She walked in, hoping that the crane gantry would remain upright for one more day.

The lobby was sweltering, and the open door did nothing to help more than a meter into the building. The air was humid from the rust-laden steam heating system.

Behind the desk sat an old brown rabbit, obese, nose running, ears drooping. The lepus' rheumy eyes locked with Evi's for about a half-second of shock. She saw the rabbit's hand moving to something concealed behind the desk. The hand stopped moving when he looked into her eyes.

The rabbit cleared his throat. "Help you?"

She walked up to the desk. "I need a room with a working comm."

"Yeah." The rabbit coughed a few times. "Outside line?"

She nodded.

The rabbit turned and began tapping at an old manual keyboard behind him. She leaned forward to see what the rabbit had been reaching for. In a holster behind the desk was a cheap Chinese revolver, a PR-14. Evi didn't even want to think about fourteen-millimeter rounds. Those things were cheap for a reason. There were a lot of them, and they were just as likely to do damage to the wielder as to the target. The only people who could fire those things accurately were the Chinese ursines.

She thought it was a stupid weapon for a rabbit. That was until she noticed a bracket sunk into the desk. A bracket with a universal joint mount on it that could provide a fairly braced firing platform for the gun.

She turned and looked behind her and saw at least one very large hole in the wall by the door.

"Room 615." The rabbit paused for a coughing fit. "How much?"

"Twenty an hour, hundred a day, half that if you got cash." The rabbit pulled a gray rag out from under the desk and blew his nose. "I don't haggle."

She reached into her pack and hoped that the Agency had left her wallet and cash in the leather. They had. She fumbled in her jacket and liberated her wallet. What remained of the roll of twenties, after the limo rental, was exactly a hundred in cash in her wallet. There was her phony ID in the wallet, but Eve's identity was compromised now.

"I want twenty-four hours and the balance credited to the comm's account." She handed the rabbit five twenties.

The cash disappeared under a balding hand. The rabbit nodded and handed her a green ramcard with the room number branded into it. "Checkout's at noon." The rabbit glanced at the Uzi. "Any shooting'll bring the wrath of God on you."

She nodded and took the cardkey.

The stairs were littered with garbage, plaster, and unconscious moreaus. Room 615 was on the sixth floor, overlooking the abandoned construction next door. The thick metal door opened on a square room, four meters on a side. The disease-green paint seemed to be the only thing holding the plaster to the walls. Black-specked yellow curtains turned the frozen white sunlight the color of urine. The color matched the room's smell. The sheets on the bed were laced with fur from the previous occupant, as was the claw-marked recliner.

Evi shut the door behind her and turned on the overhead light. The circular fluorescent pinged a few times before it lit with a nervous, vibrating blue glow. Evi pulled the recliner around in front of the comm.

The comm was anchored in a black textured plastic case. The case bore scars from cigarettes and knives but remained firmly bolted to the wall opposite the foot of the bed. She sat down in front of it and turned it on.

As it warmed up, Evi was treated to moans and heavy breathing provided by the hotel's piped-in broadcast. When the black and white low-res display focused, Evi saw a familiar-looking Pakistani canine. It might not be the same movie that had been playing on Times Square, but it certainly was the same actor. Small world.

The first thing Evi did was get on an outside line and call Diana. Diana answered the comm call immediately. *"You're where?"*

"The address is right."

Diana shook her head. "You're in the middle of the Bronx? Are you all right?"

"Yes and yes."

"Mind telling me what happened?"

"Brush with the cops and the Feds. Moreytown seemed a good place to disappear for a little while."

Diana was quiet for a while, seeming to weigh what she was going to say next. "Are you going to come back?"

"There's a lot . . ." A lot she had to do, a lot she had to think about, a lot she had to come to terms with. "I don't know."

There was no mistaking the disappointment that crossed Diana's face. "I appreciate the call. Do you insist on continuing to go it alone?"

Diana had a point. Evi might be able to survive on her own, but if she ever intended to *do* anything about the forces arrayed against her, she needed help. Price might be an option, if she could get to him. However, if she was right and Hofstadter had taken over control of the operation, Price might be as much a solo act as she was at the moment. "You still think the moreau underground might be willing to help me?"

"You're fighting the same forces the movement's been fighting for the past fifteen years."

By doing things like bombing the New York Public Library? She couldn't help picturing them as nothing more than a group of rabid terrorists. Then again, that's what she was supposed to be right now, wasn't it? "Can you tell me who to contact out here?"

Diana looked a little pained. "I haven't been close to the movement for a long time—"

Evi suddenly remembered the address Nohar had given her. It was down here in the Bronx. Maybe Nohar had had the same thoughts about the moreau underground that Diana had. And what *did* "G1:26" mean?

She typed it in on the battered keyboard and asked. "You know what that means?"

"7:26 Eastern Standard—"

"Other than that."

Diana stared at the screen and shrugged. "Hmm." After a few minutes of silence she started mumbling. ". . . after our likeness—"

"What's that?"

"Benefits of a Catholic education. Every time I see numbers separated by a colon, I think chapter and verse."

"You were quoting?"

"Genesis 1:26." Diana's voice took on a pontifical tone. *"And God said, let us make man in our image, after our likeness: and let them have dominion over the fish of the sea, and over the fowl of the air, and over the cattle, and over all the earth, and over every creeping thing that creepeth upon the earth."*

Evi sat back on the recliner and started laughing, inaudibly. That was one hell of a password for the moreau underground.

"Does that help?" Diana asked.

Evi shook her head. "I think so, thanks."

"You're welcome."

"I guess that's it."

"Good luck." Diana added, "and you really look much better without the sunglasses."

Diana cut the connection.

Evi sighed and emptied her pack. Her jumpsuit was there, clean now, as well as her leather. Most of the equipment she had started out with was trash. The magazines and extra barrel for the Mishkov were useless without the gun. All that was left was her stun rod.

She pressed the test key and a green LED winked at her.

She stripped out of the trashed exec suit and stretched. She considered sitting down, but she looked at the fur on the seat of the recliner and put the jumpsuit on first.

Since she had the comm, she tried calling David Price again. He was still locking out incoming calls. His comm was probably programmed to respond to secure transmissions from Frey's comm.

That did her a lot of good.

She sighed and ruffled through Sukiota's wallet. Not much of anything there beyond the standard ID, a few cardkeys, one with the NYPD logo. The only thing remotely interesting she'd gotten off of Sukiota was the blank white card.

"What's this?" she asked herself.

Evi plopped it into the comm's card reader. She had to hit it a few times to get it going.

The screen fuzzed in on the National Security Agency logo. After a few seconds the screen started flashing all sorts of top-secret and restricted warnings at her. She tapped on the keyboard and the database program asked for her security clearance or the card's info would be wiped.

She debated a moment on whether she should risk

her old passwords or pop the card and wait until she round a real hacker. The key word was "wait." She did not feel like she had loads of time.

Besides, clearance passwords for these files were based on security level, not individual agents. It shouldn't care if the Agency thought she was dead.

She typed a ten character alphanumeric.

The screen blanked.

There was a nervous few seconds as she listened to the laser head knocking around inside the cardreader. The green indicator on the front of the case flashed a few times.

Then the knocking from the reader ceased and the screen ran up a menu. Apparently her access codes were still good.

It was a database card, similar to the library's. Only, instead of just the raw data, this one had its own shell program. And from a brief glance at the menu, the data on this card was a lot more specific and to the point. Sukiota must have DL'd the info from Langley as soon as she'd gotten a look at the peeper's surveillance footage.

Each file was ID'd by an NSA picture. She knew the picture for Ezra Frey, David Price, Erin Hofstadter, Dr. Scott Fitzgerald, Dr. Leo Davidson. A picture of the sniper was identified with the one word in quotes, "Gabriel."

Last was a file on her. Her picture was a human-looking one where she was wearing her contacts. The human eyes made the picture look slightly wrong.

She spent a few hours perusing what the Agency's computers said about the conspirators.

Ezra Frey graduated from the USMC to Defense Intel during the hottest part of the Pan-Asian war. Advocated the unpopular position that the U.S. should intervene to defend Japan and the Subcontinent. Frey was saying that in '26, when it looked like things were going well for the Indo-Pacific alliance. A year later, New Delhi was nuked and nine bloody years followed before Tokyo suffered the same fate. In '35 he moved to the Agency, and began making the same noises about the Islamic Axis and Israel. The U.S. remained noninterventionist, and in six years Tel Aviv was blasted into a shallow coastal lake.

Erin Hofstadter had been born in the EEC, a European army brat. Oxford was the least of the schools from which he had a doctorate. He was an Agency advisor throughout his two-decade stint in the State Department. According to the file he'd been missing ever since a fact-finding mission to occupied Japan in late '53. It was presumed that he had been taken hostage by nationalistic factions attached to the NLF even though no credit was ever taken or demands made.

David Price was Pol-Sci, specialist in conspiracy theories. Sent up a few memos that suggested that some unknown agency was manipulating the U.S. government into self-destructive activities. He listed a dozen specific examples, including the U.S. nonparticipation in the Pan-Asian war, the antitechnology legislation by the Congress, up to the mothballing of the NASA deep-space probes when a launch would be cheaper than maintenance.

Dr. Scott Fitzgerald was a xenobiologist. He worked for NASA on the development of sensors on the deep-probe projects, and he had been chief of NASA's orbital ear project. That project had, Fitzgerald alleged, found evidence of intelligent signals of nonterrestrial origin. This was before Congress axed the ear and mothballed the deep-probe project in the space of four years in the early '40s.

Leo Davidson had degrees in computer science, engineering, and physics. He ran a particle collider in the Midwest, looking for tachyons, until the funding was cut and the collider was shut down. For various West Coast companies he tried to redevelop hardwired biointerfaces, build control systems for fusion-drive rockets, did theoretical work in nano-computers, along with a dozen other cutting-edge disciplines. Each one, close to midstream, ran into Congressional legislation that either stalled or killed the project, generally in the name of public safety.

"Gabriel" was a freelancer. He had worked for nationalists in the EEC, *and* the government of the EEC. He worked for a half-dozen North African countries, where he participated in three successive coups in Ethiopia alone. In South America, he worked for a number of Latin-based megacorps, removing political obstacles in Brazil, Colombia, and Peru. Hitman, assassin, demolition expert, sold himself to the highest bidder. The moral equivalent of the Afghani canines.

All of them were supposed to be dead.

Evi could see how a core of this conspiracy could have formed. Most of these men had been affected badly by the alien intervention. Frey and Price had seen an invisible hand at work in Asia, and Davidson and Fitzgerald were scientists whose research was being interfered with.

Hofstadter seemed to have no such personal stake, and Gabriel was simply a hired gun. A gun probably brought in by Hofstadter. Hofstadter was, born and bred, a creature of the intelligence community.

Hofstadter had taken over Frey's operation and was trying to clean house by putting a bullet in her.

Nyogi Enterprises was after her. Nyogi's interest was in the cadre of rogue Agency operatives. Nyogi had both her and Frey under surveillance; they'd even purchased the buildings they resided in. The veep had said it: "They want their people back."

She was sure that Nyogi's involvement with the NLF was only the tip of the iceberg as far as political machinations were involved. She had seen it before. The aliens insulated themselves within corporate fronts and used them as funnels to distribute massive assets to further their agenda. The agenda, broadly defined, being the technological stagnation of the planet. Nyogi Enterprises fit the profile. The creatures running Nyogi knew about Frey's operation and wanted the four aliens that Evi had captured in Cleveland.

When she'd found that cell of aliens running Midwest Lapidary, she had initiated Frey's conspiracy. Whatever the exact details were, a group of Agency operatives had falsified records and diverted resources to keep the aliens secret from the government. From all appearances, the conspirators still had the four aliens Evi captured, and somehow the conspiracy was exploiting them.

She sighed and turned off the comm. She was feeling the weight of events bear down on her. It seemed that every reflection brought to light a new set of players with their own agenda.

She yawned and realized how tired she was. For all the fur shed upon it, the bed looked pretty good at this point.

CHAPTER 16

She woke to the sound of the door breaking open. She grabbed the Uzi and rolled of the edge of the bed opposite the door, sending a shiver of agony down her left arm. Before she could orient herself and bring the Uzi to cover the door, machine gun fire swept the wall above her. Green-painted plaster flew everywhere, yellow plastic drapes shredded, and the window exploded.

"Toss the gun." The voice had a Bronx accent, feline pronunciation. To drive the point home, whoever-it-was started pumping shots into the bed.

Evi decided that she wasn't in a position to argue, and tossed the Uzi over the bed. The gunfire ceased.

"Get up."

She did so, raising her hands.

In the doorway was a jaguar. Black-spotted, two meters tall, and holding a vintage AK-47. The jaguar was female and wore a black beret, khaki shorts, and a black kevlar vest with a corporal's insignia on the collar. Behind the cat, in the hall, was a collection of at least a half-dozen armed rodents, similarly clad.

"Your chance to say something," said the cat. "Make it good."

Welcome to the morey underground, Evi thought. What the fuck did they expect her to say? She stood there facing them, hands raised, trying to second-guess the cat with the gun.

It was worth a try. *"And God said, Let us make man in our image."*

The jaguar nodded and didn't shoot her.

She'd assumed that Nohar was giving her a line on these people, that the cryptic "G1:26" he typed was some sort of password, and that Diana had interpreted its meaning correctly. That was two more assumptions than she wanted to make in a situation like this.

The jaguar backed out of the room, keeping her covered with the rifle. "The General wants a word with you."

At least she seemed to have made the right assumptions. Appropriate password. Moreaus had a well-developed sense of irony.

The squad of moreaus ushered her out of the building, one rat with her backpack, one rat with the Uzi. There was one point on the stairs where she could have dived out a second-story window and made a break for it. However, she had intended to contact these people. And "the General" seemed to reciprocate the feeling.

Besides, she didn't want to be stuck alone in the Bronx with only a switchblade.

The manager was nowhere to be seen as they hustled her through the sweltering lobby. Three rabbits in black kevlar preceded her out the door and to a waiting vehicle.

Evi stopped and stared at what they had parked outside of "ROOMS." She didn't start moving again until the jaguar prodded her with the rifle.

Where the hell did they get a French APC?

It was trapezoidal, splashed with black, gray and shallow-brown urban camouflage, and squatted on three axles whose tires were Evi's height. The armored personnel carrier had been through a number of refits, so Evi couldn't tell which of five models it could have been. Extra plates had been welded to the exterior. The major modification was a semicircular ring of plates sitting on top of the thing, encircling a machine-gun mount bearing an M-60.

Things like this shouldn't have been in the Bronx. It represented a big change from when she worked in the anti-terrorist wing of the Agency, and it threw a wrench into most of the scenarios she'd worked on for the Domestic Crisis Think Tank.

It did explain how they expected to get around on these rotten roads.

They squeezed her in the back with the rodents; the jaguar drove. The ride seemed to be an exercise in proving the maximum velocity of the APC. Evi swore that the jaguar aimed at every bad spot of road that they passed, and at one point the APC lurched over a huge bump that could have only been a car.

After a while, they slowed and she began to hear noise outside. She could hear gunfire, occasional animal yells, one explosion. The APC stopped, and the jaguar radioed something ahead in Portuguese, a language Evi didn't know.

After a few more fits and starts, the APC finally stopped and began powering down. The jaguar looked down into the passenger space. "Fernando, Gonzales, you come with me. The rest of you report back to the dorms."

Dorms?

The rear of the APC opened and the jaguar walked by, pulling Evi along by the right elbow. "We're going to the greenhouse. Don't bolt. We aren't enemies—yet."

Evi nodded, thinking of how much emphasis the cat had put on the word "yet."

The quartet moved out. The jaguar and two rats hustled her along unceremoniously. Evi began to realize the scope of what the APC implied. They walked out of a parking garage that was full of all manner of armored vehicles designed for urban combat. There were more French APCs on the mid-level of the garage, and the armor got heavier as they descended, until, on the ground level, she saw two T-101 Russian tanks flanking a Pakistani self-propelled artillery piece. A chunk of the second level of the garage had been knocked out to fit them in.

If these folks were careful, a satellite wouldn't have a clue.

They passed sentries that guarded the entrance to Fordham University. Unlike the Bronx she'd seen up to now, all the rubble had been cleared from the grounds. She saw bulldozers on the edge of the property, parked on a massive wall of rubble that now formed a wall around the campus. Once they walked onto the campus, she saw the rear end of two machine-gun nests embedded in the inside of the wall.

They rounded a corner and, through an opening in the wall, she could see the gray-painted walls of Fordham Hospital and makeshift landing pads that held a quartet of helicopters and dozens of aircars.

She was walking through a fully operational paramilitary base that sat only three-and-a-half miles from Manhattan. If these folks wanted to, they could simply unpark that Pakistani artillery piece and lob shells from Yonkers to Battery Park. Where the Hell were the Feds? The government should have landed on this long before it had gotten this big.

They passed a group of more sentries and a rubble-bordered freeway and walked into snow-covered parkland. As they walked, Evi realized that the snow hadn't covered the terrain naturally. The surface of the snow was artificially smooth, and the snow itself was dirty-brown.

They had buried huge ruts in the grass under the snow, hiding the vehicle tracks from the Fed's spy satellites. These people were good. Then again, why shouldn't they be? The vast majority of moreaus were designed for military use, and most of the immigrant moreys in the States were veterans.

They passed a sign directing them to the Enid A.

Haupt Conservatory. Most of the sporadic gunfire was coming from the south.

As they wove through the artificial forest of exotic trees, she kept thinking they were less than four miles from New York. It reminded her too much of Israel. One major difference: the Israeli defenders knew the Axis was there.

She wondered if these moreaus had any missiles.

The lines of the conservatory building were wrapped in overgrown vines and bushes. From the outside the place looked long-abandoned. Inside was different. The original plants and decoration had been cleaned out, walls taken down, and the floor now looked like the situation room at the Pentagon. Under diffuse white light from a snow-covered glass ceiling, there were moreaus of every stripe operating computers, radar screens, and communication consoles. The air was filled with electronic whines and beeps. Maps of New York and the United States faced each other from opposite ends of the chamber.

The rabbits stopped at the door, and the jaguar ushered her around the periphery of the situation room. They stopped at a massive oak door, and the jaguar waved her to go ahead. Evi's escort had long ago shouldered her weapon.

She looked at the jaguar, then back at the situation room behind her, and realized that she'd *better* ally herself with the moreaus. If anyone even suspected that her allegiance was still anywhere near the Agency, she was dead after seeing all this.

She opened the door and walked in.

It was a small windowless office. Behind a chipped-green metal desk sat the biggest ursine that she had ever seen.

She—the bear was female—sat on the floor and still looked down at Evi from a height of two-and-a-half meters. Her fur was a dead black, with the light picking out highlights from muscles that snaked like steel

200

belting. She wore a shoulder holster with a Chinese fourteen-millimeter automatic. The gun hung under a stump. Her right arm ended twelve centimeters from the shoulder in a mass of twisted red scar-tissue. Other than the holster, the only thing she wore was a black beret on her head with a single star as insignia.

With her one hand, she waved Evi toward the only chair in the room. "Welcome, Miss Isham." The bear's voice sounded like a lawnmower laced with molasses.

Evi sat. "You have the advantage."

The bear snuffed, apparently in good humor. "General Wu Sein at your service. Welcome to the Bronx Zoo."

"I thought we were in the Botanical Gardens."

General Wu snuffed again. "I refer to our entire complex. My people call it the Zoo."

"Oh."

"You display an unexpected amount of surprise for someone who is supposed to be working for us." General Wu opened a desk drawer and pulled out a teapot and a pair of cups. "Care for some tea?"

Evi shook her head. "You *know* the news stories are plants."

"Indeed." The general flipped the switch on the ceramic teapot, and it began to glow a little in the infrared. "But such fictions are destined to bring us together— Are you sure no tea? The humans left some very good herbs here when they abandoned the Gardens."

"No, thank you."

The general shrugged and began an elaborate one-handed preparation of her tea. They sat in silence for a while before the general spoke again. "You have questions that you do not ask."

"I didn't think I was in a position to ask anything."

"One is always in a position to ask questions." The general poured her tea. "It is just a matter of not forcing the answers."

"Then tell me what's going on here."

The general sipped. "I think you've perceived that already. An army is being trained and equipped here."

"In secret."

"Of course. If this was known, they would try and prevent us."

"Why?"

The general leaned back against the wall and finished her tea. "Why is a very complex question. Shall I be simplistic?"

"Justify it however you want."

"Simplistically, then. A few years ago a group of leaders in the moreau community, including myself, decided we should have the capability of defending ourselves."

"Defending . . ."

"Broaden your perceptions. You are too used to seeing any moreau with a gun as a terrorist." The general poured another cup of tea. "If our goal was a political statement . . . You've seen what kind of 'terror' we could utilize."

The general lifted the cup and blew the steam away from the top. "Since half the anti-moreau congressmen were indicted in that CIA scandal six years ago, things have been improving. So we sit, and wait, and hope we're not necessary."

"What would make you necessary?"

She sipped the tea. "Anything we perceive as an attack." The general put down her cup and scratched her stump. "Now. I ask questions."

For nearly an hour, that's what General Wu did. She was polite, meandering, conversational, and as thorough as any Agency debriefing. Halfway through, Evi began to realize that the general had prior knowledge of quite a lot of her story. And, while Evi was intentionally vague about the nature of the aliens because she was unsure how the general would react, the general seemed to know what she was avoiding.

Over the eighth cup of tea, the general asked, "Now, are you certain that these 'creatures' are in control of Nyogi Enterprises?"

"As sure as I can be without any direct evidence."

"You present me with a dilemma."

"How?"

"These beings, you say, bought congressmen. They wish to stagnate technological progress, correct?"

"Yes."

"There's an unfortunate side effect for moreaus. These men they buy get elected on anti-moreau platforms. They hire creatures like the Afghanis, for the humans to point to and say how bad the moreaus are. They're our enemies more surely than any human."

Evi nodded.

"You wonder why this is a dilemma?"

"Yes."

The general snorted. "You never asked who financed my Zoo."

It took a few seconds for that to sink in. "You're financed by Nyogi?"

"If what you say is true, it explains a few things. I told you 'why' was a complex question. All my people have a different reason for working with me. Some are more—hmm—direct than myself."

"You have people split off and go solo on you?"

"Too many, recently. And our financiers have been implying that funds might cease if some 'results' weren't forthcoming."

The general finished her last cup of tea.

"Why're you telling me this?"

"Because I have little choice."

"As far as I'm concerned, you have the advantage here."

"This doesn't just concern you. It concerns a few million moreaus who might suffer a human pogrom if our armed forces become a pawn of these creatures' political aims. You're going to help prevent that."

"How?"

"You are going to do for us what Nyogi wants you to do for them. You are going to help us locate and capture the four aliens you found in Cleveland."

Evi's surprise must have shown.

"Oh, you never did mention the word 'alien' did you? Or 'extraterrestrial.' "

"No, I didn't."

"Wise, I suppose. If I didn't have corroborating information, or people vouching for you, I might have problems believing your story."

"Corroborating information?"

The general nodded as she put away her tea service. Then she hit a button on her comm. Outside, Evi heard an electronic buzzer. "Miss Isham, we'll have a lot to talk about later, but now I have a meeting to attend. So I am going to leave you in the hands of an old friend of yours."

Evi turned her head as the door opened. Into the room walked a 260-centimeter tall, 300-kilo tiger named Nohar Rajasthan.

CHAPTER 17

Nohar took her to the Zoo's "guest house," an old frat building. The bricks next to the trio of Greek letters had been knocked out to make room for an anti-aircraft battery. He led her through a recycled-plywood door and to the half of the building that didn't serve as an ammo dump. The smell of machine oil and gunpowder hung heavy in the cold air.

She ended up in a small room with a sagging bed and cracked plaster wall. The window overlooked the rubble wall surrounding the campus, and the only warmth in the room was from a small electric heater.

She sat in the bed, and Nohar showed no sign of leaving.

"Babysitter?"

Nohar nodded.

Evi took stock of the changes six years had wrought in the tiger. The one thing that hit her was that the colors in his coat had faded, and the lines between black and yellow had lost their sharpness. Age, or maybe the effect of the California sun. His tail moved a little more nervously. There were one or two more scars on his back where the hair was growing back white. His expression had evolved. The white fur under his rounded chin was longer. The wrinkled grooves, growl-lines, above his broad nose were deeper. And he wore a round gold band in his ear.

That was the first time that Evi, moreau expert or

not, realized that engineered feline hands were not well designed for jewelry.

Nohar appropriated an overstuffed recliner that wasn't made for someone of his size. She heard protesting creaks and the twang of a spring giving way. He remained silent, staring out at the rubble wall.

"What are you doing here?"

Nohar sighed, a sound that began as an intake of breath and deepened to a deep bass rumble that sounded like a hostile purr. "Sitting on you so the Grand Dame Ursine doesn't lose an intelligence asset."

She leaned back on the bed, still tired. The ceiling above her was innocent of plaster, and holes had been knocked in the slats to reveal pipes and junction boxes beyond.

"When did you become political?"

"Still trying to link me to moreau terrorism?"

She turned her head to look at the tiger. He was still looking out the window. His right hand was clawing the upholstery on the chair. She was sorry for the fact that she hadn't spent enough time with moreaus to pick up on *their* scent cues. She could read humans like a book, but tigers . . .

Nohar was broadcasting powerful waves of something.

"Sounds like you don't want to be here."

He snarled. "You think I *like* all this?"

She forgot her potential nap and propped herself up on her right elbow to look at him. There was a momentary twinge from her left shoulder when she moved. It quickly faded. She hoped that the much-lauded healing powers of the Hiashu-enhanced human projects were finally at work on her shoulder.

"Want to elaborate?"

He turned toward her. "Wu and company are going to screw us over again."

Evi's puzzlement must have shown.

"I'm a moreau, I should approve?" Nohar shook his head. "Violence breeds more of the same. This is a disaster waiting to happen."

"Wu portrayed this operation as defensive." She wondered how she had gotten into the position of defending what, by most of the definitions she had been using during her professional life, was a terrorist operation. She was astounded by how little loyalty she found in her heart for either the organization or the ideals she had worked for for the past sixteen years. All this time had she been just as much a mercenary as those Afghanis?

"What happens when the government gets wind of this?" Nohar asked.

"They'll ..." That was a bad thought. There was no question about the military trying to shut this place down. That would definitely fit Wu's definition of a direct attack.

Nohar nodded, as if he heard the rest of her thought.

She could see a national wave of violence in the moreau community, igniting a backlash that could wipe out all the progress moreaus had made toward first-class citizenship. The anti-moreau forces could use that kind of conflagration to finally repeal the moreau amendment. She could see the pogrom that Wu feared.

"I was right," she said. "You *don't* belong here."

Nohar chuckled. If she didn't know moreaus, and this moreau in particular, she would have found the sound threatening. He had an unnerving tendency to show his teeth when he laughed, and his canines were the size of her thumb. "As if I had a choice. It's your fault."

"What do you mean by that?"

"My life may be in danger, the alien business may be rearing its ugly head—where else do you think a morey would go to ground?"

"What about your wife?"

"Safe." From the way he said it, she knew not to ask any further about his spouse.

"How long have you known these people?"

"Four years. From the Los Angeles chapter."

"This is national?"

Nohar chuckled again. "*Look* at this place."

She slowly dropped back to stare at the ceiling and began to reassess her world view. "Why'd you vouch for me? I worked for the Feds."

"You aren't human."

"Meaning?"

"When the shit hits the fan, species transcends politics."

She closed her eyes and tried to sleep.

General Wu finally sent for them, well after nightfall. They were fetched by the same jaguar that had snatched Evi from "ROOMS." She was no longer armed with the AK-47. Evi's standing in this community was on an upswing.

Instead of the conservatory, the jaguar led them across an unlit campus to a blacked-out building. Inside, the place was well lit. It was the windows that had been painted black. The jaguar brought them through a set of doors flanked by lepine guards in black berets and into an auditorium out of another century. General Wu stood at a podium that barely came past her waist. Behind her was a rank of green blackboards set in dark-varnished wood frames. In the audience was a collection of five moreaus. With their arrival, seven moreaus, one frank.

"Welcome," Wu addressed them. She gestured them down to the front with her stump. "My intelligence team has informed me that if we have any time to do what I plan, it is running out."

Evi walked down to the front and sat next to a lean lepus who was missing an ear. Nohar stood; the human desks weren't made for people his size. The jaguar barely fit herself into the seat next to Evi.

Wu continued, directing her comments at Evi. "The NLF team from Nyogi Enterprises must have had you under surveillance for some time. Following your personal contacts, and using you as a stalking horse to uncover the identities of your employers and coworkers. Would this conflict with any of your observations?"

"That makes sense except—"

"Why kidnap you?"

Evi nodded.

Wu tapped at a keyboard hidden by the podium. "We're assuming there was some recent triggering event that made Nyogi desperate. They intend to gain quickly now by force the information they hoped to gain slowly by stealth."

"The location of the aliens . . ." Evi whispered.

The room became very quiet. The only noises were moreys breathing and shifting their weight and the buzzing of the uncertain fluorescents. The pause lengthened uncomfortably until Evi said, "I don't know that."

That wasn't a comfortable admission. Not only because there were eight pairs of eyes looking at her for the answer, a few with blatant hostility, but because it was something she *should* know.

Nohar spoke. "Nyogi assumes that you do."

She turned to the tiger. "*I should.* I was the one who bottled up the aliens in the first place. They assumed I was an insider."

"A human," Nohar said, "would have been."

She shook her head. "Species before politics."

General Wu slapped the side of the podium, drawing the audience's attention back to her. "We need to reach those four aliens before Nyogi does. The window in which we have to act as rapidly closing. Isham and the Feds have set back their operational capability, but it is doubtful that it would take longer than forty-eight hours for a corporation with the resources of Nyogi to assemble another team to go after a secondary target. Someone else who knows where the aliens are.

"Isham, if you do not have that information, you must lead us to someone who has."

Evi looked at the moreaus surrounding her. Nohar was carefully cultivating an expressionless demeanor, though he was habitually making clawing motions with his right hand. The jaguar corporal sitting next to her was staring at her, teeth barred in a expression of silent hostility. The general stood directly in front of her, like a giant wooden totem. The one-eared rabbit to her right looked at her, nose twitching as if in curiosity. The four rats beyond showed mixtures of apprehension and hostility.

It hit her all at once, exactly how far she had removed herself from everything she had known, worked for, believed . . .

"Wait a minute." Evi stood up. "Information is one thing—"

She could feel the weight of the moreau's attention. Not only the ones in this room, not just the complex, but the weight of the surrounding community of three million . . .

"What, exactly, do you object to?" Wu asked.

What, exactly? It wasn't like she hadn't shifted allegiances before. If anything, the goals and principles Wu was offering were clearer than the ones the Agency offered.

"What I object to is a strong feeling of deja vu."

"Meaning?"

"I crossed the Atlantic in '45, before a frank had *any* civil rights in this country. The Feds said, 'Of course you'll work for us.' In a dozen years I managed to convince myself I was working on the side of right and justice, only to have the rug pulled out from under me."

"Isham," Nohar said. She turned to face the tiger, who was the only face in the room that held any sympathy. "You're too used to taking orders. You can work with someone without working *for* them."

General Wu spoke. "We aren't asking you to adopt our politics or join our organization. We're asking only that you aid us in achieving something of mutual, if not universal, benefit: Namely, capturing and publicizing these aliens."

Evi looked up at the general. Nohar was right. The one specific thing that bothered her was the prospect of owing her allegiance to another political entity that would use her as a pawn and sacrifice her without a second thought. She had played that game all her life.

It was time she owed allegiance to herself.

"I'll help you." She sat down and crossed her legs. "With two conditions—"

The jaguar spoke. "You're in no position—"

"Corporal Gurgueia," Wu interrupted. "Miss Isham has been quite cooperative. We'd do well to hear her out."

Evi waited for other outbursts from the crowd. Other than glowering stares from a pair of the rats, there were no overt objections.

"As I said, two conditions. First, this isn't to be a brute force operation. No explosives, and if there's gunfire, that means someone screwed up." She stared directly at the jaguar as she said that.

Wu nodded and the jaguar emitted a quiet growl.

"Second, *I'm* in charge of the operation."

The entire room started talking at once. Except for Nohar, who looked as though he expected her to say that, and Wu, who looked like she was above shouting down the audience.

Despite the dozen objections flying around her, Evi smiled. Yes, she did have little choice but to participate in this escapade. However, the general had little choice but to let her participate on her own terms. General Wu had said herself that the window of opportunity was rapidly closing.

It took nearly five minutes before the moreaus quieted down enough to let the general speak.

"Respectfully, General, you aren't going to seriously consider this, are you?" asked Corporal Gurgueia, the jaguar.

"I'm doing more than that. I am doing just as Isham suggests. We need a specialist in covert activity, not urban warfare. We have too little time to debate command structure." General Wu swept her gaze across the room. "Is there anyone who feels that they'll be unable to operate under these conditions?"

No one spoke.

"Good. Our first order of business is to locate and make contact with someone who has the information we need. Isham?"

"If no one's gotten to David Price ..."

David Price was the only member of the Domestic Crisis Think Tank whose outside life Evi knew anything about. He'd been the only member of the think tank with whom she'd had more than a strictly professional relationship. He was perhaps the one friend she had in there.

He had a cover identity, David King, who lived in a modular tract house in Jackson Heights. She knew the house; David had once taken her there.

Now, as she flew a matte-black GM Kestrel toward the East River, she wondered about that. He had been a part of Frey's conspiracy all along and had allowed her to be duped. Evi doubted that she had ever had any friends who weren't friends of convenience.

Except, perhaps, for Diana.

The Kestrel was a big aircar, even bigger with most of the interior seats stripped out of it. Even so, they could fit only four members of the team in it. She drove, the one-eared rabbit named Huaras sat next to her, and in the back sat Nohar and Corporal Gurgueia. The extra weight made the Kestrel handle like a wet brick.

It was exactly five after midnight when she hit the shore of the Bronx. As soon as she left shore, she raised the aircar to legal heights and switched on the lights and the transponder. Instantly, it seemed, the comm came alive with frantic instructions from La Guardia Air Traffic Control. No one commented on the aircar's sudden appearance. They wanted them to get into another air corridor, they were too close to Rikers.

She banked away from Rikers Island, and a subsonic rumble rattled the windows as a ballistic shuttle started rising on a steep ascent from the Rikers Island launch facility. The shuttle passed so close that she could see individual heat tiles on its underside.

She did a long banking right turn around La Guardia, over Flushing and Shea Stadium, and as the Manhattan skyline rotated into view in front of them, Jackson Heights slid by below. She cut the lights and began the descent.

The Kestrel put down on a shabby excuse for a back yard, raising a cloud of fresh snow. It sat in a brief blizzard of its own making. The gull-wing doors on the Kestrel flew open, shedding snow, and the moreaus stepped out. The rabbit covered the rear of the house with his machine pistol, Gurgueia tried to cover everything else with her AK-47. Nohar stood out of the way of the guns and waited for Evi.

Evi stepped out of the Kestrel, pulling on a new pair of gloves and taking the medkit and the gun Wu had provided her. The gun was a fairly straightforward Smith and Wesson ten-millimeter automatic. Her wounded shoulder was doped up on painkiller, so she could holster it without wincing.

"Gurgueia, you go cover the front. Huaras, take the rear. Me and Nohar are going in."

Gurgueia seemed to bristle a bit at taking orders from Evi, but she did as she was told. Huaras wordlessly took cover by the Kestrel. Evi ran to the back door. She spared a glance at the driveway. Price's car, an old Chevy Caldera that would have looked like a police car if it weren't for the lime-green paint job, was parked in the open garage, plugged into the vehicle feed. The snowcover on the driveway was unblemished by tire tracks or footprints. Even from where Evi was, she could see the blinking green light on the Caldera's dash that was registering a full charge on the inductors. The car'd been parked for a while.

She got up on one side of the back door, Nohar on the other. Using the doorframe for cover, she tried the lock. The magnetic keypad didn't want to open. She briefly wished for the electronic gear that'd been trashed in her pack.

It wasn't a security building, though. She saw no trace of an alarm system.

She glanced at Nohar to make sure he was covering her and grabbed the keypad-cardkey unit with both hands and yanked it off the side of the house. It came reluctantly, with a rasping noise. It hung on to the doorframe with twenty-centimeter-long bolts that pulled a chunk of wood the size of Evi's hand along with them. It took all of five seconds for her to find the right wire, strip it, and short out the magnetic lock.

A blue spark, the slight smell of melting insulation, and the door drifted open.

She led the way into the darkened house, gun drawn.

The kitchen was a mess. At first she thought that someone had beaten them to Price. Dishes were everywhere, lending the taint of spoiling food to everything in the room. The refrigerator hung open a crack, causing a dagger of light to slice diagonally across the room. She shut the refrigerator with her foot, to allow her eyes to adjust fully to the dark.

After a second of scanning the room, she realized that this was all Price's work. The pots left moldering on the stove, the coffee grounds overflowing the trash basket, the pile of slimy debris that overflowed the trash disposal—the room smelled like a compost heap, but there was no sign of a struggle, just lousy housekeeping.

When she was here before, she hadn't thought Price had been such a slob.

Something was definitely wrong here.

She stalked through the dining room, and the picture didn't change much. On the table sat pyramids of fast-food containers, old beer bulbs, pizza boxes that had been sitting around long enough to begin biodegrading. All the shades were drawn. The only source of light was from a streetlight streaming in the open door behind her.

In the living room sat Price's comm, surrounded by an audience of beer bulbs and news faxes.

On a coffee table between the couch and the comm was sitting a box of ten-millimeter ammunition. The box had ripped open, and bullets had rolled out over the table and the floor. The remains of two more boxes were on the floor. Evi kicked one, for shotgun shells.

She looked at Nohar and whispered, "If a gun goes off—"

"—somebody screwed up," Nohar finished for her.

She started up the stairs. The stairway was strewn with empty food boxes, dirty clothing, and beer bulbs. She also noticed a few bottles of harder stuff. Drunks with guns had to be one of the top items on Evi's list of unpretty pictures.

At the head of the stairs were six doors. Only one, the bathroom, hung open. From the bathroom came the sound of water dripping and an endlessly filling toilet tank. The entire second floor was permeated with the smell of cat shit. As she edged toward the bathroom, where the smell was concentrated, she saw the culprit nestled next to one of the closed doors.

If she remembered correctly, Price had at least four cats. This one's name was Lao-Tze.

The overstuffed black cat looked up at the two intruders. He addressed Evi with a questioning, "Mwrowr?" As soon as he saw Nohar, he arched his back and started hissing, backing toward the bathroom.

She looked into a bathroom and was greeted by the miasma of an overflowing litter box. The cats had long since abandoned the box and had moved on to towels, the rug, stray pieces of Price's underwear.

As Lao-Tze backed away from Nohar, Evi silently thanked him for identifying the bedroom where Price was holed up.

Once Lao-Tze had vacated the doorway, Evi waved Nohar toward it with her gun. She stationed herself by the opening side and listened. There were a number of cats in there, and someone breathing.

She faced Nohar and started mouthing a countdown.

"Three ... Two ... One ..."

Evi threw open the door and dived into the room, rolling and taking cover behind an overstuffed recliner. A displaced Siamese hissed at her. She braced the gun in both hands, aiming over the arm of the chair.

Price lay on the bed, fully clothed, oblivious.

It took a few seconds for her to realize he was alive. But he *was* breathing, and he was radiating faintly in the infrared. He was sleeping off what looked and smelled like a substantial drunk. There were more beer bulbs scattered around this room than the rest of the house. Lying at the foot of the bed was a Vind 10 Auto that had been improperly broken down.

Curled up next to the barrel was a black-and-gray tabby. She had remembered Price calling that one Meow-Tse-Tung.

What worried Evi was the fact that Price had a sawed-off double-barreled shotgun clutched to his chest. His finger was resting on the trigger. It wasn't pointing at anything, but if Price was startled out of unconsciousness, he could blow a hole in the wall by accident. Evi would like to avoid the police involvement a gunshot would bring.

She waved Nohar into the room to cover her. She holstered the gun and opened the medkit on her belt. She pulled out the airhypo and slipped in a trank cartridge.

Damn. She almost cursed out loud. She couldn't risk the trank on someone who smelled like a brewery. The drug might put Price into a coma, the state he was in.

She put the trank away and started creeping up on the bed. Easy, she told herself, the shotgun wasn't even pointed at her. She just had to get the weapon away from the drunk before he became aware of his surroundings. Easy.

She was only a half step away from Price, when she found cat number four. The cat had been under the bed with only its tail sticking out. She'd been so intent on watching Price for any reaction, she hadn't kept a good eye on her footing. Her boot came down on the cat's tail accompanied by the loudest and most grating screech she had ever heard.

Price's eyes shot open and Evi dived for the gun. She did the only thing she could think of: she slammed the edge of her right hand in front of the shotgun's hammers as they cocked.

She lay on top of Price, and two nails of pain were driven into her hand as the hammers pierced her glove, and then skin.

But the shotgun remained silent.

A huge furry arm extended over Evi's shoulder and pointed a grotesquely oversized automatic at Price's forehead.

"Don't," said Nohar.

Price froze and Evi gently removed herself and the shotgun. She unhooked the shotgun's grip on her hand, gratified to find that her hand retained its mobility. Even if clenching it into a fist now felt as though she were trying to rip the side of it open.

"Damn it!" She said in a harsh whisper. She broke open the shotgun and dumped the shells on the floor. Then she really broke it by bending the barrel much farther back than it was supposed to go. There was a quiet snap as a connector gave way, and the gun fell to the ground in two distinct pieces.

Price's eyes kept darting from her to Nohar, then back again.

"Cover him," she told Nohar, "I'm going to check the rest of the house."

Nohar nodded as a yellow tabby crawled out from under the bed and began to weave between Nohar's legs.

Of the four remaining doors, three were empty bedrooms. The last was a linen closet.

Evi was closing the door to the closet when she heard three distinct gunshots in rapid succession. She darted into Price's room, but the tableau remained unchanged. Nohar looked as surprised as Price did.

Someone outside had screwed up.

CHAPTER 18

"Grab him," she told Nohar. "Get him back to the car."

Nohar picked up Price and draped him across his shoulder. Price still seemed too stunned to say anything.

More gunshots, definitely from outside this time. Corporal Gurgueia was trigger-happy. The shades rippled and shredded as a few shots tore into the bedroom window. Evi ducked on the ground with the cats.

A spotlight swept by the window washing it with a white glare and black abstract shadows. She edged up to the window so she could get a good look at the front of the house.

Another Chevy Caldera had slid to a stop diagonally across the street in front of the house. This one *was* a cop car, flashers going, spotlight sweeping for Gurgueia, two cops huddled behind it.

Evi ducked as the spotlight swept by again.

She hit her throat-mike. *"Gurgueia!"*

"Corporal—" Gurgueia paused to lay down more fire. "Gurgueia here."

"Cease fire, back to the car."

"But—"

"Now! I'll cover you."

"Acknowledged."

The cops would stay cautious for a half-minute or so once the firing stopped. Evi peeked over the ledge of the window; neither of the cops looked injured. If they were smart, they'd stay back behind the cop car until reinforcements arrived.

She wanted to give them something to take up most of their attention.

She braced her automatic, two-handed, on the sill, aiming out the busted window. There was a feeling of pressure from under the bandage on her left shoulder. That was her shoulder's way of telling her that if it weren't for the painkiller, she'd be blacking out from the pain.

She didn't aim at the cops but at a small area between the trunk and the back seat.

The cops looked as though they were about to become adventurous, so she emptied the magazine. Nine shots, and at least one hit a charged inductor. She could smell it from here. Smoke began to pour from the remains of the trunk, and the spotlight began to flicker erratically.

She ran for the back door.

Everyone had backed toward the aircar. Nohar was already inside, his arms wrapped around Price. Evi was starting to hear distant sirens.

She dived into the Kestrel, followed by Huaras and Gurgueia. "What the fuck happened?"

They'd left the engine going, so all she had to do was engage the fans. The fans started with a high-pitched whine, and snow began flying around them, caught in the downwash of air.

Gurgueia spoke. "They slowed down and started sweeping that spotlight—"

Evi shook her head and took a few deep breaths as she made sure that the lights and the transponder were off. "So you opened fire."

"I think—" A perceptible growl evolved in Gurgueia's throat. Evi looked at the jaguar, and, eyes locked on her, maxed the acceleration of the Kestrel straight up.

"Never engage without clearing with your commands." Their eyes were locked on each other. The Kestrel kept rocketing upward.

Gurgueia broke eye contact. "You're right, of course, Commander."

Evi turned to look where she was going. The Kestrel was about to hit its maximum ceiling, and they seemed to have made it out of the area without a cop tail. She pulled a long turn and decided not to bother with the transponder.

Behind her, Price asked in a weak voice, "What's going on?"

"Dave, just shut up for now, okay?" She looked back at Price and couldn't help thinking of Chuck Dwyer, and how Chuck had looked at her when he saw her real eyes. It wasn't a rational connection to make. For one thing, Price had always known she wasn't human. For another, Price wasn't even looking at her. He was squeezed in the back with Gurgueia and Nohar and seemed to be dividing his attention between the two big cats.

Huaras spoke up in a heavily accented English, "Where we put down the car?"

Good point. It was not a good idea to put down anywhere near the base. Even without a transponder, Air Traffic Control would have a radar fix on them and would see where they landed. The cops by Price's house would have called them in. It wouldn't take a genius to put two and two together.

Evi could almost feel Sukiota breathing down her neck.

The Kestrel passed by La Guardia, and the comm lit up like Times Square on New Year's with incoming calls. The Kestrel's onboard computer was picking up two aircraft tailing her. One had an NYPD transponder. The other didn't have a transponder at all. So much for not having a cop tail.

"The question, Huaras, is do we put down at all."

She wished she were at the controls of that veep's

Peregrine. At least that thing could maneuver. "What do ..." Price began to say as Evi pointed the nose down at the East River. Altitude screamed by them as the Kestrel accelerated faster than the fans were ever designed to do.

"Nohar, look out the back. On the scope I have an unlabeled aircraft at a hundred meters and closing. Seven o'clock." She had to shout over the scream of rushing air.

Her knuckles were whitening on the wheel, and the plastic was splitting under her fingers. Pressure was building in her left shoulder. The Kestrel was flying down so fast that the snow around them was falling up. Below, Evi could see the landing lights at Rikers flying up to meet them.

"Helicopter, I think." Nohar yelled back.

"Make?"

"You kidding?"

When she could read the logo on the wing of a parked ballistic, Evi flattened out the descent, slamming the forward fans on full. A brick slammed into her stomach, and an invisible giant dug his thumbs into her eyes. She'd just lost a thousand meters in under ten seconds, and once she pulled that high-G turn, Rikers rocketed away behind the Kestrel. She flew the aircar down the East River, barely thirty meters above the waves and going over five hundred klicks an hour.

Both blips on the radar passed above Rikers, and fell way behind them. She hoped she'd slipped beneath their radar.

She slowed the Kestrel and banked to the left. It took a while to find the Bronx. She had overshot and had flown a few kilometers into Long Island Sound. No one talked. She flew low along the Cross-Bronx Expressway from the wrong end and eventually put the Kestrel down on a familiar stretch of pavement in front of a place called "ROOMS."

"F—Finally," Price stammered. He was shaking, and he'd lost most of his color, if he had any to begin with. It was the first time Evi had spared more than a moment to look at him. Price's hair was tangled in knots, he had at least three days of beard, his shirt was wrinkled and sweat-stained, and he was wearing one shoe.

Evi popped the doors and stepped out. She reached in and grabbed Price, who seemed more than a little unsteady. He stumbled out of the car, leaning away from the two big cats who followed him.

Evi held Price up by the upper arm. "Good a place for an impromptu questioning as any. Huaras, take the car back and give the team our location. By the time you get back, we should have what we need."

Huaras lifted off, dusting them with snow.

Price had the confused look of a dog who didn't know why its owner was kicking it. Evi shook him. "Are you with us, Price?"

"Wha? Evi?"

She grunted in disgust and handed him to Nohar. "Hold him."

Evi reached down and grabbed a handful of snow, the chill dulling the throbs of her injured hand. She looked at Price, who still seemed to be looking through an inebriated fog.

"Are you with us?"

"What?" Price said too slowly.

Evi slapped the handful of snow across Price's face. "Earth to David Price, you awake?"

Price sputtered, blinking his eyes. Gray slush dripped down his face, and his eyes seemed a little wider.

Evi picked up another handful of snow. "With us yet?"

"Stop it—" Price began, and got another face full of snow. He spat out a mouthful of slush and said,

"Stop. I'm awake." He put a hand unsteadily to his forehead. "*Christ,* am I awake."

Evi felt little sympathy. She led the trio into the sweltering lobby of "ROOMS." With Nohar and Gurgueia behind her, it didn't take much to remind the rabbit proprietor that she still had a paid room upstairs.

They got to the room, which still smelled slightly of gunfire, and deposited Price on the bed. Evi turned the chair around to face him while the two cats guarded the door.

"You have a lot of explaining to do."

David Price backed up until his back was to the scratched-varnish headboard. His face was wet and streaked with dirt. "W–what's going on?"

"For one thing, I've been played the fool for half a decade."

Price ran a shaking hand through his tangled hair. "Evi, wha—what're you talking about?"

Evi leaned forward. Price wouldn't meet her gaze. "Dave, you're an academic, not an operative. Without a script you're a terrible liar. What was I involved in?"

"Ask him about—" Gurgueia started to say.

"Nohar, would you shut her up?"

The tiger put one hand on the jaguar's shoulder. "I think we should leave them alone." He ducked out the door with Gurgueia before she had time to object.

Evi turned back to Price. "So, Dave?"

"You have to understand." He cradled his head in his hands and Evi supposed that he was having one hell of a hangover. She hoped he wouldn't lose his lunch—though he didn't look like he had anything solid to lose. He was quiet long enough for Evi to consider getting more snow. Eventually, he said, "I was against keeping you in the dark."

"How'd you feel about sending this Gabriel character to blow holes in me?"

Price looked up, rubbing his forehead. "You know

that? Y–you must know how crazy it got. Davidson proved his hy–hy–hypothesis—"

"No, I don't." Evi drew her automatic from its shoulder holster and rested it on her knee. "And you are going to explain it, step by step, until I do."

"Don't need the gun." Price shook his head and rubbed his eyes. He looked a little more coherent, but that didn't say much. "I'm out in the cold too." He smiled weakly. "Do I look like someone in the loop? I've been waiting for Gabe to show for *me*—"

"Start at the beginning."

Price took a deep breath, glanced at the gun, and told her.

The aliens had never gotten past the Aerie back in that August of '53. Frey had been the one running the show, and he saw implications that went far beyond what Midwest Lapidary's corporate front was doing. He saw the petty influence buying in Cleveland mirrored on a much larger scale. He saw, couldn't prove but saw nonetheless, the alien hand in the American nonintervention policy in the Pan-Asian war. Beyond that, he saw their hand in the war itself.

And he saw no way he could trust his own government.

"You see that, don't you? Those four aliens controlled over a hundred congressmen—"

"They were indicted." Evi stood up and walked over to the window. Snow was blowing in, the glass hadn't been replaced. "Most of them anyway."

"That mattered? These creatures want political chaos. *You only found four.*"

Frey had bottled up the aliens, and with a little electronic legerdemain he had written himself and his people out of existence. Then he began to recruit people. People the alien's activities had adversely affected, people with skills he could use, people who would be sympathetic to him.

Like Scott Fitzgerald, whose orbital ear had picked

up on the existence of the aliens and was quickly thereafter quashed by Congress.

Like David Price, whose conspiracy theories no one took seriously.

Like Erin Hofstadter?

"Frey was nutty about Asia. H–Hofstadter was an Asia expert." Price paused to take a few deep breaths and massage his forehead. "Asia expert and the most fascist bastard—" Price closed his eyes and muttered, "Oh, Christ," a few times, and Evi had to prod his foot with the gun to get him to continue.

"His fault that Gabriel and Davidson got on board."

"What's the matter with Davidson?"

Price shook his head. "Two years in, waist-deep in tech crap. Hofstadter gets Davidson. Worst kind . . ."

"You'd call Davidson a fascist?"

"Leo Davidson in a lab coat and the rest of us, white mice."

According to Price, it all started out as a private enterprise to pump the captive aliens for information and develop contingency plans to guard against further alien interference. The Domestic Crisis Think Tank was legitimate. It just worked for Frey instead of the Agency.

"You *would* have been brought in if it weren't for H–Hofstadter. He's pathological about nonhumans."

"And you couldn't let me go because I knew about the aliens." She stepped up to the bed and placed the barrel of the automatic under Price's chin. She pushed up so he was finally looking her in the eye. "So why wait so long before you start shooting at me?"

"It isn't me." His breath fogged the barrel of the automatic.

She was being unfair, she knew. Still, she was so damn angry. Price might be a potential ally now, but for six years he had strung her along like everyone else.

Price stared at Evi. Straight into her eyes as the

odor of fear sliced through the crystal January air. "Frey was losing control a month after Hofstadter came on board."

Hofstadter had quite a different view of the aliens. Where Frey saw the aliens as a threat, the German economist saw the threat as the governments that could be so easily exploited. Hofstadter was interested in *correcting* such vulnerability by building a post-democratic government on the ruins of the old. A human-only government. Leo Davidson was equally anti-democratic. He saw politics as an engineering problem.

Price sucked in a breath. "Then, a few weeks ago, all hell broke loose."

"Explain."

According to Price, the probe launch that the aliens went to such effort to prevent had gone forward with the captured alien finances and Dr. Fitzgerald's help. Frey called them the first recon units into the enemy camp. That was five and a half years ago. Which meant that the first probe was just entering the neighborhood of Alpha Centauri. According to Leo Davidson, if the aliens were out there, with an eye locked on Earth, they would have started detecting the radiation on the probe's main engine within the past month.

"Davidson was right," Price said. "They have."

She pressed the gun into the flesh of Price's neck. "Don't play me for a fool, there's no way anyone could know that. Alpha Centauri is over four and a half light-years—"

"Tachyons." Price croaked.

She lessened the pressure on Price's neck. "D–Davidson said the aliens had the ability to have a t–tachyon communicator. One-way, massive planet-based particle accelerator to transmit. But the receiver could be compact—"

She lowered the gun. *"That's* why everything is happening *now."*

227

Price was stammering on, breathlessly. "The project went defensive when Davidson whipped out his tachyon receiver. Untranslatable signals from Alpha Centauri. Whatever aliens were out there to receive—"

"Would know that those four aliens didn't liquidate themselves when they were supposed to." Evi holstered the gun. "So, why were you locked in your bedroom with a shotgun?"

"I'm an academic, not an operative. I could see the operation shifting under Hofstadter's control. That tach receiver came out of nowhere, at least a million in R&D money out of nowhere. I warned Frey, but he didn't believe me, so I went to ground and waited for a knock on the door. Frey didn't believe, not until it was too late—"

"What convinced him?"

"You did."

In the distance, out the broken window, she began to hear sounds of traffic. An aircar, maybe an APC as well. Huaras was coming back with the rest of the team.

"Now the big question. Where is the project keeping the aliens?"

CHAPTER 19

Someone, thought Evi, someone in Frey's band of conspirators had an appreciation for irony. Only someone with a diabolical sense of humor would have stashed the aliens in the old UABT complex. United American Bio-Technologies was the reason moreaus had any rights in the States. It was also why there was a domestic ban on macro-genetic engineering.

UABT *started* by working on human genetics, but when the UN passed its ruling, UABT dutifully switched to nonhuman genetics.

The interference in UABT's production didn't stop there. Atrocities committed in Asia caused a legislative backlash in the U.S. that led to the most schizophrenic decision in constitutional history, an amendment that banned domestic genetic engineering on a macroscopic scale while granting the intelligent products of nonhuman experimentation the protection of the Bill of Rights. UABT dutifully switched to algae and bacteria.

That wasn't as profitable as the Asian market for military hardware.

When UABT was indicted for the continued production of engineered animals and, worse, engineered humans, the government shut the operation down, and all of UABT's assets fell down a bureaucratic black hole.

One of those assets was a large block of medical real estate parked midway between the UN Building and the Queensboro bridge. Somehow, that block of buildings had fallen under the Agency's purview, and from there it was co-opted by Frey and company.

It was within walking distance of Frey's condo. The aliens were hidden under everybody's nose: Nyogi's, the Agency's, and hers.

At three-thirty in the morning Evi's gray Dodge Electroline van hit Manhattan.

The bridges across the Harlem River looked like hell with abandoned cars and the concrete NYPD traffic barriers. Some of that was camouflage. As Evi wove the van across the 138th Street Bridge, she saw that at least half the cars, despite the burnt-out appearance, weren't abandoned. A half-dozen times Huaras got out of her lead van and walked to a burnt-out corpse of a car, and slipped into the remains of its driver's seat. The engine started, and Huaras would open a gap in the wreckage wide enough for Evi's convoy of three vans to pass by, single file.

The last barrier was one of the concrete NYPD roadblocks. A large chunk of one block was taken out by a cab from a cargo hauler. The wreckage neatly filled the gap between two of the concrete barriers. It didn't look like the truck's cab could be moved, even with the help of a skyhook. However, Huaras climbed into the charred cab, and the truck obediently started backing away, scraping on its rims, revealing a gap between the NYPD barriers large enough for an APC. The civilian vans passed through without any trouble.

Huaras got into Evi's van, and van number three split off to head toward a satellite uplink somewhere in Greenwich Village. That left Evi with her van, Huaras, Nohar, and Dave Price, and the second van with Gurgueia and a rat with a vid unit.

If Price could still work the security at the UABT complex, they wouldn't need to fire a shot, and the country would receive a big wake-up call.

The two vans shot through a light snowfall down a

lightly trafficked Park Avenue. New York City never slept, but between the hours of three-thirty and four-thirty, it rested a little.

The glass-metal canyon of Manhattan got deeper as they traveled south. The blue-lit spire of Nyogi towered over the smaller skyscrapers, dwarfing them by an order of magnitude.

When Evi hit 56th, she turned away from the sight. It made her nervous.

They closed on the UABT complex, a scattering of onyx dominoes, flat to the ground and stacked at random. Half a block away, she could tell something was wrong. She got on the comm.

"Gurgueia."

"Gurgueia here." There was a pause. "Commander."

"Have Fernando hit the IR enhancer on his gadget, look at the buildings."

Evi slowed her van to a stop, half a block away from the complex as she waited for a response. Over the comm she could hear the two moreys in the tail van confer in Spanish.

"Fernando says there's a hot spot in the building to the right of the parking lot—" Gurgueia was interrupted by more chittering Spanish from the rat. "It's a fire, something's burning in there."

"The cars in the lot?"

More Spanish.

"Half-dozen. A van and a truck with the engine going—" The rat cursed in Spanish. Gurgueia continued. "Fernando sees at least two canine moreaus. Afghanis. Japanese firearms, silenced."

Evi slammed her fist into the dash.

Nyogi had beat them. What the hell could they do now?

What else was there to do?

"Gurgueia."

"Yes?"

231

"You're going to fall back. Watch the buildings. If they come out with the aliens, follow them. But don't engage them, understand? No heroics."

"Understood."

Evi cut the comm circuit.

"And we do?" asked Huaras.

"We go in." She looked back at her passengers. "Except you, Price."

She gave Price control of the base comm unit and led Nohar and Huaras toward the complex.

On the way, Nohar whispered, "You trust him?"

Without turning her head, she responded. "I don't trust *you*."

One thing Nyogi's canines did, they made it a lot easier for Evi and her two companions to break through security. The fence surrounding the property was dead, and the front gate hung open, unguarded. Unfortunately, the front gate led directly to the parking lot and a pair of Afghani moreaus.

Evi, Huaras, and Nohar made it to the front gate without attracting the attention of the two canines, who were more intent on the buildings. Evi's team hid behind an illegally parked limo that sat near the entrance to the UABT complex.

"Price," Evi whispered over her throat-mike, "is there a way into the complex out of sight of the parking lot?"

"Not without blowing in a window," Price's voice chirped over her earpiece.

"What about the roof?"

"Still have to break in."

Huaras shook his head. "No time but to go in front," he whispered. The one-eared rabbit drew a long knife from a sheath he wore on his back, made a quick slicing motion toward the parking lot, and resheathed it in one fluid motion.

"Gurgueia," Evi whispered over her mike, "does Fernando still see only two canines?"

"Still only two." She wondered if the growl she heard in the jaguar's voice was just interference.

She wished that she'd brought a sniper weapon. The closest they had was the AK-47 hanging off of her shoulder. It would cover the distance, but it would tell everyone they were here. She looked down at Huaras, "Go."

Huaras slipped away, moving downwind of the canines. The brown rabbit seemed to vanish into the landscaping. Despite the fact the weapon wasn't silenced, Evi braced her AK-47 on the hood of the illegal limo and aimed at the parking lot, waiting for Huaras and hoping she wouldn't have to fire.

She could see the two canines. One stood in front of a cargo hauler, watching the front doors of the largest building in the complex. The other paced in front of the rear doors of the trailer, letting his Mitsubishi point at the ground. She could probably disable both of them with one sweep across the length of the vehicle, if she had to.

"How do you feel about humans?" The rumbling whisper from Nohar was unexpected. She forced herself to keep sighting down the gun. She had no idea where Huaras was.

"What kind of question is that?"

"Hate would be easy . . ."

"So?" *Huaras, where are you?*

"Do you?"

Did she?

"I'll get back to you on that."

"I'm not the one who needs to know."

She only got a brief moment to reflect on that. She saw Huaras slip from behind a parked sedan and slip under the cargo hauler. She didn't see any reaction from the canines. She strained, focusing on the cargo hauler. Huaras was sliding on his stomach toward the rear of the trailer.

The canine paced past Huaras, and the rabbit slid

out from under the trailer. The Afghani started turning and Huaras jumped. The rabbit's left arm snaked around the dog's muzzle, and the knife seemed to slide out of nowhere, even as the two fell to the asphalt.

Evi moved the AK-47 to cover the forward canine. He knew something was wrong behind the truck. He walked along the side of the trailer, toward his fallen comrade. Huaras came out of nowhere. He fell on the dog from the top of the truck. The dog looked up just in time for the knife to slash his neck.

"Score two for the good guys," Evi whispered.

"Believe that?" Nohar asked.

"No." She activated her mike. "Gurgueia, any more activity going on by the truck?"

"Fernando says that if there's anything going on, it's in the buildings."

"Okay," Evi told Nohar, "we go in."

The two of them ran up to the parking lot. Huaras had stripped the canines of their silenced Mitsubishis and as Evi made it to the trailer, Huaras tossed her one. Evi passed the AK-47 to Nohar. "Could hide bodies," Huaras said, "But dogs, they know, smell them—"

Evi nodded; she had smelled the blood from the dogs as she'd run up. She gave her attention to the van that was parked next to the cargo hauler. The van could hold ten dogs. The truck . . . "Nohar, open the back of the truck."

He reached up and operated the door. When the hydraulic door slid aside, a blast of heat drifted out in a cloud of steam. With it floated the odor of sulfur.

Evi backed up until she could see in the trailer. Inside, it looked like a cave. A stonelike substance crusted the walls, rounding the corners of the interior of the trailer. Greenish-red lights were set in the far corners, casting an evil glow. It smelled of sulfur and ammonia.

"Deluxe accommodations," Nohar said.

Evi couldn't help but wonder how many other unmarked cargo haulers were crisscrossing the country with this kind of cargo. Fortunately, that meant that they didn't use the trailer to ship in the troops. Only enough canines to fill the one van.

"That's what I needed," Evi said, "We have ten to twelve dogs in there, probably in teams of four—"

One of the onyx domino buildings, the one where Fernando had put the fire, erupted in a ball of yellow flame that rolled out the windows and shot upward. As she turned toward it, the shockwave hit her with a blast of heat that threw her against the side of the trailer. As she watched, a secondary explosion shook the parking lot and shattered windows throughout the complex.

"Price!" she screamed over her throat-mike, abandoning any attempt at stealth.

"Yes, I see—That's the computer and administration complex. The creatures are in the *main* building." Price added, weakly, "Shit."

"I hate explosives," Evi whispered.

Nohar and Huaras picked themselves up off the ground. Nohar looked at the burning administration building. "Afghanis don't share the sentiment."

"Main building." Evi waved her Mitsubishi at the doors. She clicked it on full auto and started running.

The doors to the main building were glass, and riddled with bullet holes. She closed on them and could smell human and canine blood. In the hall beyond the door fluorescents flickered erratically. She saw two security guards draped over the desk in the reception area. She kept low; nothing offered her cover from the lobby.

She stayed in a crouch, next to the doors, looking into the lobby through a hole where a picture window used to be. Wind rattled the remains of a set of black lacquer venetian blinds. She swept her gaze past the overturned chairs, over glass-covered carpeting, past the massive concrete planter that was the centerpiece of the room, past the desk with the dead security guards ...

Out of the corner of her eye she saw some movement.

Evi dived through the window, seeking cover behind the concrete planter. She hit ground on top of a pile of black lacquer slats as bullets tore through plastic foliage. Before she could get oriented, the firing ceased, punctuated by a solid thump and the rustling of fake foliage. The smell of fresh canine blood filled the air.

She cautiously got up and looked around.

Laying face-first in a fake palm was an Afghani merc missing most of the back of his skull. Walking into the building behind him, was Huaras clutching the other commandeered Mitsubishi.

She looked at the one-eared rabbit and asked, "Where'd he come from?"

Huaras gestured at the rank of elevators lining the wall to the right of the lobby. "Got here, just. Think maybe he check on why other two dogs no longer talk on radio. No?"

"Think he got word to the other dogs?"

"No way we know. Think not."

Nohar followed Huaras into the lobby. "Where from here?"

Evi walked over to the desk. "We stay here for a few minutes. Cover the elevators, both of you."

On the desk were two dead security guards. She rolled the bodies off the desk as she moved behind it. The guards never even had time to draw their weapons.

"Price," she asked over her mike. "Where're the aliens being kept?"

"Sublevel three."

She looked over the vid displays set into the desk. Many showed snow. She kept hitting keys, changing cameras, until she got a picture showing Afghanis on it. "Sublevel three," the camera said, "maint corridor five."

It was a war. The camera was aimed down the length of a concrete corridor, toward a steel vaultlike door. Trapped in front of the door were easily a dozen humans, security guards and scientists, wielding handguns. The humans were using crates and overturned lab carts as cover. Three of them were on the ground and looked dead.

Pinning the defenders down were six or seven Afghani canines. The dogs had ripped a fire door from somewhere and were bracing against it as they swept wave after wave of machine-gun fire past the humans.

As she watched, a human wearing a lab coat jerked backward and sprayed blood on the vault door from a wound that sprouted in his chest.

"Price, I'm looking at a camera pointed down maintenance corridor five straight at an airlock-looking door."

"That's them," came the response over her earpiece. "Fitzgerald wanted them in their own environment, 2.25 atmosphere—"

"All I want is another way in, Price."

"Blocked?"

"Yes, damn it, it's blocked!"

"Let me think—"

"We don't have time—"

"Isham," Nohar yelled back at her. "One of the elevators is moving!"

"If it's a dog, shoot it." She looked at that end of the lobby as Nohar and Huaras leaned up against the wall on either side of the moving elevator. The elevator was coming from the sublevels. "Price," she yelled.

"I don't have the floorplan memorized. Give me a minute."

Evi looked up and the elevator was on sublevel two. She looked down at the monitor and saw that another human had fallen, as well as one canine. She began switching cameras at random, looking for another way down there.

"The methane jet." Price said over the radio.

"What?"

"There's this massive flame-jet set up in the center of the alien habitat. All the works for it are a level below—"

"How do we get there?"

"Same as the air lock you're looking at, but a floor below."

She punched up a camera and looked at a view labeled. "Sublevel four, maint corridor five." It was the twin of the one where the battle raged, but empty of people, canine or human. If they could get there before the Afghanis plowed through the humans—

The elevator dinged.

She ducked behind the desk and covered the doors with her Mitsubishi. The elevator doors slid open reluctantly. Nohar and Huaras were leveling their weapons when Evi could see inside the elevator.

It wasn't carrying a dog.

Erin Hofstadter bolted out of the elevator. Huaras and Nohar both hesitated as the round German economist ran past them. He didn't seem to see either of them as he headed straight for the doors.

Evi leveled the Mitsubishi and yelled. *"FREEZE!"*

She could feel her finger tighten on the trigger even as Hofstadter stopped moving. It took a great effort of self-control not to shoot her old boss.

Hofstadter turned around, "Isham?"

"Grab him, Nohar."

Hofstadter started to back away from the advancing tiger. "What the hell is this Isham?"

She couldn't help grinning. "It's poetic justice."

"You work for the Feds." He was turning red. From exertion or anger, Evi couldn't tell. "What're you doing with a gang of moreau terror—"

Nohar put a massive tawny hand on Hofstadter's shoulder. The economist gasped when it happened. It looked as if he tried to shrink away from the contact, but the tiger kept a solid grip on him.

Evi walked around the desk. Fear, that was the overriding smell that floated off her old boss. He was sweating, and the white shirt he wore was drenched. From him, she could smell traces of bile and ammonia. With all the anger that was swelling in her, all she could think to say was, "Any nonhuman with a gun is a terrorist to you."

The fear got worse, and Hofstadter's face was purpling, "You've turned."

She took her right hand off of her weapon and slapped him across the face as hard as she could. His soft flesh crushed under her hand, and he was thrown against the tiger, spitting blood.

"How dare you!" She yelled at him. "You turned against your government, and then you turned against your own conspiracy."

Hofstadter was on his knees, sputtering. The left side of his face was discolored and swelling and it looked as though he might have a broken cheekbone. She could smell urine. Hofstadter spat up blood. "So you're—" he gasped and clutched his chest. "Kill me, too?"

"I should—" She leaned in and realized that Hofstadter did not look good.

"Time, it is short, yes?" Huaras said from behind her.

No time for personal business. "Hofstadter, look at me."

He turned. His eyes were bloodshot, and he had trouble breathing. He still clutched his chest.

"Are the aliens still in the habitat, Hofstadter?"

He started laughing. It started as a giggle and moved up the scale to a desperate grasping wheeze. Then he started choking, doubling over as he clutched his chest. He collapsed at Nohar's feet. Evi dropped her gun and turned him over. Hofstadter stared up at her with an expression somewhere between a smile and a pained grimace. He sucked in a shuddering breath and whispered, "Ten minutes and no aliens."

Evi stopped as she was unbuttoning his collar. "That there's a methane—"

"Yes." Hofstadter wheezed and closed his eyes.

Evi looked up at Nohar. "I hate explosives."

CHAPTER 20

"Not good, we leave, yes?" asked Huaras.

"Damn," Evi said. "Drag him out of here. Wait back at the vans."

They picked up Hofstadter, who had lost consciousness. As they left, Nohar looked back over his shoulder. "Isham?"

"Move!" she yelled back at them. She headed for the elevators.

Hofstadter said they had ten minutes. She was confident she could disarm any explosive that Hofstadter could have rigged. The problem was getting there and finding it.

"Price," she called over the mike as she waited for an elevator to reach her. "Give me the access codes for the sublevels."

Price gave her two sets of six numbers, one for the elevator and one for the air lock on sublevel four. "I don't know if they'll work. They're my codes and I—"

"They'd better work, Price."

An elevator dinged into place. The door slid aside, stopped as the lights in the lobby flickered, and resumed opening the rest of the way. "Price, before I drop out of radio contact, where would you hide a bomb around that methane jet?"

"What?"

The doors started closing.

"Never mind," she said as she slipped inside the elevator. The voice of the elevator was repeating the phrase, ". . . stairs in case of fire. Elevators should only be used by emergency personnel . . ."

The voice pickup was dead, so she keyed in her destination manually, along with the six-digit security code. The elevator descended.

She passed the third sublevel and the lights flickered again and went out. Emergency lights came on. Apparently the fire in the administration building, probably Hofstadter's work, had finally nuked the power grid for the complex.

If Hofstadter had been right, she had all of eight minutes left.

She wedged her fingers between the doors to the elevator and pushed them apart. Her left shoulder felt it, even under the anesthetic. With the door open, she could hear gunfire on the third sublevel. The lower halves of the elevator doors leading to that sublevel were riddled with bullet holes.

She kneeled and tried to separate what she could see of the doors for the fourth sublevel. They came apart reluctantly. The ceiling of the fourth sublevel only cleared the floor of her elevator by a meter. She rolled out.

Emergency lights cast a stark white light on the bare concrete corridor. To her right the corridor shot a straight twenty meters to an airlock door. Above the airlock a red light was flashing some kind of warning.

She looked to the left. Ten meters away she saw a canine coming out of the door to the fire stairs.

Evi rolled back to take cover in the shaft. She grabbed one of the elevator doors and swung inside. The bottom of the elevator brushed her hair. She didn't hear any shooting. The dog might not have seen her.

She hugged the wall of the shaft, one hand holding on to the door for dear life, her left hand clutching the Mitsubishi. Her feet were half-hanging off of the girder that ran across the shaft, level with the corridor's floor. She looked down the shaft behind her and saw three more sublevels before it ended in a flat slab of concrete.

She was breathing hard and beginning to sweat. Her pulse throbbed in her neck, and the copper taste of panic soured her mouth.

This dog could be point for a recon team, looking for another way in to the aliens. There could be as many as five of them if her original estimate was correct.

The smell began to drift toward her. She could distinguish two separate canines before she heard the fire door swing shut.

Six minutes left.

She could hear a dog talking on the radio, in Arabic. "... similar air lock design, no defenders. We're going to—"

Her eavesdropping was interrupted by the abrupt return of power. The elevator began to descend.

She began crouching as she lost clearance. Her footing began to slip.

With a meter and a half left, she bolted. She leaped back into the corridor, turning to swing the Mitsubishi with her bad arm. She sprayed the corridor and prayed that she hit something.

The silenced Mitsubishi made a sound like someone jackhammering mud. Both dogs were taken by surprise. She managed to get one in the abdomen. Then she landed on her ass, and as she slid on the concrete floor, her remaining shots hit the ground at the other's feet. One canine folded, collapsing in a heap, while the other took cover behind a large pipe that ran floor to ceiling. That one crouched and snapped off a burst.

She still slid across the floor. As the dog shot at her, she felt something like a sledgehammer hit her left arm. The impact tore the gun from her hand and rolled her over. She came to rest by the wall opposite the elevator in a slick of her own blood.

The elevator dinged and its doors closed.

The wound was a burning pressure in her bicep. Most of it hid under the effects of the painkillers that already doped her arm. But she knew it was a bad hit, because she couldn't move her arm any more.

The canine was getting out from behind the pipe he was using for cover. He pointed the Mitsubishi at her as he crept over to his partner. She supposed she looked dead.

He turned to look at his downed comrade.

Evi used that break in the dog's attention to draw the Smith and Wesson from her shoulder holster and pump three shots. Two hit the canine in the face. The dog hit the ground before the cannon shot echoes died.

Five minutes.

She didn't have time to look at her arm. She got to her feet and ran for the airlock door. She had to holster her automatic to operate the keypad. "The code better work, Price." Price didn't hear her; the few tons of concrete above her had killed her radio.

After she entered the code, it took the computer an inordinate time to respond. After a short eternity, the door slid aside, revealing a square chamber beyond, with a smaller door on the opposite wall. Red lights flashed at her from the corners of the air lock. She stepped inside and the door started sliding shut.

It stopped when the power died again.

"Shit," she whispered.

Next to the opposite door was a glass-covered recess. Beyond the glass was a red lever. The writing on the glass said "emergency release." She punched in the glass and pulled the lever.

The door cracked open, filling the air with a high-pitched whistling. Wind razored by her, trying to scour her skin with wind-blown sand. She had to hang on to the lever to remain upright as the door continued to slide away. She closed her eyes and turned away.

The air that blew by her, trying to force her down, was hot and moist. It would have been saunalike if not for the smells that seared her nose. Bile, ammonia, sulfur, brimstone, lava. Molten smells, diseased smells.

She hung on to that lever for thirty seconds as the pressure equalized between the two environments. When she could face into the chamber beyond, she had only three minutes to find Hofstadter's bomb.

The chamber beyond the air lock was cylindrical. The ceiling sloped upward into an irregular concrete cone. At the apex of the cone was a roughly circular hole about two meters in diameter, beyond which shone red-green light. A massive network of pipes snaked upward in the center of the room, terminating in a flared nozzle that stopped about a meter short of the hole in the top of the cone. The methane jet.

No fire shot out the top of the nozzle though. Instead, Evi heard a steady low hiss. The wind from the pressure equalizing must have blown it out. The nozzle was now pumping methane into the room.

Where did he stick it?

When she didn't see it immediately, she had a fear that Hofstadter had planted it on the floor below, where the pipes seemed to originate. She told herself that if she didn't find it in sixty seconds, she'd run and take cover in the stairwell.

When she circled the base of the pipes, she saw it. A small brick of plastic explosive and a small electronic timer/detonator. The timer said that Hofstadter had overestimated the amount of time they had.

The display had already rolled over to under a minute. She had forty-eight seconds to turn the thing off. She ran up to the pipe and instantly realized that Hofstadter was taller than she was. The bomb was out of her reach.

She could see it clearly, nestled between a thin pipe that seemed to be part of the ignition system and one of the big gas pipes. She grabbed the smaller pipe and pulled herself up to within reach.

It was a standard timing element. An idiot-proof detonator mass-produced for the defense department. Nothing exotic, but she had expected as much from Hofstadter. If Hofstadter had been an operative and not an economist, she wouldn't be down here risking this.

The trigger didn't even have a motion sensor. The extent of its booby-trapping capability was the ability to send a triggering spark into the explosive block if the wires were pulled out prematurely.

The little timer window rolled over into the thirties.

She tried to find footing, but her feet kept slipping on the base of the pipes. Damn it, all she had to do was hit the reset button on the thing. It wasn't brain surgery. All she needed was to get her hand free.

The timer hit twenty-nine.

She looked down at her wounded left arm. The jumpsuit was wet with her blood from the shoulder down. She tried to move it.

The painkillers lost their effectiveness. Not only her shoulder burned, but there was a white-hot poker twisting in her bicep. Sweat stung her eyes, but she saw her arm move. She raised her shaking arm as lightning flashes of pain shot up her arm to settle into her gut. Every pulse of her heart ground a branding iron into her upper arm.

It seemed to take much longer than twenty seconds to raise her arm to the bomb. However, when her hand reached it, the timer still had nine seconds to go.

She blinked the sweat from her eyes and saw that Hofstadter had broken off the reset button.

"You BASTARD!"

Six seconds. Evi wrapped her hand around the detonator and hoped that Hofstadter's primitive method of protecting his device meant that he wasn't technically adept.

Five seconds. She knew she was going to die. She could taste it in her mouth, feel it breathing on the back of her neck.

Four seconds. "If this doesn't work, at least I'm the one who did it."

Evi ripped the detonator from the block of explosive. When she did so, her grip slipped and she fell backward. Even as she was in the air, she knew that it had worked.

To booby-trap the detonator the operator had to crack the case and wire a jumper inside. Hofstadter didn't have the time or the technical inclination to attempt that.

The detonator beeped at her as she hit the ground and blacked out.

The first thing she became aware of was the pain. It felt as if someone were squeezing her arm, and every squeeze sent a wave of fire across her shoulder.

It took a second to realize that someone *was* squeezing her arm. Her eyes shot open. The first thing she saw was the peeper. She tried to reach for her automatic. Her right arm didn't move.

There were three canines on her. One held down her right arm, one her legs, and one seemed to be doing first aid on her wounded arm. The peeper was leaning against the piping, holding the detonator.

"Evi Isham," he said. "Finally."

She looked with alarm at the dog who was tending her arm.

"Don't worry, Sharif is an excellent combat medic."

The dog jabbed something into the wound. Fire exploded inside her arm, burning out the inside of her skull. Her back arched, and when the pain receded, she could feel the ache of stressed muscles from her neck all the way down her spine.

The peeper gave her a lopsided smile. "I thought you'd like to experience the full effect of that wound."

The peeper pulled the collar of his khaki shirt away to reveal a puckered red scar in his neck, under the Adam's apple. "Like I did."

The world had finally fallen in on her.

"Ironic," the peeper said as he hefted the detonator. "You probably saved my life. I doubt the Race's little beasties could patch me up after an explosion. It's one of the ways you kill *them*."

Sharif silently ripped what felt like a meter of barbed wire out of her arm. She turned to look at him tossing aside a few dozen strands of carbon fiber from her jumpsuit.

"What are you going to do with me?" She asked. She was ashamed of how weak her voice sounded.

"If it was up to me," he said, looking down at her and his smile disappearing, "I'd cut out your eyes and toss you naked into the Bronx."

Sharif finally finished his job. Evi felt the pressure of an airhypo injecting something into her arm. Then Sharif wrapped her arm in a dressing.

The peeper went on. "Unfortunately, for both of us, the Race has an interest in you, beyond the re- trieval of their—" He hesitated and said the last word with distaste, "people."

Sharif backed off of her arm and the peeper told her, "Get up."

The canines retreated, letting her stand. The world felt oddly disjointed, as if she were watching events from a distance. She wondered if it was an effect of the pain, or hitting her head, or what they'd doped her with. They'd shot her up with something, and it wasn't painkiller. The fire in her arm was a razor- sharp sensation, while the rest of the world seemed fuzzy and indistinct.

"Who are you?" The words came out in slow mo- tion, as if they had to fight her tongue to get out. "NLF?"

"Move first. We've outstayed our welcome."

He prodded her and she started walking. She knew enough to realize she was drugged. She walked through air that felt like molasses, and she couldn't bring herself to resist the peeper's commands.

The three dogs escorted her out the air lock and down the corridor, the peeper in the lead. The power had died, and they walked under the periodic spotlights of the emergency lights. The peeper kept talking, his voice a small rattle in a gray-cotton silence. "Dimitri's what *they* call me. NLF was Hioko's little boondoggle, before his brain had an argument with a bullet . . ."

When they reached the fire stairs, she had a brief fear that she had forgotten how to climb them. She stopped short, confused, as the peeper's, Dimitri's, voice faded in her awareness. Someone pushed her from behind and she had to struggle to move. It took an inordinate amount of concentration, and Dimitri's voice kept fading in and out of her awareness.

". . . never trusted the Race, smart move though it killed him . . ."

". . . don't kill you is because what the Race'll do instead . . ."

". . . need folks like you. What they give is almost worth it . . ."

Somehow she made it to the ground level. She was briefly curious about how long she'd been in the bowels of the UABT complex, but her time sense had left her. All she knew was that it was still dark outside, and the cargo hauler was gone.

Where was her backup? Gurgueia, Huaras, Nohar, and Fernando with his video camera who was supposed to document the aliens and the conspiracy. She remembered that she'd told the jaguar to follow wherever the aliens went; she must be following the truck.

The administration building still burned. The roar of the fires seemed to heighten in volume in time to her pulse. For some reason she couldn't focus on the fire; her eyes kept darting after random motions, following smoke around in circles.

Someone prodded her, and she realized she had stopped moving. Dimitri's voice faded into her awareness. ". . . not get distracted. Once you're in the van, your attention can wander all you want."

She nodded. It made a lot of sense at the time.

Once she settled into the seat in the van, she allowed her gaze to drift again. It took too much effort to focus her attention on any one thing. She cradled her arm and looked out the windshield. Dimitri talked on in the background, but she couldn't keep a grip on what he said. As she faced the windshield, the van shook. That was briefly of interest, since no one had started the engine.

Glass fell from the windows of the main building, looking like black ice. Blue-green fire rolled out from the lobby, upward. It struck Evi that something had ignited all the methane that had been pumping out of that jet. She turned her head to the rear window, where, in the distance, she saw red and blue flashing lights. Police, she thought. NYPD or Agency impersonators? She didn't know, or care.

Dimitri climbed over her and into the driver's seat. She followed him with her eyes and her gaze rested on the back of his neck as he turned on the van and slammed on the accelerator.

As the van rocketed forward, she recorded a brief amazement at the fresh red scar under the edge of his close-cropped hair. It was obviously the exit wound from the bullet she'd placed in his neck less than seventy-two hours ago. Nothing healed that fast.

The van hit a bump and her head rolled aside. There were four Afghanis in back here with her. She wondered what these shaggy dogs thought about her. She was responsible for the death of a lot of their fellows. This breed of moreau was the least "human." The Afghani dogs were pack oriented and had little concept of individuality. They were so well engineered for combat that they couldn't adapt to any other environment. No room in their psyches for personal vendettas. They took orders, killed people, and usually died violently.

As the van shot through the gate and a space that used to hold a parked limousine, she closed her eyes and wondered if she should try to force her thinking into a more coherent pattern.

CHAPTER 21

The ride in the van was a long sequence of disjointed imagery. Evi tried to force her mind on one track of thinking. The effort had the edge of desperation, and she embraced it. The feeling of desperation helped to fight the sense of apathy that enveloped her like quicksand.

If she closed her eyes and concentrated, to the exclusion of the outside world, she could think straight.

The first coherent thought she had was that there was no way she could escape this situation while she was drugged. But the fact that she could force herself to think coherently meant the effects of the drug were waning. Her metabolism tended to race such things through her body. If she got lucky, Dimitri wouldn't know that.

One consolation about her capture. It looked as if they assumed she was still working solo, or with Frey's people. They didn't seem to be aware of the moreaus; that was good. If Gurgueia followed her orders, they would track the cargo van to its destination. With Fernando, they'd complete some of the mission, getting some record of the aliens' existence on video.

Only surveillance footage of aliens being transported from point A to point B wouldn't be as effective as their original idea of broadcasting straight from the alien habitat itself. However, it might still shake something loose.

Unfortunately, for her that was all moot now. She

had hoped the plan would nullify the reasons everyone wanted her, dead or otherwise. With a public broadcast, Hofstadter couldn't keep his secrets by killing her, the Agency couldn't save itself embarrassment by disappearing her, and, if they'd done it right, Nyogi would have other problems than kidnapping her.

Now, it seemed, Nyogi wanted something from her, beyond getting their people back. From what she remembered of Dimitri's speech, whatever that was, it wasn't pleasant.

The van came to a stop and she opened her eyes. The world became disjointed again, but it was easier for her to concentrate. The van had parked in a huge elevator, easily the size of Diana's entire loft. There was the whir of distant motors, and the ceiling was receding above her. She found herself focusing on a concrete beam in the ceiling above that must have had a cross section larger than the van's.

She forced her gaze down, into the van. The only residents were herself and Dimitri. Dimitri was covering her with an unsilenced Mitsubishi.

Where were the Afghanis?

Dimitri seemed to notice her looking. "The canines aren't allowed where you're going. Few creatures are, other than the Race themselves."

"Race?" She managed to slur.

"What *they* call themselves."

She found that, with a considerable effort, she could keep her gaze locked on the peeper. "Why," she forced herself to say, "you work for . . ." It took too much effort, she let the question trail off.

"Why'd a human turn on his whole planet?" Dimitri smiled. "Why'd a nonhuman work for a bunch of humans?"

That sliced through the fog. "I never had a choice." Her voice actually sounded coherent that time.

"We all have choices, Isham," Dimitri said. "Sometimes we make the wrong ones to save our asses."

The elevator came to a halt, and Dimitri pressed a button on the dash that opened the rear door.

It wasn't until the door opened that she realized that the air conditioning in the van had been going full blast. Heat slammed into the van in a wet, rancid blast. She turned to look out the rear doors and saw a massive room beyond. The room was a warehouse. She could see crates, robot forklifts, and cargo haulers in a massive loading dock, everything in the room disturbingly normal.

The normalcy was disturbing because the construction of the room itself was alien. The entire warehouse area was a squashed sphere, ovoid in cross section. The ovoid was maybe a hundred meters in diameter and easily twenty meters tall at its highest point. Cones projected from the walls at regular intervals, shooting blue-green jets of fire that added to the ranks of red lights that were sunk into smooth depressions in the ceiling.

This dwarfed anything she'd seen in Cleveland.

A small robot golf cart rolled up to the back of the van. Dimitri gestured with the gun. "Get in the cart."

Dimitri stood back in the air-conditioned van and watched her from behind his submachine gun. The heat started her sweating and made her dizzy. By the time she had dragged herself to the cart, she wanted to pass out.

It had to be forty degrees down here, she thought. It felt as if she were buried under a burning compost heap.

She closed her eyes when she collapsed in the back of the cart. She could hear Dimitri walk up to her. This was the time to make a break for it, she thought. She opened her eyes and saw Dimitri standing in front of the cart as it started moving. He faced her, never lowering the barrel of the gun. She tried to sit up, and the wave of disorientation she felt when her head moved told her that at the speed she was operating,

Dimitri would put three shots in her chest before she got halfway to her feet.

The cart rolled through the cavernous warehouse. The lack of right angles or straight lines in the room made it hard for her to judge distance. Holes collected in the walls in irregular groups of eight. She couldn't tell if the openings were small and close by or huge and impossibly far.

They passed through one of the holes long before she expected to. Suddenly she was slipping through a nearly spherical concrete tube that was of a much more manageable scale. It could have been a storm sewer if it weren't for the red lights sunk into the ceiling in organically smooth pits. The concrete walls were polished to a sheen that reflected light like wet marble.

They traveled through miles of sameness. The concrete tubes had branches that resembled the inside of a stone giant's circulatory system, and the ovoid openings that broke into the sides of the tube resembled ulcers. Most of the doors showed only darkness beyond, but behind at least one she saw a pulsing white amoebic form.

The farther they went, the hotter it became.

The cart pulled to a stop when the tube emptied into another squashed spheroid. This room was much smaller than the warehouse, twenty meters across. It was big enough for the cart to pull in and circle halfway around the perimeter, around a hole in the center of the floor.

She noticed eight corridors that slipped out of the room at regular intervals in the walls. Still in a drugged fog, she couldn't pick the one the cart had come from.

"End of the line," Dimitri said. "Everybody out."

As he spoke, there was a sucking sound, and a blast of cool air came from the center of the room. She looked in that direction and saw a metal lid opening in the room's central pit. It reminded her of a trapdoor spider. Light came from underneath it, a more reasonable white light.

"That's where you're going."

She looked at him. He was sweating profusely. It might be possible . . .

She stood, and the wave of vertigo made her reconsider. She climbed out of the cart, trying to be careful of her footing, and slowly walked across the too smooth floor toward the blessedly cool pit.

When she reached the edge, she looked down. It was a steeply angled tube that quickly slipped out of her sight. It was clear she was intended to slide down it.

Dimitri waved his gun. "Go."

She quietly told herself that, if Dimitri and company wanted her dead, they would have killed her long before now. Then she stepped into the hole, protecting her arm with her body.

Her slide down the chute was much faster than she'd expected. The vertigo returned with a vengeance, heightened by the fact that the tube was smooth and uniformly white, giving her eyes no landmarks to lock on.

The dizziness was so intense that she didn't realize she'd passed out.

Evi opened her eyes and found herself looking at a bearded man in his early fifties. She recognized him from the surveillance footage from the peeper's, Dimitri's, Long-Eighties. He was the professor type, Fitzgerald, the xenobiologist.

"Are you all right?" he asked.

The quickness with which she grabbed his lapel told told her she'd been out long enough for the drug to work its way out of her system. *"All right?"* she yelled at him. *"What do you think?* After you, and Frey, and everyone else screwed me over." She pushed him away, hard, and sat up. No waves of vertigo hit her this time; for that she was grateful.

She got off the bunk she had come to on, and looked around. Fitzgerald backed toward a regular *flat* wall. Two bunk beds sat opposite each other in the rectangular room, and the lighting came from recessed fluorescent tubes. An air conditioner thrummed low in the background, and cool breezes flowed from vents high in the walls.

She stood in a room normal-looking enough for her to briefly think that her travel through that alien environment had been a drug-induced hallucination. It hadn't been. She could still smell the taint of sulfur and burning methane that filtered through the overworked air conditioner.

If she had any other doubt, the fact that the only entrance to the room was a circular hole on the far wall between the bunks showed that what she'd seen was more than a hallucination. The drug might have played with her sense of scale, but what she had seen of the alien habitat must've covered several acres at least.

Fitzgerald took a tentative step forward. "Miss Isham?"

"WHAT?" She advanced on him, feeling three days worth of adrenaline course through her blood. "What, by the name of all that's holy, what could you possibly have to say to me?"

Fitzgerald sputtered, "But—"

"Are you going to tell me how sorry you are? You folks didn't *mean* to keep me in the dark. You didn't *mean* to make me a traitor!" She pushed him to the wall with her good hand. "Or are you going to apologize for being the one to hand your own conspiracy back to the damn aliens. You were the one, weren't you?"

"I—"

"How about Gabriel? How did you feel about him trying to blow me away?"

"He's dead." Fitzgerald said in a hoarse whisper.

"What?" She realized that she had wrapped her right hand around the professor's throat. It dawned on her that she could have killed the man. She backed away and began deep-breathing exercises. "Who's dead?"

"Everyone," Fitzgerald croaked. "Gabriel, Davidson, Frey. Hofstadter tried to blame it all on you—"

She thought back over what had happened to her.

"How did Davidson and Gabriel die?"

"Their car crashed on the Southeast side of Manhattan."

The aircar, she thought, the one that had chased her into Greenwich Village. "I'm sorry I jumped on you."

He shook his head. "Did you kill Frey?"

"No!" She could still smell Frey's blood, still feel the panic she'd felt then, when she first began to realize the scope of what had happened.

"Gabe and Davidson—"

"Were trying to kill me."

"You have to understand." Fitzgerald wrung his hands. "This was never supposed to become violent. It was research—"

She snorted.

"—first contact with an alien species. Do you have any idea what that means?"

Evi sat down. "I have a pretty damn good idea." The air-conditioning vents were too small, the tube was an impossible climb, and the walls were solid concrete. She was stuck here with the professor.

"It was my life," he went on. "Can't you realize—"

"Your *profession*," she snapped. "*My* fucking life."

Fitzgerald lapsed into silence.

The quiet got on her nerves. "So, in six years of research, did you find out *anything* useful?"

He walked over and sat down on the bunk across from her. "What do you want to know about them?"

"Everything."

Fitzgerald obliged her.

The Race had developed on a nearby world, a massive, hot, tectonically active ball of rock circling a dim reddish sun. They had populated a number of planets, between six and a dozen of them, including a planet orbiting Alpha Centauri A. They were very aware of Earth and the creatures populating it.

They needed the resources of the planets they'd colonized, and Earth was a potential rival. Once Earth reached out of its solar system, there'd be a costly war for territory on those new planets.

As Earth turned on, into another millennium, the Race had a political dilemma. How to prevent a seemingly inevitable conflict. The decision, after a long-distance study of Earth's culture, was a covert operation. The aliens on Earth would prevent any force on the planet from gaining the technical expertise or the inclination for interstellar travel for as long as possible.

"It's interesting," Fitzgerald said, "to see how mankind isn't the only species capable of hypocrisy and self-delusion."

Evi ignored the subtle racism implied by the word "mankind." Fitzgerald probably hadn't even noticed it.

"You see," he continued, "the Race has a long history, as bloody as any human account. They now have a culture that prides itself on the 'honor of nonconfrontation.' Direct violence is anathema to them."

"What do you mean?"

"I think of it as 'the hand on the knife' syndrome. The Race's culture puts the highest taboo, not on the knife going in the back, but on any honorable person having his hand upon it."

259

"I find it hard to believe that these things are nonviolent."

"That's the irony. *They* believe they're nonviolent. Ever since they landed on this planet their *modus operandi*, if you will, has been to employ politically active 'locals' who are instructed to carry out their agenda. It doesn't matter if the 'local' is a member of parliament, a military commander, or a terrorist. If a few people die as the 'locals' are carrying out the alien's agenda, the Race feels no responsibility."

Fitzgerald leaned forward and smiled. "In fact, if people get killed, the Race simply considers it an example of our own moral degeneracy and a justification of their mission here."

She thought the whole thing was twisted enough to be human.

Then Fitzgerald went into a catalog of what events could be traced to the Race's interference, and what started out being ironic and twisted became truly frightening.

Fitzgerald said that it was almost certain that the Iranian terrorists that slaughtered the Saudi royal family in '19 were backed financially by the Race. That had been the sparking incident that led to the Third Gulf War and the formation of the Islamic Axis. The fundamentalist Axis made sure that the only real technical progress the region made was in the area of warfare. Embryonic space programs in Saudi Arabia, Egypt, and Pakistan all died on the vine.

Funds from the Race led to the rise of a rabid anti-Islam regime in India and a fascist technocracy in Japan. The rise of tensions between India and the Islamic Axis, and Japan and Socialist China broke in 2024, when the first shots in the Pan-Asian war were fired. In '27, New Delhi was nuked. In '35, Tokyo followed suit.

It took only a few years for the Islamic Axis to

finally turn its attention to liberating Palestine. In '41, Tel Aviv was nuked.

By the time Fitzgerald reached Tel Aviv, Evi was shaking. Forget the war itself. Forget a trail of blood that ran across two decades. Forget everything but those three cities. New Delhi, Tokyo, Tel Aviv ...

Those three names represented the only grave markers for nine million people.

"It seems that the Pan-Asian war was so successful in keeping us earthbound that the Race is trying to foment a civil war here in the States. The Asian war left the U.S. with the only viable space program looking beyond the solar system."

She raised her head. Images of what she had seen when she passed through Tel Aviv were still fresh in her memory. She had to pull herself out of that private horror to pay attention to what Fitzgerald was saying now.

"With one hand," he was saying, "they try to get anti-technological, anti-moreau politicians elected. You uncovered one of those operations."

"With the other?"

"With the other, they finance radical moreau groups. One group plays against the other, and the resulting explosion keeps people too busy to look beyond the local gravity well."

She thought of General Wu and her military hardware. It looked like it was getting damn close to an explosion. She could only imagine what would happen if command weren't in the hand of that cautious, serene bear but rather in the hands of a hothead like Corporal Gurgueia.

She thought of the probe that was, "even now," Price had said, entering the neighborhood of Alpha Centauri. The whole reason the Race was here was to prevent that. That had been what triggered the shit hitting the fan.

However, it wasn't just her. It was a national shit, and the fan was the size of a continent.

She looked at the scientist, who had seemed to shrink even as he conducted his animated discussion about the Race. She leaned toward Fitzgerald. "Did you think of the reaction you'd provoke if you launched those probes?"

"What?"

"The reason all this happened is because of those probes. It isn't just us, or Frey's little group. You've given the Race—" She snorted at the pretentious name. "—incentive to push even harder to drive this country over the edge."

"No one anticipated that they had faster-than-light communications—"

"Except Davidson. And all that means is you would have had, what, another four years or so before the aliens here got word of the launch?"

"By then we would have—"

"What? Gone public? I doubt it. Know the Race better? I think you had what you needed to know six years ago."

"You don't understand—"

"I understand that for six years you sat on this. You studied it, got involved in your own political rivalries, and became enamored of your own discoveries." She stood up and jabbed her finger into his chest. "And none of you did anything about it."

"Frey wanted—"

"Frey was too damn paranoid. He couldn't trust anything that wasn't under his own control. He was so afraid of betrayal that it became a self-fulfilling prophecy."

"The Race had bribed so many—"

"If you had gotten word to enough people in enough departments, they couldn't have suppressed it. They *aren't* omnipotent, they *aren't* all-knowing—"

There was a hiss from behind her and foul air

drifted in from the opening that led to the chute. A cable descended from the hole. She heard Dimitri's voice echo above. "Time for your audience."

There was a handle on the end of the cable.

She turned back to Fitzgerald. "Did you force yourself to believe you were doing the right thing, or did you simply ignore the question?"

She picked up the handle, and the cable drew her up the chute before she heard him respond.

CHAPTER 22

"Sorry to keep you waiting," Dimitri said as the cable pulled Evi through the trapdoor. The cable was dangling through a hole in the ceiling and seemed to operate under remote control. During the ascent, she had thought of swinging up when she cleared the hole, and throttling Dimitri with her legs, much as she had the first dog she'd killed.

Her friend the peeper must have anticipated her thought. He stood well out of reach and covered her with the Mitsubishi.

The cable stopped and she swung herself to the side and stood. "Now what?"

Dimitri tossed her a pair of handcuffs, "Put those on."

She managed to catch them with her right hand. She looked at her left arm and winced at the thought of cuffing that wrist.

Her left hand was clutching her stomach inside the remains of her leather jacket. The heat was getting to her. She was sweating profusely, and she realized that one of the reasons she'd been about to pass out on the first run through was she'd been too drugged to think of shucking the leather.

She peeled off the ruined jacket and got a good look at her arm.

The dog had given her a decent field dressing. But under the shreds of her jumpsuit, the bandage was ripe with her blood. The heat was making it itch.

"Hurry up, Isham. Important people are waiting." Dimitri said "people" like some humans said "moreau," or "frank."

She fumbled with the cuffs, trying to get them around her left wrist without moving that arm. Even with the effort, she had to grit her teeth and endure fiery daggers cutting deep into her shoulder.

When she had the cuffs around her wrists, she gasped. She'd been holding her breath. She looked up from her work to see that Dimitri had used the time to fetch Fitzgerald and have him cuffed.

"Into the cart." He waved them ahead of him, always keeping the gun on Evi.

She watched him as closely as he watched her, and she never saw an opening. Fitzgerald climbed into the back of the golf cart, and when she followed she tried to do it without using her arms. Humidity had condensed on the runner of the cart and she slipped, slamming her left shoulder into the cart.

Pain washed out her vision as a white nova exploded in her arm.

She was on her knees next to the cart, and Dimitri was laughing. She turned to look at him, the smoldering pain turning to rage. She looked at him. He made no move toward her, and the gun never wavered.

He stopped laughing. "Get in the cart."

The heat and the pain made an anger that had been three days festering erupt into a full-blown rage.

She was going to kill this man. She no longer cared about anything but bringing the house down on the people, the things, *the Race,* responsible for the last three days, responsible for the betrayal of the last six years, responsible for the destruction of her homeland. And she would start with Dimitri.

She stared into his eyes. The gun didn't move. She was too far away. She was quicker than he was, but she wasn't quicker than a bullet.

Slowly she stood, nodded at him, and carefully

climbed into the back of the cart. There would be a moment when that gun would lower, and then she would move.

"Don't worry about that arm," Dimitri said. "In a few minutes it's either going to be good as new, or else it isn't going to matter."

The cart started rolling through a new set of tunnels, larger ones that grew even larger as they moved away from the cell. Other tunnels emptied into the main one until the tube they were traveling through became ten meters in diameter.

The stench of bile and ammonia, not to mention burning methane, became much, much worse.

The tunnel didn't end so much as have the walls roll back into another ovoid chamber.

The chamber they drove into was another squashed sphere, thirty meters across. In the center was a two-meter tall, polished-concrete cone that belched a jet of methane flame.

The chamber was taller in proportion than most of the rooms Evi had seen down here, and the reason was obvious. A spiraling two-meter wide ramp snaked around the edges of the chamber three times.

The room was a small auditorium, and the ramp provided seating for the audience.

And the audience was the Race.

The aliens.

There were over a hundred white pulsing forms sprawled on the gradual slope of that spiral ramp. The mass of them exuded a bile-ammonia smell that made it hard for her to breathe. No two of the Race held exactly the same shape: some were conical, some spheroidal, some cylindrical. Most had erupted white tentacles the length of a human arm, in some cases three or four of them, and waved them at the cart that was trundling in the only entrance. They all undulated to a pulsing rhythm she couldn't hear.

The cart pulled to a stop just inside the chamber.

"Get out," said Dimitri. "You're about to be honored."

The gun was still locked on her, so she did as she was told. Fitzgerald followed her, a look of awe on his face.

The three of them seemed to be surrounded by acres of white featureless flesh. A leprous wall of pulsing wax that made soft bubbling sounds that echoed throughout the chamber.

Polyethylene bags of raw sewage, she thought. They smelled like they'd been scraped off the floor of the john in that porno theater.

She hated every last one of them.

But Dimitri would not move that gun off of her.

Fitzgerald walked toward the end of the room opposite the one entrance. The ramp terminated near the ceiling there, and at that point of precedence was a Race that had taken a rough humanoid form. It had a soft, blubbery body, four limbs, and a head built around a hole that formed a mouth of sorts.

This one didn't go to the lengths that the ones in Cleveland had gone to. The ones there had worn fake plastic eyes and dentures and had taken to human clothing to rein in cascading flesh. This one did none of that, and there was no way, even with its token humanoid form, that it could be mistaken for an earthly creature.

Evi rounded the cone, following Fitzgerald. Dimitri stayed a good distance behind her, the gun tracking her every move.

"Welcome," said the lead creature. "In the name of the Octal and the Race."

"Some fucking wel—" she started to say. She stopped because she could now see a concave depression in the floor between the cone and the far end of the room. The cone had blocked it before. The depression sank for two meters, and had stopped Fitzgerald's progress toward the lead creature.

Sitting in the center of the pit was a creature that was neither Race nor anything from Earth.

The thing was a pulsing amoebic form, like the Race. It formed a rough spheroid. Unlike the Race, it was a dull red in color. And rippling across its body were hairlike tentacles that resembled red grass waving in the wind.

The smell of rotting meat hung over the pit.

"Show some respect," Dimitri said. "That's about to become your mother."

Evi couldn't repress her shudder.

"Evi Isham," the leader continued in its bubbling monotone. "You show an aptitude that we find useful when you work for us."

She looked up from the pit. "You've got to be kidding."

The creature went on. Either it didn't understand her or it was ignoring her. "We find few natives useful enough for us to offer what we offer you. You are much more effective than the canines we employ. More effective than Dimitri, the last one we offer this."

She was dumbfounded. After what she had gone through, after what these things had done to her and her planet, they were asking her to . . .

"No," she whispered. "I'm not going to work for—"

"You don't have a choice." Dimitri said from behind her.

The creature kept going on, ignoring her, as if it were reciting a memorized script. "You join with us, bond with us, become one of us. Commune with Mother."

"What the *hell*?" She looked into the pit that smelled like rotting meat. The red spheroid undulated on, oblivious.

"Mother," Dimitri whispered at her. "Race have trouble with English." He laughed. It sounded more ironic than anything else. "Wonder why I keep walking? After a bullet through the neck?"

Evi looked over her shoulder at Dimitri. The gun was still locked on her, he was still too far away, and he was smiling. "I didn't kill you because they're going to do to you what they did to me."

She looked back into the pit. The lead creature went on, but she was only listening to Dimitri now.

"Mother lays eggs," he said, his voice low, almost seductive. "Lays them in any living tissue. The microscopic larvae bond to your cells. They'll do just about everything to keep you alive, until they mature, of course."

She was feeling sick to her stomach.

"Up to that point, you're as invulnerable as the Race are. Fire, acid, electricity, that's it. Only two problems."

"What?" she found herself asking, unable to tear her eyes off the creature in the pit. She was focusing on it now, letting it fill her field of vision. She could see that the cilia that waved across its back were actually hair-thin hollow tubes. The tubes were pointed at the end and resembled hypodermic needles. That must be what they were, ovipositors, designed to inject microscopic eggs into a host.

Thousands of those injectors, millions of eggs.

"Problem is," Dimitri said, "you have to eat *their* food, or the little beasties die off and take you with them. The other is, you have to take the Race's suppressant drugs or the larvae mature."

And the Race thought of themselves as nonviolent.

"You'll embrace Mother, Isham," Dimitri said. "Then, if you don't work for the Race, you'll be eaten alive."

Rage, that's what she felt, that and a fear bordering on panic. She was going to be used, again. Used in the worst possible way. She looked at Mother and could only think that she was about to be raped, and she was panicking because she couldn't see how to fight it.

If only she could do something. If it weren't for that damn gun.

"Scott Fitzgerald," she heard the creature say.

It crossed her mind that it was about to go through that whole speech again for the professor.

Not even close.

"You help in locating our four others. For that you are thanked. Your purpose for the Race and the Octal is served. We allow Dimitri to deal with you as he sees fit."

She got a ten minute speech. Fitzgerald got barely ten seconds. She supposed that it was poetic justice. She'd been duped; Fitzgerald, apparently, had sold everyone out.

Fitzgerald backed away from the pit. He opened his mouth but didn't say anything. He began to shake his head violently.

"No!" was what finally came out. "Not after all—" He broke off, choking on his own words. Evi turned toward him and began to realize what must be going through Fitzgerald's head. His life's work had led up to this point, and he'd just been dismissed as so much extra baggage.

He might have *wanted* what the aliens were offering her.

If she could, she'd trade places. Alien larvae or not, she thought she could take Dimitri in a fair fight.

Fitzgerald was backed all the way to the cone. "I will not let you do this to me." Then he surprised the hell out of Evi by jumping Dimitri. The doctor was still in the air as Dimitri turned the Mitsubishi around to empty half a clip into his chest. Fitzgerald jerked and fell face-first onto the smooth concrete floor with a dull wet thud.

The bubbling around the perimeter of the chamber increased in volume.

Evi was primed for action. The second that Dimitri turned the gun away from her and began firing, she jumped. She was much faster than Fitzgerald, faster than Dimitri. She got behind him and lowered her arms over his head, to pull the chain on her handcuffs across his neck.

Dimitri was trained. He saw her arms lowering and in the split-second he had, he raised the Mitsubishi up to his neck. Her arms met the hard resistance of the submachine gun's short barrel, and the impact sent a shuddering flame of agony down her left arm. Dimitri's right elbow slammed into her abdomen, awakening deep bruises left there by Sukiota's interrogation.

She slammed him face-first into the concrete cone. She felt an explosion in her left wrist; the cuffs were becoming burning brands.

Dimitri jerked against her, rotating. He was now turning to face her, and the gun had come loose. She was no longer clamping on the vulnerable portion of his windpipe; her hands were feeling the back of his head.

They were too close together, leaning by the side of the conc. Dimitri was pushing against her with his knee, trying to clear a space to point the gun at her.

She glanced up at the jet of burning methane shooting out the top of the cone. He glanced up there, too.

"No," he said.

Evi clamped her forearms tight on either side of Dimitri's neck, under the jawline, her hands entangled in his hair. The effort of tightening the muscles flamed up her arm and blurred her vision. She wanted to scream or pass out. She let herself scream.

She put everything she had into the lift and the swing, all the rage, all the pain, all the strength she could squeeze out of her genetically engineered muscles. She could almost hear the bicep in her left arm tear as Dimitri's hundred kilos left the ground. As her forearm brushed the lower edge of the methane flame, every nerve in her shoulder was flayed open and ignited as her shoulder redislocated.

When Dimitri's chin caught on the lip of the gas nozzle, she couldn't hear his screams over her own.

She hung on to the back of his neck, arms on either side of the concrete cone, as Dimitri's face was forced into the fire. His arms flailed widely on the other side of the cone, clawing at her arms. He stared at her through the blue-green flame, and she stared into his eyes as his face reddened, blackened, melted . . .

Evi closed her eyes.

Dimitri stopped struggling.

It took her five minutes or longer to disengage herself from the body. She had to slowly pull her arms over Dimitri's head, and that hurt, especially because the insides of both forearms were badly burned. The only reason she didn't burn herself worse when disengaging herself was because, when she pulled on the back of Dimitri's head, it nodded forward and plugged the hole. That put the flame out.

Once she got the handcuff chain over the back of Dimitri's skull, she slid off of the cone and landed on her ass next to Fitzgerald's corpse. Dimitri fell off of the cone in the opposite direction.

The room filled with the sound of hissing, flameless methane.

She sat down, clutching her arms to her stomach, breathing heavily. She wanted to throw up, but her stomach was empty.

She sat there for a long time it seemed, only aware of the pain in both her arms. She forced herself to look up. The Race were still there, unmoving, bubbling, pulsing, unaffected by the little drama that had played out before them.

"You freakish bastards. You just don't give a shit do you?"

The leader, the one at the head of the spiral ramp, spoke in its underwater monotone, "Personal native arguments do not concern the Octal. We appreciate now that you step in and embrace Mother.''

Evi got to her feet, clutching her stomach with both arms. Her laugh broke from her in racking silent spasms. "Fuck you."

She backed away from the pit and the hissing gas jet. "You'll have to kill me first." She was grinning, and that scared her. She was losing it, and it was a bad time to lose it.

"The Race does not kill. Lesser species kill."

She had backed to the cart at the entrance. There seemed to be a shuffling movement along the ramp. The bubbling was deepening in intensity and increasing in volume. Both her arms were burning, the wound on her left arm had burst open and she was bleeding all over the place, and she couldn't help laughing. "Bullshit."

"Evi Isham, you embrace Mother for your own good. You are wounded. You die without Mother's aid."

She looked down at her arm. That *was* a hell of a lot of blood. There was a clear trail from her all the way back to the hissing cone. She clamped her right hand over the wound to stop the bleeding.

The bubbling was reaching a crescendo and the leader continued. "We leave you here to decide as we handle infrastructure problems."

One creature, the one nearest the bottom of the spiral ramp, descended toward her, the cart, and the exit.

Evi looked at the creature, then to the cone back in the center of the room. Flameless methane still hissed into the room.

No wonder these things were acting nervous. Fire was one of the things Dimitri said could hurt the Race. This whole room was about to become a bomb.

She turned to look at the robot golf cart. Electricity was another . . .

She raised her foot and kicked the cowling off the rear of the cart. The plastic cracked off, revealing the inductor housing and the lead wires. She bent over it and grabbed an insulated wire in each hand, even though it hurt like hell. She pulled the wires away from the engine, which sat under the cart, and something out of her sight gave.

She fell on her ass with about a meter of wire in each hand. Even though the pain in her arms whited out her vision, she managed to keep the red wire from touching the blue one. She managed to croak out, "Stop moving. I think there's more than enough juice in this to liquefy you."

When she opened her eyes, the creature had stopped short of the end of the ramp. She got to her feet, hands shaking. More blood was streaming down her arm, and now she couldn't put any pressure on it. Her left hand had stopped hurting, even though she thought her wrist was broken. Felt like it had fallen asleep.

Slowly she turned toward the other end of the room. Yes, she had enough play in the wires to cover the end of the ramp from where she stood. If aliens started bailing from the ramp in other parts of the room, they could make it out the other side of the cart, but it didn't look as if they were built for jumping. "Wrong answer," she told the head alien. "Try again."

"You bleed to death without Mother—"

"You have a one-track mind. Get the picture. *I'm taking your worthless asses with me.*"

The room, not just the leader who'd been addressing her, but the entire room, became silent. The bubbling quieted. Tentacles stopped waving. Undulation ceased.

The only sound was the hissing gas from the methane jet.

"This makes no sense. Such an ending when other options—"

"You've been fucking with this planet for so long that you don't understand revenge?" She couldn't believe she was grinning at the thing. She was feeling light-headed and giddy. Her entire left arm was asleep now.

There was a thudding plop and Evi turned around. One of the Race had jumped from the ramp. It wasn't going to be much more of a standoff. They were going to rush the exit now.

The ground shook under her feet. "What?"

She looked back down the tube of the corridor, and she thought she could hear a crash or an explosion back in that direction.

She turned back to the alien that had jumped the ramp. It wasn't moving toward the exit. It had turned grayish and was pulsing quietly.

The leader spoke again. "We reconsider our offer. Put down the wires and we discuss other options."

The leader sounded weak and was turning gray, too. In fact, all the creatures near the top of the chamber were becoming grayish. As she watched, a dull gray pulsing cone with five tentacles collapsed into itself and rolled off the edge of the ramp, hitting the edge below, pushing aside two grayish fellows.

Damn, Evi thought, *this might* look *like home to these guys, but I bet, back home, their volcanic vents don't go out.*

The room was filling with methane and they were asphyxiating. A wave of dizziness hit her. *I could use some oxygen myself.*

That started a silent laugh that degenerated into a gasping wheeze.

She thought she could smell smoke under the sulfur-ammonia smells now. She wondered if she really heard gunfire in the background or if it was just wishful thinking.

275

"We give you what you want," said the lead creature. The pseudo-humanoid form it wore seemed to be melting into a gray slime. "Name a wish, it is yours."

"I want my life back, I want my country back, most of all—" She paused to catch her breath. "I want to see you dead."

"Isham." Where the hell did that voice come from?

"Isham." The voice came again as the alien spokesman slipped off its perch and slammed into the ramp below. She looked around the room and at first saw only collapsing aliens. Then she saw Dimitri's corpse move.

"Oh, shit."

Apparently Dimitri could still hear, because a blackened skull turned toward her. Empty sockets looked for her as Dimitri's hands groped about him. "Kill you." It came out as a moan.

There was no way that this man could still be alive. His face was burnt off. Despite that, he was on his hands and knees groping around.

Dimitri's right hand brushed the Mitsubishi.

Evi looked from the gun to the methane jet to a few dozen gray asphyxiated aliens, dropped the wires, and ran.

She was twenty meters down the hall before the thought struck her that if Mother's larva were bonded to *all* of Dimitri's cells, then she needed total immolation to kill him, not just burning his face. Thirty meters down the tube and she was sure she could hear gunfire ahead of her. Forty meters down the tube and she heard gunfire from behind her.

She felt her feet leave the ground as a pressure wave blew by her. A flaming hand slammed her into the ceiling. Her last coherent thought was how much she hated explosives.

CHAPTER 23

Evi woke up in a hospital. They kept her drugged and at the fringes of consciousness for days. By the time she was conscious enough to take full stock of her surroundings, she had been there for at least a week.

The place was an Agency hole. Evi could tell. Her room was private, windowless, and—when she managed to get out of bed once—locked. No comm. Her only contact with other people were with the doctors and nurses, none of whom talked to her.

Go from the frying pan to the fire, Evi thought. *Where do you go from the fire?*

No answers.

Someone had to have gotten to her within five minutes of the explosion, or she would've bled to death. From the looks of things, the Agency.

She had started off in bad shape, but they gave her a lot of time to recover. One thing about an Agency hospital, they knew more about her engineered metabolism than any civilian medics—even though they pretended not to know English.

Or Spanish . . .

Or Arabic . . .

Or any other language she came up with.

At least it gave her a chance to think. And those thoughts brought a whole raft of mixed feelings. On the one hand, she'd been willing to give her life to see those aliens go down, and somehow she'd managed to see that happen and live through it. On the other hand, it was the Agency who'd done it, and that was uncomfortably familiar—not to mention that she was a de facto traitor.

She was also their prisoner.

Evi wondered why they even bothered with fixing her up if they were going to just disappear her.

The more she thought about it over her days of recuperation, the more she wondered about the Agency showing up. It was so convenient, even if it had saved her life. Evi had the uncomfortable feeling that she'd been used, *again*.

When the bones had knitted together, and she'd become ambulatory, she had a visitor who confirmed some of her worst suspicions.

Evi was in the midst of a hundred push-ups—she knew if she tried anything medically objectionable, the silent doctors would come in and stop her. She'd long ago determined that even the bathroom was under constant surveillance—when the door opened. Instead of a doctor or nurse, the door let in Sukiota.

She wanted to ask why she was still alive.

Evi stopped her push-ups, stood up with the help of a crutch, and said to Sukiota, "Someone had to have gotten to me within five minutes, or I would have bled to death."

Sukiota shook her head. She was dressed in an anonymous androgynous suit; the only sign of authority was a ramcard clipped to her lapel. "We got to you in less than thirty seconds, if you're counting from that explosion."

Evi shook her head, somewhat gratified to have someone here respond to her. She'd half expected Sukiota to pull the same mute act that the doctors did. "Now what? Am I under arrest? Now that I'm almost healed, am I about to disappear down some Agency hole?"

Sukiota smiled. "Actually, I'm here to thank you."

"What?"

278

Sukiota's smile was surreal, as if Evi was looking into a distorted mirror. Physically they were so much alike. Evi didn't like the fact that Sukiota's smile looked so much like her own. "You gave my operation a chance to crack Nyogi. I've been trying to get approval to take them down since I started investigating the Afghanis."

Evi shook her head. She didn't like the way Sukiota's talk was drifting. "Last time you were throwing words like 'traitor' at me."

Sukiota's smile never wavered. She took an opaque evidence bag from her pocket and began to toss it from hand to hand. "I suppose so. If it weren't for certain expediencies on my part, the Agency would have considered you part and parcel of that extra-Agency conspiracy. The Domestic Crisis Think Tank you called it. We finished mopping it up weeks ago."

Evi realized that she had been here a long time.

"Everybody?"

"We're checking the records, but I believe we have all but one accounted for. Of the people you fingered, Frey, Gabriel, and Davidson are on slabs, Fitzgerald is so much carbon, Hofstadter was dumped at a critical care unit in upper Manhattan in the late stages of a stroke and is vegetating two floors below us . . ."

"Price?"

"He's the unaccounted one."

Sukiota was still smiling, and it was getting on Evi's nerves. "Did you set me up?"

Sukiota tossed the white evidence bag up, following it with her eyes. "I was pissed with you." She caught the bag and tossed it to her other hand. "But I needed you. You served your purpose."

"That whole scene in the subway—"

Sukiota shrugged and caught the bag.

"You bastards set me up!"

"You didn't do anything that you weren't about to

do anyway. I saw a good chance you'd go straight to our target—"

"Damn it," Evi yelled. "You knew about Nyogi all along. You could have stormed the place any time you wanted too."

"You know better than that, Isham. The Feds give the Agency major latitude in domestic covert ops, but Nyogi is a major corporation with major congressional and Executive support. I couldn't get approval to go in."

"But you went in."

"After you."

"What?"

Sukiota laughed. "I told you I carried out certain expediencies on your behalf. Before we let you escape, I resurrected your Agency file."

Evi just stared.

"Different rules apply to hot pursuit, especially when an active duty agent is involved."

"You used me as an excuse?"

Sukiota nodded. "And after we did that, we couldn't very well let you die. That would have been embarrassing."

All of a sudden she had just come full circle. She was right back where she had started, an Agency creature. And, again, as always, she had no choice in the matter.

Evi sighed. It might have been fatigue, but she felt that she had used up all of her anger. Her emotions were one vast plain of resignation. "What about the aliens?" she asked.

"I'd say that's on a need to know basis, but that'd be a fraud. Rest assured, the Feds are sifting through the UABT complex, the buildings at Columbia, and underneath the Nyogi tower. We've captured a number of aliens—" Sukiota seemed uncomfortable with the word— "and enough people and agencies are involved this time that no one is going to bottle this up." Sukiota shook her head. "Everyone from the Biological Regulatory Commission and NASA to Defense Intel and the Department of the Interior . . . The Agency handed the alien problem off to everyone else. We've got other problems."

"Like what?" As if the aliens weren't enough. What the hell could take precedence over that in the Agency's agenda?

"You should know. We had a tracking device on you all that time. RF, audio, limited video . . ."

It began to sink in, exactly what that meant.

The Bronx.

The entire military setup. Evi had waltzed through all of it, handed it all to the Agency.

It must have shown in her expression because Sukiota nodded. "I see you *do* know what I'm talking about. That's why I'm here, really. I resurrected your file, and I have to release you, but I'm retiring you. You're not going to interfere with any future operations."

"I'm not—"

"No, you're not, even though I think you have an inclination otherwise; it would be embarrassing. And since it would be inconvenient to threaten you—" Sukiota tossed the evidence bag at Evi. It sprung open on the foot of the bed.

Evi leaned over on her crutch, grabbed the end of the bag and upended it. Out fell a pair of velvet-lined handcuffs. The same ones she had liberated from Diana's bedstand. They still had a splattering of blood on them from the veep.

"It would be very nice for Diana Murphy if you led a nice quiet life as Eve Herman from now on."

Sukiota left her.

Evi stared at the cuffs.

When Evi hobbled through the threshold of Diana's loft, she was the recipient of a shocked expression, then of some very tall hugs. The reunion was so teary that it took nearly ten minutes before either of them was close to being coherent.

"I thought I'd never see you again," Diana said, wiping her eyes.

"I never thought I'd see anyone again," Evi said. "Can I sit? The leg's still kind of bad."

Diana helped her over to the couch, peppering Evi with questions. How was she? What happened?

Evi shushed her. She hadn't realized how much she had missed Diana until then, how she had worried. She finally told Diana *everything*.

Diana's reaction was unexpected. "Damn, until now I thought the whole thing was some kind of silly hoax."

"What was a hoax?" Evi asked. She hadn't expected to be believed so readily.

"The broadcast—"

"What broadcast?"

"That's right, you've been incommunicado. I recorded it. I'll try and find the ramcard . . ."

Diana moved up and switched on her comm. She sifted through the pile of ramcards as the thing warmed up. Then she inserted the card and fell back next to Evi on the couch.

"I really missed you," Diana whispered.

Evi stroked Diana's hair, for the first time with her left hand, and watched the comm. There, centered in a frame that was obviously shot from a hand-held camera was David Price.

Behind him was a familiar-looking cargo hauler, and lined up by the end of the trailer behind Price, were four blubbery-white aliens. Evi watched as David got very chummy with Corporal Gurgueia. The Jaguar was holding an AK-47.

"They hijacked the damn truck," Evi whispered.

Diana whispered into Evi's ear. "What?" Evi could feel the warmth of her breath.

"They hijacked the damn truck!" Evi shouted, smiling from ear to ear. They had done it. By everything that was holy, they'd completed the objective . . .

She realized that she was being unreasonably happy. Sukiota had told her, almost point blank, that the shit was about to hit the fan.

Even so, Evi couldn't help grinning. It was a small battle, but she had won it.

They had won it.

A battle, but the war was still out there.

Evi hit the mute on the remote sitting on the table in front of her. Then she hugged Diana back. She was free. Sukiota had retired her, and now she owed her allegiance to no one.

Evi looked up into Diana's human eyes and realized that that wasn't quite true. She also realized that she hadn't worn sunglasses or contacts for nearly two weeks.

"Diana."

"Mmm?"

Right now Evi was holding Diana about as close as she could while staying a separate person. She finally had choices. If she wanted, she could divorce herself from everything the Bronx would bring.

"You know," Evi told Diana, "I've become unreasonably close to you in a short time."

"Feeling's mutual."

Evi had choices, but Sukiota had pressed the point home that, if she chose not to remain aloof, she would drag along someone she loved. "I have a decision to make." Evi whispered. "One I can't make without you."

"Later," Diana said, kissing her.

S. Andrew Swann

☐ **FORESTS OF THE NIGHT**   UE2565—$3.99

When Nohar Rajasthan, a private eye descended from genetically manipulated tiger stock, a moreau—a second-class humanoid citizen in a human world—is hired to look into a human's murder, he find himself caught up in a conspiracy that includes federal agents, drug runners, moreau gangs, and a deadly canine assassin. And he hasn't even met the real enemy yet!

☐ **EMPERORS OF THE TWILIGHT**   UE2589—$4.50

New York City, sixty years in the future, a time when a squad of assassins was ready to send an entire skyscraper up in flames to take out one special operative. Her name: Evi Isham, her species: frankenstein, the next step beyond human, her physiology bioengineered to make her the best in the business whether she was taking down an enemy or just trying to stay alive. Back from vacation and ready to report in to the Agency for a new assignment, Evi suddenly found herself on the run from an unidentified enemy who had targeted her for death. Her only hope was to evade her stalkers long enough to make contact with her superiors. But she would soon discover that even the Agency might not save her from those who sought her life!

Science Fiction Anthologies

☐ **FUTURE EARTHS: UNDER AFRICAN SKIES**   UE2544—$4.99
Mike Resnick & Gardner Dozois, editors
From a utopian space colony modeled on the society of ancient Kenya,
to a shocking future discovery of a "long-lost" civilization, to an inge-
nious cure for one of humankind's oldest woes—a cure that might cost
too much—here are 15 provocative tales about Africa in the future and
African culture transplanted to different worlds.

☐ **FUTURE EARTHS: UNDER SOUTH AMERICAN SKIES**
Mike Resnick & Gardner Dozois, editors   UE2581—$4.99
From a plane crash that lands its passengers in a survival situation
completely alien to anything they've ever experienced, to a close en-
counter of the insect kind, to a woman who has journeyed unimaginably
far from home—here are stories from the rich culture of South America,
with its mysteriously vanished ancient civilizations and magnificent
artifacts, its modern-day contrasts between sophisticated city dwellers
and impoverished villagers.

☐ **MICROCOSMIC TALES**   UE2532—$4.99
Isaac Asimov, Martin H. Greenberg, & Joseph D. Olander, eds.
Here are 100 wondrous science fiction short-short stories, including
contributions by such acclaimed writers as Arthur C. Clarke, Robert
Silverberg, Isaac Asimov, and Larry Niven. Discover a superman who
lives in a *real* world of nuclear threat . . . an android who dreams of
electric love . . . and a host of other tales that will take you instantly
out of this world.

☐ **WHATDUNITS**   UE2533—$4.99
☐ **MORE WHATDUNITS**   UE2557—$5.50
Mike Resnick, editor
In these unique volumes of all-original stories, Mike Resnick has created a series of science fiction mystery scenarios and set such inven-
tive sleuths as Pat Cadigan, Judith Tarr, Katharine Kerr, Jack Haldeman,
and Esther Friesner to solving them. Can you match wits with the
masters to make the perpetrators fit the crimes?

Buy them at your local bookstore or use this convenient coupon for ordering.

PENGUIN USA P.O. Box 999, Dept. #17109, Bergenfield, New Jersey 07621

Please send me the DAW BOOKS I have checked above, for which I am enclosing
$_____ (please add $2.00 per order to cover postage and handling. Send check
or money order (no cash or C.O.D.'s) or charge by Mastercard or Visa (with a
$15.00 minimum.) Prices and numbers are subject to change without notice.

Card #_____ Exp. Date _____
Signature_____
Name_____
Address_____
City _____ State _____ Zip _____

For faster service when ordering by credit card call **1-800-253-6476**

Please allow a minimum of 4 to 6 weeks for delivery.

DAW
Tanya Huff

VICTORY NELSON, INVESTIGATOR:
Otherworldly Crimes A Specialty

☐ **BLOOD PRICE: Book 1**   UE2471—$3.99
Can one ex-policewoman and a vampire defeat the magic-spawned evil which is devastating Toronto?

☐ **BLOOD TRAIL: Book 2**   UE2502—$4.50
Someone was out to exterminate Canada's most endangered species—the werewolf.

☐ **BLOOD LINES: Book 3**   UE2530—$4.99
Long-imprisoned by the magic of Egypt's gods, an ancient force of evil is about to be loosed on an unsuspecting Toronto.

THE NOVELS OF CRYSTAL

When an evil wizard attempts world domination, the Elder Gods must intervene!

☐ **CHILD OF THE GROVE: Book 1**   UE2432—$3.95
☐ **THE LAST WIZARD: Book 2**   UE2331—$3.95

OTHER NOVELS

☐ **THE FIRE'S STONE**   UE2445—$3.95
Thief, swordsman and wizardess—drawn together by a quest not of their own choosing, would they find their true destinies in a fight against spells, swords and betrayal?

DAW

Eluki bes Shahar

THE HELLFLOWER SERIES

☐ **HELLFLOWER (Book 1)**   UE2475—$3.99

Butterfly St. Cyr had a well-deserved reputation as an honest and dependable smuggler. But when she and her partner, a highly illegal artificial intelligence, rescued Tiggy, the son and heir to one of the most powerful of the hellflower mercenary leaders, it looked like they'd finally taken on more than they could handle. For his father's enemies had sworn to see that Tiggy and Butterfly never reached his home planet alive. . . .

☐ **DARKTRADERS (Book 2)**   UE2507—$4.50

With her former partner Paladin—the death-to-possess Old Federation artificial intelligence—gone off on a private mission, Butterfly didn't have anybody to back her up when Tiggy's enemies decided to give the word "ambush" a whole new and all-too-final meaning.

☐ **ARCHANGEL BLUES (Book 3)**   UE2543—$4.50

Darktrader Butterfly St. Cyr and her partner Tiggy seek to complete the mission they started in DARKTRADERS, to find and destroy the real Archangel, Governor-General of the Empire, the being who is determined to wield A.I. powers to become the master of the entire universe.

Coming in HARDCOVER in February 1994:

FOREIGNER
by C.J. Cherryh

It had been nearly five centuries since the starship *Phoenix*, came out of hyperdrive into a place with no recognizable reference coordinates, and no way home. Hopelessly lost, the crew did the only thing they could. They charted their way to the nearest G5 star, gambling on finding a habitable planet. And what they found was the world of the atevi—a world where law was kept by the use of registered assassination, where alliances were not defined by geographical borders, and where war became inevitable once humans and one faction of atevi established a working relationship. It was a war that humans had no chance of winning and now, nearly two centuries later, humanity lives in exile on the island of Mospheira, trading tidbits of advanced technology for continued peace and a secluded refuge that no atevi will ever visit. Only a single human, the paidhi, is allowed off the island and into the complex and dangerous society of the atevi, brought there to act as interpreter and technological liaison to the leader of the most powerful of the atevi factions. But when this sole human the treaty allows into atevi society is nearly killed by an unregistered assassin's bullet, the fragile peace is shattered, and Bren Cameron, the paidhi, realizes that he must seek a new way to build a truer understanding between these two dangerous, intelligent, and quite possibly incompatible species. For if he fails, he and all of his people will die. But can a lone human hope to overcome two centuries of hostility and mistrust?

☐ **Hardcover Edition** UE2590—$20.00
